For Brenda

TOOTH AND TALON

STORIES

JAMES WALTER LEE

2ND
SIGHT PRESS

2ND SIGHT PRESS
www.2ndsightpress.com

Book and cover designs by James Walter Lee

ISBN 978-0-9966058-0-9
ISBN 978-0-9966058-1-6 (ebook)

CONTENTS

TOOTH AND TALON

DEVIL BENEATH

"Try it now," he yelled from the dark crawl space.

Marion White went from the open window to the kitchen electrical panel and flipped the breaker. The lights in the kitchen and living room came on.

"Oh yeah, Herb, you got it," she shouted.

She then heard the heavy wooden doors close, first the left, then the right. Moments later, the sound of well-polished steel surfaces sliding and clicking as the padlock came together. From the backdoor she heard the tread of heavy work boots shuffling against the mat. The screen door opened and in walked Herbert Wallace, an average man just under six feet tall and one hundred and seventy-two pounds. He had played basketball in high school and those long distant memories seemed to keep him going. Now at seventy-eight, staying active was the only thing his doctor seemed to talk about. Dr. McGee had been his wife's trusted medical counsel for over twenty years, but he thought it would be nice to get a little more out of your physician than the obvious.

"Marion, I think you're all set. It was just the two wires that were worn. Looks like squirrels might have gotten to them," he told her.

"Thanks, Herb. Would you like some ice tea?" Before he could answer she poured him a glass. It was toward the end of June and already getting hot. She saw the sweat on his brow and knew he had to be thirsty.

"Thanks, that would be nice," he replied.

"Haven't seen too many squirrels around—are you sure?" said Marion. She took a seat at the small kitchen table with the two glasses of ice tea.

Still standing, Herbert raised an eyebrow. "Well, if not that it might be a raccoon or possum."

"Sit down, Herb, I know that heat's getting to you. It sure has me tired and I haven't hardly started my day." He sat down across from her and drank some of the ice tea.

"Jean has glasses just like these. Tapered with flowers on them," he said with a cocked head, inspecting the glass as if he was having difficulty focusing his eyes.

"Well, Marion, I have to mow my lawn, but I can run you to the store later if you like."

"That would be nice," she said with a smile and a nod.

Since Herbert's wife, Jean, had died four years ago, and Marion's Lester was missing, they both were left with each other. Herb was always respectful, not knowing what had become of Lester. He wanted to help Marion, but at the same time avoid having her think that he was trying to take old Lester's place. The situation just seemed to bring them together, if nothing more than for practical purposes. Herb's cooking abilities were limited and Marion needed help around the house. Before Lester vanished they would invite Herb over for dinner from time to time, knowing he could use the company and a nice cooked meal.

Lester trusted Herbert, even though Lester was a truck driver, spending most of his time on the road making deliveries cross-country. Lester needed someone to look after his wife that he was comfortable with.

Another hot day passed and as the night came so did a cool breeze through Marion's bedroom window. She lay in bed staring at the ceiling, still too warm to drift off to sleep. Below her she could hear rustling. There was that faint scratching again. How the hell was that damn animal getting inside her crawl space? She thought she heard it the other night. Now she was definitely hearing it. Better not tear up my wires again, she worried. Since Lester disappeared this house had become more than a handful. The cleaning and minor fixes were enough to keep her occupied. The scratching noises grew louder, then dropped off.

"Damn bugger, you're going to keep poor old Herbie busy, aren't ya? Well, if there's no damage tomorrow, I'm still going to have him take a look anyway to see how you're getting in."

The noise stopped abruptly, like a squirrel pausing to listen for threats. With no more ruckus Marion trailed off to sleep.

With the heavy wooden doors placed aside, Marion peered down through the crawl space opening. Inside she could only see Herb's work boots as he was on his knees crawling on the dirt floor.

"Well, it didn't touch the wires I replaced yesterday," she heard him say as he tried to project his voice out of the shallow space.

"Don't see any holes anywhere either," he added.

She could see the beam of his flashlight as he directed it around the inside perimeter.

"I want to check inside the house too, if you don't mind," he said.

She dreaded the thought that the animal was actually inside one of the walls. If that were the case, maybe it was trapped there? She agreed with Herb and wanted to be thorough.

After closing and locking the crawl space doors, he mentioned that he saw some markings on the floor joists near some of the plumbing.

"If the animal was small enough, perhaps it made its way up and into the house," he said, sounding concerned.

"Well, now it seems like I have more to worry about," she replied.

It was one thing to have the noises on the other side of the house, but having them closer to her bedroom made her uneasy.

"Now, now, let's just have a look; I'm sure everything is fine," he comforted her.

Inside he would look under her kitchen sink and in some of the closets where he knew pipes would be present.

"I found nothing in the closets, and there were no small gaps around the pipes, so that's good," he explained.

While under the kitchen sink he noticed the drainpipe was a little loose, but the gap there was too little to be concerned with. Maybe only a small mouse could make it through that, he thought.

"Well, Marion, looks good to me," he told her.

Still a bit nervous, she just shrugged and nodded.

"You have dinner plans?" she asked, already knowing the answer.

Usually he spent his evenings alone, but an old buddy of his was in town. They agreed to meet for drinks and maybe bowl a couple of games at Shuster's Bowling Alley.

"Sorry, Marion, but an old friend is in town," he apologized rather than just thanking her for the offer. He felt bad due to her worries about a possible animal in the house.

After a quiet dinner, Marion wanted to break the silence so she went into the living room and put on the TV. After all it was time for her favorite game shows. The ones Lester hated, but then again he wasn't a very educated man and not knowing the answers just frustrated him. She chuckled to herself thinking she could have just set up a snack tray and sat in front of the TV as her husband did to watch the news or one of his favorite nature programs. One thing she loved about him was that he wasn't much of a sports fan, so there never was much of a struggle for the remote. She sat in his old chair and stared at the TV momentarily before turning it on.

"Where the hell are you, Lester?" she mumbled, staring into the glow of the TV set.

She knew he hadn't run off with another woman, so his disappearance was maddening.

Police in three states had him listed as a missing person. After a two month intense search, priorities shifted to the missing Jensen twins, along with their baby sitter, Grace Stevens. They were two-ten-year old girls and Grace was only seventeen. Marion understood the change of focus to the three girls, but she still called the police every day for a month inquiring about Lester.

"No, Ma'am, nothing new. We've got our best men on the case, and will let you know as soon as we find him." That seemed to be the going response. Most departments had his case being looked after by detectives that she felt were only half committed. Probably due to the fact Lester was in his seventies and a truck driver, which maybe to them added up to another woman. Also, Lester was a likable guy with no enemies that she knew of. That first week when he didn't come home, she drove the expressways accompanied by Barbara Gladwin, an old friend from her church. Lester's friend Mike Connors who scheduled the deliveries gave Marion the location of Lester's last delivery as well as any ideas for routes he might have taken. The guy at the Coca-Cola distributing warehouse in Davison only confirmed that Lester made his pickup, but nothing beyond that. She knew the crates of soda never made it to their destination as his truck was found with the trailer fully loaded. No signs of struggle, nor any signs that the truck broke down, only that it was parked on the shoulder of Interstate 78, a half mile east of a rest stop. Marion and Barbara did visit that rest stop, but there was no need for Lester to go there, his truck had plenty of gas, so she doubted that he had stopped there.

The light from the TV flashed against Marion's face and as she started to fill with sadness from the thoughts of Lester, only the barrage of questions from the game show brought her back to the moment. She answered most of the puzzles correctly, as she often did. During a commercial break she thought she heard a thumping noise coming from the kitchen.

"Herb, I wish you were here," she said in a low voice.

After turning the TV volume down, she walked slowly and paused in the doorway to the kitchen. No new sounds. She thought that perhaps whatever animal was under the floor or in the wall heard her coming. She looked around, carefully scrutinizing every crevice for any kind of movement. Not that she was capable of removing the intruder, but she still wanted to know what she was dealing with.

Her eyes were tired of staring, but she remained in the doorway. Before she could take a glance at the clock, a loud thud came from under the kitchen sink. She jumped at the sound, which reminded her of old loose plumbing being jostled around. Two more softer thuds followed and she took a single strong step forward, yelling, "Get out! You get out of here!"

She was afraid of getting too close, with the fear that the doors under the sink would burst open and some animal would bite her. Trying to think quickly, she grabbed a chair and pushed it up against the sink doors. Although her kitchen table was much smaller than the one in the dining room, still it was an old farm-style table and the chairs were heavy oak.

"That ought to hold you, until Herb can deal with you," she shouted. Then the scratching of claws came, as if they were trying to carve out a hole. She backed up against the opposite wall.

"Get out, I said!" she yelled towards the sink. The clawing slowed, then stopped.

Marion stood there staring at the sink doors, then tears filled her eyes. I don't need this aggravation, she thought. After seventeen minutes of silence, she grabbed her dishtowel and wrapped it through the sink door handles and tied it the best she could. She then took her other chair and placed it next to the first one. Satisfied with her effort, and now confident that it would keep things at bay, she turned off the TV and went down the hall. Looking back briefly before closing and locking her bedroom door, she was too exhausted and afraid to clean up, so she just changed into her nightgown and slipped under the covers of her full-size bed. She lay on the side where Lester normally slept, as she often did when he was on the road. After his disappearance she always found herself on his side of the bed, maybe hoping that he would wake her one evening, finally making it home. I'm sure he would have some tale to tell, and it better be a good one, making her worry so much, she thought as she drifted off to sleep.

Marion awoke to faint slow scratching noises coming from beyond her bedroom door and down the hall. In a small, quiet house, especially one with no other occupants, every sound was amplified. At first she thought she was dreaming of the animal working its way from the crawl space into the cabinet under her kitchen sink. Her clock radio read just past ten p.m. Is this going to go on all night? Just as she finished that thought the sounds died down as quickly as she had been awakened by them.

"That's right, getting tired of digging and scratching," she whispered, and hoped it were true. While still in a groggy, half-sleep stupor, she contemplated going to take a look.

Her steps were slow and soft down the hall, arriving at the opening to the living room. Glancing around, nothing caught her eye, no movement of shadows, no silhouette of any small wild beasts. As she crossed the room and peered into the kitchen she noticed that the sink cabinet doors were open. The doorway framed the sink, the small window, and cabinet below; the rest of the room was cropped from view. She moved with caution to the doorway and looked around, refraining from turning on the light for fear the creature would bolt toward her. No movement or sounds of any animal foraging for an evening snack. Her gaze froze upon a standing figure in the corner of the room. She almost missed it with the lights off. Her heart hammered in her chest and she tried not to scream. What was this person doing in her home and why was he standing in the corner? If he was going to rob her, why was he not in the living room or the bedroom going through her things? Her mind raced and she grabbed for a knife from the block on the counter. The figure did not move as she held the carving knife in front of her. She realized that he was facing away from her. As quiet as she was, maybe he was unaware that she was there. Could he be on drugs? she thought. Her mind raced, wondering whether to speak or run back to the bedroom and lock the door.

A low, dry whisper came from the shadowy corner, "Marion," it spoke her name. As if from a distant memory the voice she knew to be Lester's.

"Lester?" she half cried out.

The figure turned slowly, trembling, one hand bracing the wall like an old man with unsure legs. She slid her hand up the wall to the light switch. As the ceiling light came on, the figure vanished, absorbed by the shadows that moved as fast as the light displaced them.

"Lester!" she cried out.

This time she heard her own voice, loud and firm, but no one was there. She slumped down against the cabinet just inside the doorway. She trembled, causing tears to tumble from her eyes like fruit being jostled from a tree.

From a dream state she heard a muffled voice calling her name, followed by a distant pounding against heavy wood. The knocking did not let up. As she surfaced from sleep she realized that someone was at the front door. She sat up and rushed to put on her robe and slippers. Trying to leave the room, she was unable to turn the knob, forgetting that she had locked it the night before.

"Coming," she yelled after getting the bedroom door open.

She knew it was Herb by his voice. The only other visitors who knocked on her door this early in the morning were the local door-to-door religious salesmen of the Jehovah's Witnesses persuasion.

As she passed the open sink cabinet doors to let Herb in, she felt a chill, causing her to grasp at her robe near her chest.

"Marion, what happened? Looks like you fought off that animal last night." She just stared at him, then hugged him abruptly.

"Gee, Marion. Are you ok?" he asked.

She just murmured, "He was here last night—Lester." Herbert moved the chairs from near the sink and helped Marion sit at the table.

"Now tell me what happened here, and what about Lester?"

She explained all of the late-night commotion in the kitchen that brought her to investigate, only to find this man, who she thought was her husband Lester.

She stood and moved to the corner where she saw the dark figure and with open hands motioned downward.

"He was here, right here," she said.

Herbert looked at her with confusion and concern.

"He even said my name, but when I turned on the lights, he was gone. I know I'm not crazy, I saw him," she declared.

"Ok Marion, I believe you, but let's think about this. You said that he just disappeared? What happened with the cabinet?" Herb tried to be supportive yet rational.

The sink doors being open did raise a question, which unsettled and confused Marion. She just stared at the open doors and thought, had Lester come from the crawl space?

Herb got on his knees to inspect under the sink.

"There sure is a large hole here, one with quite a few claw and teeth marks. A small child could probably crawl up through there, or one large raccoon," he said.

From the marks, he thought it was a very determined animal.

"I want to check the crawl space," he said. Marion nodded.

After Marion spent fifteen minutes of staring down the shadowy entrance to the crawl space, Herb finally appeared to give her the news.

"Looks like a bigger animal than I hoped for. I'm going to get some scrap wood from my place and patch that. Then I'll see about picking up a trap at Marty's Sporting Goods."

She took some comfort from his intentions. "I just hope it doesn't keep me up all night again," she said.

"Well, at least it won't make its way into the house again," he assured her.

He still wondered how she saw Lester and was concerned that she might be having a nervous breakdown.

"I don't want to make you feel more uneasy, but if you like I could sleep on the couch?" he stated without any romantic intentions.

"Herb, I wouldn't want to put you out," she said.

He put up his hand to assure her that there was no inconvenience. As he left to retrieve the wood from his place she felt more at ease.

After Herb secured the hole in the crawl space, they both sat at the kitchen table eating some leftovers.

"No animal should be able to claw through that, unless they spend a good three months at it," he told her between bites.

He could see the appreciation on her face, but he was still worried about her mental state. He wanted to talk more about her seeing Lester, but thought better of it. All she needs is ghosts on top of trying to take care of this damn house. Instead of dwelling on the thought, he just tried to enjoy the meal. After some lighter talk about the coming Forth of July holiday, Marion asked if he would like to watch some TV.

"Just in time for some of my favorite game shows," she said.

Unlike Lester, Herbert Wallace enjoyed some of the same programs that Marion did. Like Lester he was not an educated man, but he was a good sport when he got the answers wrong. They laughed a bit and Herb complimented Marion on her knowledge.

"You could be on that show," he told her.

As the evening set in and they finished watching the news, she went to the closet and got Herb some bedding.

"As warm as it's been, this sheet and pillow should do."

She put the bedding down next to him on the couch.

"Thanks. Sure that'll be more than fine," he said.

"What time was it last night when you started hearing noises from the kitchen?" he asked.

"Well, it was just after the news, so right about now," she said.

With the TV off, Herb walked into the kitchen. The room was quiet and held a strange stillness even after he turned on the light. He bent down in front of the sink cabinet and slowly opened the doors. The carved-out hole around the pipes looked terrible, but the wood he nailed from underneath was well in place.

"Looks solid; guess I don't have to worry about something trying to bite my face off," he smiled and told Marion, who stood just inside the doorway with her hands knit together. She returned an uneasy smile, still grateful that he was there.

"Well, Herb, I'm off to bed. Guess we'll know sooner or later if our little friend has returned," she said.

He looked around under the sink a bit more before closing the doors and heading to the couch to make his bed.

Marion lay in bed staring at the ceiling, waiting for some audible confirmation, but after an hour and a half she finally eased into sleep. Herb lay on the couch, fully dressed minus his boots. He looked at all of the Whites' little collections. Marion liked birds; she had several porcelain pieces on the mantle. A couple of small bowling trophies of Lester's, as well as a framed photo of him and Herb with their catch from a weekend fishing trip several years ago, decorated the right side of the mantle. They had no children, so there was a lack of family photos. Herb felt sad for them as he knew Lester shot blanks and would have loved to have had children, although Marion never seemed to mind. Herb's two kids were all grown and lived out of state, and since his wife Nancy's passing, with Lester at least he had a fishing and bowling buddy. Memories brought about sadness as he knew something bad must have happened to old Lester. *He would have told me if he was up to something.* Then again, he never had a bad word to say about being married to Marion. *Well, I'll take good care of her,* and with that thought he drifted off to sleep.

The wind did pick up that evening and the night held its collection of sounds. Herb woke to the sound of the wind and scratching, but on glass, not wood. He sat up rubbing his eyes and looked at the wall clock—it was past midnight. Even without the lights on he could see into the kitchen, lit well enough from the moonlight. He lumbered to the doorway and looked around. The sink cabinet doors were undisturbed. The glass he used earlier was washed and in the drying rack. He got himself some water from the tap and looked outside. There was a figure standing on the lawn next to the old apple tree. It remained still, casting doubt as to what Herb was seeing. He rubbed his eyes and quickly looked again. The shape either disappeared, or maybe it was just part of the tree's shadow.

Herb went and put his boots on and stepped outside through the kitchen door, being careful not to make too much noise. Standing on the bottom step, he scanned the yard looking closely at the apple tree. Strange shadows seem to move against the side of it. The wind animating the branches only added further confusion as to what he was seeing. He stepped off the porch step and walked toward the tree. Halfway across the yard and now in the open, he realized that he was unarmed.

"Anyone out here?" he asked.

His voice just loud enough to carry over the wind. As he got closer to the tree he could see something moving on the side of it.

"Hello," he said.

"If you're one of the neighbor kids, just go home, I won't chase after you."

No response, so he stepped forward. He could now see more of the shape, some cloth given life by the wind. It was a shirt, big enough to fit him. Dried dirt filled the fabric and it smelled of musty leaves. Who left this here? he wondered.

As Herb walked back to the house he noticed the crawl space doors ajar. The padlock was still in place but the hinges were loose, as if something had pushed against the doors from the inside. He pulled the doors from the bottom and noted the space they allowed for.

"Couldn't get to your meal so you decided to take a hike," he said as he inspected the doors.

"I'll fix these tomorrow and then you'll have to dine elsewhere."

He pushed the doors up and inward as best he could to straighten them, then took a weighty rock to keep them in place. Confident that would keep any smaller animals out, he went back inside. After dropping the dirty shirt on the floor under the coat hooks, he took another look under the sink just to double-check his work. Satisfied, he went to lie down. Marion's door was still closed so he would tell her about the shirt and crawl space in the morning.

* * *

Herb awoke to the sun-filled living room. Sitting up, he noticed Marion's door was still closed. It was almost half past eight in the morning. He folded the sheet, putting it aside with the pillow, and went into the kitchen. Looking through the cupboards he found the coffee and set about getting some brewed. As the water in the coffeemaker was heating up, he went to inspect the shirt he had found. Holding it up at the shoulders, it was definitely a man's work shirt. There was a folded piece of paper in the left breast pocket. It was soft and appeared to have been soaked in water. Now dry but clumped together, he could still make out the Connors Freight logo. Could this be Lester's shirt, and why was it stuck in the tree? Did Marion really see Lester? If she did, how come he doesn't just walk through the door? Too many questions spun through Herb's mind.

Having made the coffee, he went to check on Marion; her door was still closed. "Marion? Are you awake? I need you to come on out, I think I found Lester's shirt," he spoke through the door. He knocked, but still no reply.

"Marion, you have to get up."

He turned the knob and cracked the door to peer inside, he saw that her bed was empty. Looking about the room he found her in a fetal position in the corner opposite the bed.

"Marion!" he said as he rushed over and crouched down next to her.

Her nightgown was disheveled and she was shaking. He pulled the blanket from the bed, wrapped her in it and held her. In a soft, comforting voice he asked her what had happened. She was unable to push any words past her trembling lips, and just stared ahead, rocking gently in his arms. After a moment, he helped her stand and walked her to the couch in the living room.

Herb held out a cup of coffee. "Here drink this."

"He was here—Lester," she muttered. "I first saw him outside my window, then he was in the room," she continued.

He felt her forehead; she was cold and clammy.

"I better take you to see Dr. McGee, you feel like you're coming down with something," he said.

Although Dr. McGee was Herb's doctor, she was glad that Herb had brought Marion in; that saved them a trip to Philipsburg to see Dr. Peterson, who normally looked after the Whites' medical ailments.

"Her blood pressure is very low, let's get some fluids into her," Dr. McGee told the nurse.

The immediate care facility was only set up for minor medical needs, but did have a four-bed unit for those awaiting transfer to the hospital. Since Marion seemed weak and lightheaded they opted to put her in one of the beds. As she slept, Herb talked to the doctor in the hall.

"Herbert, just what happened to her?" Dr. McGee asked.

"She's been under a lot of stress lately. I might have told you that her husband, Lester White, went missing, and now she's contending with some animal trying to get into her house," he replied.

Before Dr. McGee could ask further questions, the nurse came from Marion's room. "Doctor, I need you for a moment, can you please take a look at something?"

Herb waited in the hall.

A few nurses came and went from the room, until Dr. McGee finally emerged.

"Herb, tell me more about that animal. Was she attacked?"

"No, not that I'm aware of; we were doing a good job at keeping it at bay. I was supposed to get a trap today. Is she ok?"

Dr. McGee told Herb that they found bites on Marion's back and shoulder.

"We have to get her a rabies shot, and I suggest that you stay out of that house until you can get an exterminator," she advised him. "We'll keep her here overnight; she needs rest and fluids. You can go on home. I'll have the desk call you tomorrow."

It was only two in the afternoon as Herb sat at the bar in Shuster's Bowling Alley. His hand shook a bit as he took a sip of his beer.

"You ok?" Ronny Shuster asked.

"Yeah, just old age creeping up on me," Herb said with a subtle smile. He felt it best to avoid going into any details.

Young Ronny Shuster was only twenty-three, on summer break from the local community college, playing barkeep for his folks, who owned the place. They let him run things until five; afterwards the place sometimes got a bit rowdy. With his beer only half drank, Herb paid Ronny and headed to Marty's Sporting Goods.

Having purchased the store's last animal trap, Herb sat in the parking lot in his ninety-three GMC Jimmy. His hands shook on the steering wheel. He was both upset and angry that Marion got hurt.

"Let's get this done," he told himself and drove on to the Whites' house.

When he pulled into the driveway he half cursed himself, having forgotten about the crawl space doors, which could use new screws and possibly hinges. *If I can just get rid of this animal, then I'll fix the doors tomorrow,* he thought. He was curious about finding Lester's shirt. Herb was convinced that he knew the man well enough to believe that if he were alive, he would just walk in the front door. As for Marion, he thought she was just seeing ghosts.

Herb set the trap just inside the crawl space, using some corn for bait that Marion had left over, and hoped that tomorrow his little nemesis would be behind bars. After loosely closing the crawl space doors, the stage was set.

Back inside the house he went to Marion's room to have a look. He checked in the closets, under the bed and even moved the dresser to peek behind it. There were no signs of the animal, or any indication of how it got into her room. He left the bedroom door open, and looked around the rest of the house.

"Nothing," he said. "Well, hide all you want, you're going to have to contend with me face-to-face sometime," he added.

He ate one of the frozen potpies from Marion's freezer and afterwards sat in the living room to watch the news. *No sense going home, I'll check the crawl space in the morning, then head back to my place for breakfast and gather some things to repair those doors,* he thought.

Almost falling asleep lying on the couch, he turned off the TV before the ten o'clock news was over. Looking at the ceiling and around the Whites' living room, he contemplated taking the shirt he found to the police. Not sure it would help them find Lester, that piece of the puzzle raised more questions than answers, he thought. I can only imagine all of the nightmares running through Marion's head. I better not start seeing his ghost, or she and I will be headed for the nut house. Imagining Lester's whereabouts, Herb closed his eyes and gave in to sleep.

It seemed like hours had passed. An uneasy silence surrounded him. He thought that he had opened his eyes, but recalled no new visual memories; blackness seemed to prevail. His body felt paralyzed, swaddled by cold earth. There was pressure against every inch of his body, a feeling of encasement, like an insect trapped in amber. None of his limbs seemed to work, nor was he able to twist his torso. After several exerted attempts, he finally could move his arm slightly. Gripping his fingers he could feel the texture of the dirt that held him. My God—I'm buried alive, he thought. He tried to cry out, but was silenced by dry earth that tumbled in and filled his mouth. He forced his arm upward with all of his strength, the loose dirt poured into the empty spaces where his arm once was. Finally he was able to wiggle his fingers; they were free and touching air. He struggled with his hands to work the layers of weighted soil away from his body. He managed to get most of the dirt off of his chest and from around his head, while his lower body remained buried. After clearing off his face and expelling the dirt from his mouth, he opened his eyes to darkness and gasped for air. His mind told him that he needed to breathe, and that the air would bring him back to life, but he was unable. His chest heaved and his mouth remained open attempting to draw breath, but nothing happened. Within the dim light he witnessed the movement of his arms and hands.

"I'm alive," he thought.

He pushed aside some of the dirt over his legs and managed to get free.

There were several slivers of light coming from above. He tried to stand, only to be forced back onto his knees by the low ceiling. What is this place, he thought, and how did I get here?

He heard footsteps above him, prompting him to cry out, "Help me—I'm down here."

There was no indication that the person above him heard his plea. He pounded his fists upward and without thought of the surface above him. His knuckles made a dull thud as they hit against a wooden surface. He paused to listen for any reply, instead he heard steps moving away. He hammered his fists upward several times more, only to stab his hand on a downward exposed nail. The pain shot up through his arm and seemed to sit on his shoulder. He could feel wet beads descend down his forearm. He drew his arm across his chest and cried out again for help, but only silence was returned. His hand pulsated with ever-increasing pain.

Herb cried out a final time, jarring himself awake, his one arm cradled across his chest. The moonlight lit swaths across the room from the windows. Before Herb could recover from his nightmare, a shadowy figure emerged from the dark corner of the room, and moved to the end of the couch at Herb's feet.

"Only one man in this house," a slow, whispered voice came from the darkness.

"Lester?" Herb muttered.

The figure stepped forward and Herb fell from the couch. He moved onto his back and rose up on his elbows, then fixed his gaze on the ghost.

"Lester?" Herb pleaded again for some confirmation. As the figure moved closer, Herb could see that the man was bare-chested, and the smell—he smelled of a muddy ditch full of wet, decaying leaves.

"Lester, it's you—you're alive?" Herb cried out.

"Leave this house, fornicator," came a dark, demanding voice, projected forth by this thing appearing to be Lester White.

Herb rolled forward and attempted to get to his feet, but Lester's hands were already around Herb's neck, thrusting him upward and driving him into the wall. Lester's grip was cool, wet, and unyielding. Herb was unable to speak; he just stared into Lester's eyes—empty, dead eyes—then the darkness came.

Sunlight came from the kitchen, projected into the living room, and fell across Herb's lap. He awoke on the floor, seated against the wall. He touched his neck, which was tender, and tried to speak.

"Lester, what's become of you?" His words were reedy and strained.

Looking around the room there was no evidence that Lester had even been there last night, but the pain in Herb's neck said otherwise. He stood, moving slowly, and worked his way down the hall to the bathroom. Gruesome red bands circled his neck.

He could make out the shapes of palms and fingers; he was physically marked with a warning.

The white of his left eye was now mostly red, filled with blood. Where the hell has Lester been all this time and why did he attack me? he thought as he worked the faucet. He splashed water on his face in an attempt to revive himself and bring clarity to his thoughts. When he walked into the kitchen he noticed the sink cabinet doors were ajar. Looking inside, the boards he had nailed in place were now just lying on the dirt floor of the crawl space. He knew well that no animal, at least not of the four-legged variety, could have pried all of that wood loose. He stepped outside and inspected the crawl space. The animal trap was empty. From his angle near the opening, he could see that the dirt was disturbed near where the boards lay. He secured the doors as best he could and drove off to his place.

Herb heard the phone ring from inside his garage and hurried to the house to get it. A nurse from Dr. McGee's office called to ask if he could take Marion home. He told her that he would be over before noon.

When Herb arrived at the clinic, Marion was already dressed and sitting in the waiting room.

"How you feeling? Hungry?" he asked.

"Better, and yes, I could eat a horse," she said.

After a quick lunch, they sat in the Denny's parking lot and Herb told her about finding Lester's shirt in the backyard, as well as being attacked by him in her living room. She was amazed and frightened by both confessions. He demanded that she stay at his place tonight until they could figure things out.

"We need to find him and help him," she pleaded.

"Marion, he wanted to kill me. His eyes were vacant. He did looked like Lester, but—," he replied, unable to look her in the eye. "I've thought about calling the police," he added.

"If we tell them that he's come home, then he can't be listed as missing. Do you want him arrested for assaulting you?" she asked in an challenging tone.

"No, I suppose not, but I've never seen him get violent, and now he clearly doesn't want me in your house," he countered, wanting her to offer suggestions.

"Let me deal with him. I appreciate your concern, but you can take me home now," she said, crossing her arms, letting him know that there was to be no further discussion.

As he drove her home, he convinced her that he could at least fix the crawl space doors. She told him the rest could wait, which meant the hole under her kitchen sink would remain. Although he would need more wood to again seal the hole, he thought it strange that she was comfortable letting it go until later.

Early evening was approaching and he had just finished installing new hinges on both crawl space doors. They now aligned properly and were better than the old ones. She thanked him, as she was always grateful, but withheld any offer for him to stay for dinner. Tired, Herb put his tools in the back of his truck and headed home. He hoped that Marion knew what she was doing, and contemplated driving by later in the evening to check on her.

* * *

It was almost a quarter to ten in the evening and Herb was sitting at his kitchen table eating a microwave dinner. He shook his head thinking of Marion, and wondered what to think of Lester. "I couldn't even talk to him. Did he have some sort of mental breakdown?" Herb mumbled to himself. Not knowing if Lester could be a threat to Marion, Herb slammed his fist on the table and committed himself to driving over to the Whites'.

Marion lay in bed on top of the covers, in her summer nightgown. She dreamt of walking in a dark, undefined space, where every direction was the same. The floor felt like earthy clay under her bare feet. A distant voice called to her. Her eyelids opened in a trancelike state. Shadows played across the ceiling of her bedroom and parted to the corners of the room. The moonlight now revealed a dark figure pinned to the ceiling above her. She was unable to cry out or move, still swaddled within a dream state; all she could do was watch the figure descend toward her. As it got closer, she could see that it was Lester.

"Did you hear me calling you?" he asked in a sweet, seductive tone, one she never heard from her husband before.

He was a gentle man, but one not known for sweet words, the kind a secret lover would impart. Her body trembled as he floated just above her. A heavy chill stiffened her torso and limbs, like opening the door to bitter snow and wind. Her body remained frozen; not even her eyes moved as his cool, porcelain lips moved across her cheek.

The Whites' house was dark. Did Marion go to bed already? Herb wondered, as he sat in his truck parked just off from their front yard. Without looking, Herb touched the headless hickory axe handle sitting across the passenger seat. He hoped that he could avoid cracking open Lester's head, but at least he had something to defend himself with. He sat there for thirty minutes before he stepped out of his vehicle. He then closed the door just enough for the dome light to go out and the lock to engage. As he stood there for a moment and surveyed the yard, the moonlight provided enough illumination to confirm that no one was creeping about. He took a few steps into the yard to test his stealth, before making his way across the open span to the nearest tree. When he got to the second tree, he could finally see into the master bedroom. A dark figure lay over Marion. It moved strangely, almost floating over her, while her body remained motionless. Herb's breath went out of him at the vision, and his knuckles turned white as he held the axe handle, not knowing if Marion was alive.

Being careful not to be seen, Herb hurried around to the back of the house to the kitchen door, which he was relieved to find unlocked. He paused just inside, holding the axe handle upward and ready for anything. As he crossed the kitchen, he noticed the sink cabinet doors were open. No one was in the living room, and he could see Marion's bedroom door was open at the end of the hall. He hurried as quickly as he could without giving away his presence and arrived at the bedroom doorway. Marion lay inside on top of the covers, exposed, as her nightgown had been torn down the middle and opened up across the bed. He could see her naked body in the moonlight, her arms were open and inviting; a splash of darkness near her neck and left shoulder stained the blanket. She did not move, just wore a vacant stare toward the ceiling.

The rest of the room was dark and without movement. He swiveled smoothly like a deer hunter, not wanting to spook his game. The living room was also dark. A grave stillness seemed to fall over the entire home. He crept up alongside Marion's bed, touched her arm, and whispered, "Marion?" She remained motionless and there was a chill to her body that made Herb tense. He touched her cheek. "Marion?" Her eyes remained vacant and transfixed toward the ceiling. Inspecting the wet area near her head, he found it was sticky, and had little doubt that it was her blood. Herb pulled the sheet over her body, but did not cover her face. He needed to believe that she was still alive.

Before he could open his mouth to let out a sigh of grief, he felt a cold iron grip on his shoulder and then a second on his neck, lifting him. He was thrown into the corner of the room, propelled as if tossed from a moving vehicle. His body smashed into Marion's wooden rocking chair, busting it into pieces. He lay barely conscious, first facing the wall, then rolling onto his back. His ribs ignited with pain, and he could feel the debris from the chair poking upward into his flesh. With eyes half open he could see the dark figure of Lester on the other side of the bed. Herb trembled and fumbled his hand on the floor, feeling for the axe handle. The shadowy figure did not move. Herb rolled onto his hands and knees, only looking down briefly to grasp the axe handle, then using it to help him to his feet.

Lester moved almost dreamlike around the bed. As he came closer, Herb swung with all his might, intending to take Lester's head off if he could. But his best efforts were easily thwarted as

Lester caught the axe handle, and with his other hand began to crush Herb's shoulder. Herb cried out in pain, his clavicle feeling like it would snap in half any second; his knees gave out and he went to the floor. As he looked up at Lester all he could see were black pools of infinite darkness where his eyes used to be.

"You're not coming with us," he told Herb in a dry, forced whisper.

Herb released the axe handle, and as Lester tossed it aside, he reached for anything on the floor to use as a weapon. Finding part of the broken chair leg he thrust it upward as Lester descended upon him. The splintered wood impaled him. Lester stepped back, bringing his hands to his chest, and looked down at the foreign object projecting from it. Herb braced himself against the wall and managed to get to his feet, he then lunged toward Lester. He grasped the end of the broken chair leg and drove it deeper into Lester's chest. It went in like a stick into dead leaves and swamp muck. Both fell to the floor, but Herb rushed to get on his elbows and push away from Lester's grasp.

Herb sat up against the wall and watched as Lester curled into a fetal position. His darkened mass slowly slipped under the bed, like a dying animal crawling for shelter. When it finally ceased to move, Herb's chest heaved as he tried to catch his breath and comprehend what had happened. Marion lay dead and he could have joined her, but that was little comfort for killing another man; that is if Lester still was one. It seemed like hours passed as he sat against the wall, his body stiff and achy. The stress and exhaustion overtook him and he passed out.

* * *

Herb awoke; the sunlight that poured in from the bedroom window was blinding. He rolled onto his hands and knees and pushed up, bracing against the wall. Standing there, he felt like he had just climbed from a car wreck. With the severe light no longer in his eyes, he looked upon an empty bed. Marion's body was gone. The blood-stained sheets were all that remained. Herb stumbled forward, grabbing the corner bedpost to keep from falling. On the floor were Lester's shoes and pants, but no body. He knelt down to pick up the pants; ash poured from the legs, and the shoes were filled with ash as well. Herb felt that he was losing his mind. He stood and made his way to the bathroom. Splashing water on his face, he winced at the cut across his forehead, and was confounded as to what to do next. Would the police believe him? He just knew that he had to get out of there.

Driving back to his place, Herb wondered what Lester meant by him not coming with them. Where the hell did they go? he thought. After looking into Lester's eyes, perhaps it was Hell. He pulled into his driveway and lumbered into the house. After a hot shower and a cup of coffee, he sat in the kitchen to think. Not convinced of what he saw this morning, he decided to return. He went to his closet and retrieved his Remington 308. Although he had not hunted for years, he still kept the rifle in good working order. He took five rounds from the box, loaded four into the internal magazine and one in the breach, thumbed the safety on, and put three more rounds in his left pocket.

After sitting on the couch for an hour and a half, trying to regain his wits, he picked up the rifle leaning against the armrest and thought, okay, you can do this.

* * *

He parked away from the Whites' house as he had done the night before. The loaded rifle sat across his front seat, an upgrade from the axe handle, neither of which he ever wanted to use against another human being, but now things had gotten so far out of hand, he was left with little choice.

After entering through the kitchen door, he stood silently listening for anyone or anything. He noticed the sink cabinet doors were closed, but failed to recall if they were when he left earlier. The house was silent with a dead stillness. He looked down at Lester's old muddy shirt; it remained where he had left it prior to taking Marion to the clinic. Now he wondered if he should have just taken it to the police. Could they have saved her? he wondered.

He crossed the kitchen and through the living room. An eerie feeling came over him—was this what criminals felt when they returned to the scene of the crime? The room was as he left it, Lester's pants and shoes still on the floor, the bed with the large bloodstain, now dried into the blanket and sheets. In the corner was the broken rocking chair. Herb took a deep breath and braced himself in the doorway, trying to make sense of it all. He went to the couch and sat down, leaning the rifle against the armrest, his shoulder and back still sore with pain. He closed his eyes and tried to rest his thoughts.

Herb could hear a soft, distant voice calling his name. It had a sweet, childlike, singing quality. He opened his eyes, but the room was dark. Reaching for the table lamp, which was no longer there, brought him out of his haze. He was still in the Whites' house—how long had he slept? he thought. Leaning to the opposite side, he found the lamp; it barely lit the end of the couch.

"Herbert," a soft whisper came from the kitchen. A silhouette filled the doorway.

"You came back for me. I knew that you cared." The soft, feminine voice caressed him like a warm breeze.

"Mare—rion," Herb could hardly speak her name.

She entered the room, stepping slowly towards him, her naked body moved fluid and dreamlike. The gray in her hair was all but gone, her flesh appeared full and firm; he had not seen her look this good in years.

"Marion, you're alive." His statement sounded more like a question.

He sat in amazement, pinned to the couch. She leaned over him and watched his eyes follow her neckline to her breasts.

"Do you want this body?" she asked as she drew her leg over his, half straddling him. He just stared at her with an open mouth.

"I have so many things to show you," she told him.

She raised her head, brushing her hair against his face. Her eyes opened to blackened pools of infinite darkness. Herb drew back, pressing hard into the couch. He put his hands on her hips and tried to push her away, her soft lips opening to bare sharp, penetrating teeth, a devil's smile. Straddling him fully, before he could bring his hands upward, she embraced him, her cool lips against his cheek.

"Take me, Herbert. I know how much you long for me," she whispered into his ear.

"God help me," he cried out and with all his strength he threw her to the side. She landed on the couch next to him and hid her face.

"You were supposed to take care of me. Don't you want to help me?" she questioned his commitment.

He stood, grabbed the rifle, and moved up against the wall.

"You're not right, Marion, I don't know how to help you," he pleaded.

"We could have been together and still can," she said, now rising from the couch.

Herb raised the barrel of the Remington 308 as she stepped toward him.

"Don't make me, Marion, I don't want to—"

He fired as she lunged for him and the round went through her, penetrating the wall beyond. The blast filled the space, and he could now only register her expression, but could not hear what she was saying. It was a look of sadness and dashed hope. She moved closer as he worked the bolt to chamber a second round. The barrel now sat between her breasts.

"Herbert, don't leave me alone, it's very dark here," she pleaded.

Her vacant eyes and the bloodless wound from where the round entered, only confirmed that this entity was no longer Marion. Herb pulled the trigger. The barrel jumped but again the blast did nothing. The only proof that he had fired the rifle were the holes he put in the back wall, and the ringing in his ears.

They struggled with the rifle; Marion managed to bring the stock up, hitting him in the head with the butt. Herb's knees folded and he slid down the wall fighting desperately not to black out. It was a feeble attempt.

Herb opened his eyes, expecting to see Marion over him, but instead found himself surrounded by darkness. He blinked his eyes several times to make sure they were indeed open. Cool, soft earth was against his back and he could feel loose dirt between his fingers. A jagged halo of light came from above. The tomb reminded him of his dream, which terrified him. He lay there for a moment, expecting to hear footsteps from above, but none came. As his eyes adjusted, the little light was enough to reveal his surroundings.

He was lying in the crawl space of the Whites' house. She must have dragged me here, he thought. His head swam as he sat up. He moved slowly, careful not to hit himself on the floor joists above. Crawling to the doors, he found the animal trap. It was still set, like a stupid joke told hours before, lingering in his mind. He moved it aside and pushed against the doors, which only flexed slightly. Sliding on his back he kicked both feet against one of the hinges. After several attempts the screws gave some, but did not break free.

"Dammit Herb, the only animal you successfully trapped was yourself," he said in an exhausted tone.

He crawled under the hole. Looking up, sizing the opening, he considered the alternate escape route. He sat down to rest and take in his situation. Dirt was piled up in the darkest corner of the crawl space. After a moment he moved to inspect the mound. His hands sunk into the loose soil; something was buried there. Brushing away the dirt he saw it was a woman's leg. He removed more of the burial, revealing her shoulders and head. "Marion," he gasped. He started to weep, but his sadness quickly turned to dread as her body started to move. His heels dug into the earth and he crawled backwards to the hole, not taking his eyes off of her. It would be a tight fit; standing brought his head and shoulders through the hole.

He pushed the sink cabinet doors open, which brought in more light and a strange view of Marion's kitchen, perhaps seeing what her cleaning supplies might have seen when she opened the doors. Struggling to push up on his elbows, he could feel the raw, splintered edges of the hole. His weight seemed to double causing him to sink back into the hole only to be caught and held under his armpits. His legs felt bound. He tried to push off with his feet, but was pulled downward into the hole and landed hard on his ass. Marion held him by the ankle, her dirty naked body looked like an exhumed corpse. He kicked his leg to try to break free of her hold on him, and her hand and forearm started to smolder. She drew her hand back, cradling her arm against her chest. The light from above separated them. The illuminated barrier seemed to keep her at bay.

"I won't let you leave; you belong to me," she spoke in a dry, reedy voice.

Herb lunged toward the crawl space doors and began kicking them again. Marion watched him for a moment, considering his attempts futile. After several forceful blows the hinge he loosened earlier broke free. A blade of light penetrated the dark space. As he went to the next hinge, he saw her move from the corner of his vision. Her body moved fluidly, swimming within the shadows, across the ceiling. He kicked with all his might, with the last blow he felt movement under his boot. She was now over him, clawing at his neck and shoulders; he drew his hands up in a defensive posture. Her nails dug into his flesh, baring her teeth she bit into his forearm. Thin streams of blood ran up his arm.

He cried out but continued to kick the doors, the second hinge broke free, a swath of light fell immediately on them. She screamed as her skin smoked and her hair caught fire. As she tried to crawl back into the darkness, Herb grabbed her around the waist and pulled her to him. He turned his head away as her body smoldered, then turned to ash. Her remains fell through his arms like dry autumn leaves.

Herb wondered what evil had consumed this house and its owners. He wanted to burn it to the ground, but instead swung the broken door open, climbed out into the daylight and drove home.

CLOSET MONSTER

Jeremy pulled the blankets up to his eyes and fixed an unblinking gaze on the bedroom closet door. The hood lamp of his small five-gallon aquarium dimly lit the room. Two gold cichlids hid in the bottom corner, leaving only the soft narrow stream of bubbles trailing upward to give life to the watery microcosm.

The bottom third of the door to the right of the fish tank was visible, that and a small portion of the floor was lit like a tiny stage waiting for the presence of performers. The remainder of the room was dark and would give any audience held breaths of anticipation.

It had been two years without any disturbances. Two whole years of peace, but guarded sanity, Jeremy counted. Last night came the distant sound of talons drawn across rough wood. He envisioned spiral wood shavings being carved out and spun up from sharp points. Rough wood not easily yielding, now accepting the new patterns across its back. Within the walls of his bedroom, Jeremy imagined a dark beast circling, like a large wild cat, only he was inside the cage and the beast was peering in.

Hollow rustling within the walls, movements stopping and starting, taunting him to cry out. Around the wall to the darkened corner of his room, his eyes shot in the direction, but no light fell there. He knew his little red chair was there along with his stuffed monkey Tony. Both sat there in the hellish dark along with the beast. The dreaded silence created voices in his head, he could hear the inanimate objects pleading for their lives.

His focus was broken by the sound of the closet doorknob as it turned. His eyes first shot back and forth between the two before becoming tightly fixed on the knob. The knob plunger now fully retracted allowing the door to move forward. It moved seemingly millimeters at a time, but grew gigantic within his vision.

The edge of the door caught the light as it opened, sharp black talons curled around the edge, points digging into the paint and wood. Eyes peered outward into his eyes. They were golden and illuminated like a wild animal seen at night with a flashlight. Jeremy's grip on the blanket shook uncontrollably, lowered to reveal an open mouth unable to speak or scream. His eyes filled with tears and an expression of impending doom came over his face. A great vulture-like beak with rows of small black sharp teeth came forth slowly out of the shadows, breaking the envelope between light and dark. The smell of rotten flesh reached Jeremy's nostrils. He retched as he had two years ago, when he and Jimmy MacDonald found a corpse of a deer, blackened and ripe as it lay in the July sun.

A blade of light appeared under the door to the hallway, soft footfalls approached and the door opened. The hall light burst into the room. He turned toward the half open doorway, and his mother stood there.

"Sorry honey, I didn't mean to frighten you," she said.

His expression was the result of a far greater terror. His eyes returned to the closet door, but it was closed.

"There's a monster in the closet," he cried out, now finding his voice.

She opened the door further and looked around.

"Oh Jeremy, I thought you outgrew that; are you sure you just didn't have a nightmare?"

Frustrated but compassionate, Mrs. Wheeler inspected the closet and calmed him down. She hoped that their last move, almost two years ago, would have cured her son of his night terrors. This night she left the hall door open and the light on.

Marc Fenton, the playground bully, was making his rounds collecting protection money. It was a daily routine and the service provided would generally guarantee that he wouldn't pummel you that day. No matter how much lunch money was given, there was no certainty whether his services would include the next day, and definitely not the entire week.

"Alright, Jeremy, let's have it," Marc calmly demanded.

Being two grades above Jeremy, really three since he had been held back, Marc was not to be disappointed.

Jeremy shook his head. "I only have fifty cents; my mom packed my lunch."

"I'll do you a solid, let's have it and you'll be covered," Marc promised.

Jeremy handed him the two quarters, only to receive a punch in the shoulder, and then in the thigh.

"Hey, look at his leg wobble, I bet I gave him a nice charlie horse." Marc laughed and looked around to make sure everyone else was also laughing.

"Your lousy fifty cents only means I don't break your face open, got it!" Jeremy held his shoulder and nodded, trying to contain his tear-filled eyes until Marc moved on to his next customer.

Jeremy silently sat at the dinner table with his mom. His playground battle wounds hidden tonight due to Marc Fenton's generosity not to give him a black eye or fat lip, which occurred all too often. Being the child of a single parent, especially one with meager financial means, meant mostly packed lunches and little protection money.

The pains he suffered today paled compared to his fear of what might come to visit him again. The uncertainty of when, always loomed over him. It wasn't every night that the darkness came. It liked to play with him, an unknown cancer festering, then pouncing when his guard was down. Regardless of when his number was up, there were preparations to be made.

The battalion of 30 troops was lined up three rows deep awaiting instructions. Fire team bravo: infantrymen composed of riflemen, a couple of grenadiers and a single heavy machine gunner, were to be positioned at the forward left flank. The two flamethrowers and bazooka specialists would be on the right flank. Lining the windowsill ledge would be five snipers. Two tanks would sit atop the chest at the foot of the bed, along with a single half-track with mounted machine gun support. Tonight would test the most hardened of men; they were, after all, made of almost indestructible plastic. He had proved this point when he taped one of the snipers to a firecracker last summer. Only fire could deter these men from their mission. Although the intent was blurred between madness and silliness, fear made the ritual of placing the plastic army men a serious matter. The line must be held.

Three nights passed and the men held their posts, with the exception of the right flank, where they were often displaced due to Jeremy's mom's room inspections and laundry detail. As their commanding officer Jeremy was not weary, but anxious. He knew in his heart that the demon hunting him would not easily go away. After all, it had followed him to their new home.

Tonight, Friday night meant he could stay up a little later and sleep in on Saturday. With his homework out of the way the sky was the limit, at least for a seven-year-old. Mrs. Wheeler allowed him to watch the new *Transformers* movie, which finally made its way to network television. After that it was bath and bedtime.

Soaking in a sea of bubbles, his toy amphibious transport floated in front of him, empty.

"Captain, no men to transport tonight, they're all dug in at fixed posts, First Mate Jeremy Wheeler reporting, sir."

He stared at the plastic green craft, thinking of his men positioned in the bedroom waiting for the war to begin. Long empty feelings came back, memories of the days when his dad was stationed in Afghanistan. That empty feeling forever trailing, even when the army returned his father's body. He still expected him to come back, smiling with lots of hugs, the cycle of deployments and brief visits ceased, but was not accepted.

Jeremy wore his *Transformers* pajamas which gave him an extra level of protection; after all their armor was bullet-proof.

"*Bumblebee* is my favorite," his mom told him, sitting at his bedside.

"I like *Optimus Prime*, he's their leader," he replied in a soft voice, smiling.

He pointed to his chest where *Optimus Prime* was printed on his pajamas in a fighting stance. She just nodded and smiled, then kissed his forehead. "Sleep well."

"You too, mom … I love you."

The aquarium light cast caustic patterns across the faces of the green soldiers. All held eternal stony expressions, tonight even more so. Jeremy lay on his side in a semi-fetal position. The combination of the movie and warm bath had taken its toll.

Wood under intense pressure creaked and whined, and the closet door bulged from the force, pushing into the room. The handle plunger catching, metallic parts resisting, flexing the wood that held them. Jeremy tossed in his sleep, a nightmare dreamt, now real. He grabbed at his covers and kicked his feet until his body was wedged tightly against the headboard. Elbows digging deep into his ribs, his fists clenched the blankets up under his nose.

The doorknob plunger broke free and the door swung wide open, it banged against the small dresser and jostling the aquarium. The cichlids fled to the far end of the tank, in the direction of the wave that sloshed over the top.

Light from the aquarium now only illuminated the facing door. The darkened interior of the closet appeared like an endless void. Jeremy felt himself being pulled toward the closet. Pushing harder against the headboard of his bed, he strained trying not be drawn in, into the dark place where the beast was waiting.

Sharp black talons slid around the edge of the door frame, like something trying to climb out of a pit. The razor tips penetrating the wall as a second claw appeared at the top of the opening. The golden glowing eyes became slits of impatient anger that floated in a black sea of shadows.

Husky overlapping voices tormented Jeremy. "Hey, look at his leg wobble." … "Your son is a daydreamer and destined for academic failure." … "Your dad was a loser, he got killed by a kid wearing pajamas and flip-flops."

Jeremy covered his ears and cried out, "No!"

The only voice that filled his head was that of his dad's. "Take care of your mom when I'm away, be respectful, be a man."

With that he sat up in his bed and shouted, "I'm not afraid of you, I'm the man of this house."

He heard the sound of an enormous jaw snapping shut and the eyes and talons faded back into the darkness. The hallway door swung open and light poured in, along with his mother.

"What's going on?" she cried out.

She saw the closet door was wide open.

"I banished the monster," he said, crying as she held him.

Returning home that Sunday from church, Jeremy felt galvanized by Friday night's battle. He vowed to himself that he would stand up to Marc Fenton the coming Monday, even if it meant a bloody nose. That of course wouldn't be anything new, but this time he would at least hit back.

When Monday finally arrived, Marc had not been at school, which left Jeremy to return home relieved but also half disappointed.

"What are you moping about?" his mother asked.

"Oh nothing," he told her.

He watched cartoons while his mom put in a load of laundry in the basement washer. The afternoon news came on and before he could change the channel, there was Marc Fenton's picture next to the talking head of the news anchor.

"A Washtenaw boy, Marc Fenton, age ten, was brutally stabbed to death Sunday evening. His father, Joseph Fenton was arrested that same evening," the news lady said.

The local police chief now appeared on the screen.

"Mr. Fenton is not yet formally charged and no weapon has been found. He is being held for questioning."

The news anchor spoke over footage of the Fenton's home. "It appears whoever murdered the boy tried to hide his body in the bedroom closet. We hope to bring you more on this story in this evening's news."

SEVENTIES

I have forgotten my days. Is it Wednesday? Maybe Thursday? Do I have someplace special to be today? Maybe tomorrow? Just curious, I suppose, like a bored friend, calling everyone to see what they are up to. My skin itches, or at least feels like it does. I scratch my forearm, but the irritation feels deeper, like bugs crawling through my veins. I use to get winter dermatitis. The air outside feels dry; it is March after all—I think?

Tonight I have found myself sitting on a strange couch. It is a cream color with a floral print, which makes me want to puke. Thank God, my stomach is empty. Thank God? The question makes me feel like a kid who has missed the morning school bus, left wondering what to do. Should I return home to an empty house, empty because my parents are at work, or should I just remain standing at the bus stop, a sort of nowheresville. Ville? Mar-ga-rita-ville? Lost my shaker and salt? Why is it my own damn fault? These questions seem to come from nowhere.

The odd pictures in their frames, sitting on the fireplace mantle, break my train of thought. I remember now that my parents have been dead for years, but when did they die? Who are these people? The man has medium brown hair and a bushy mustache. Is it the

Seventies? The woman has long brown hair, darker than the man's. There is a boy in the foreground. They are all smiling. I squint at the picture, but they all still look like cutouts, one layer partially covering the other—man, woman, then boy.

I hear a puckering sound, followed by the delicate rattling of glass jars, then the light in the room where I'm sitting increases for a moment, then back to black. The sound of liquid filling a glass, and brief suggestions of silver against china come from the other room.

Bare feet scuff the floor. I watch the figure of a man cross the room. I can see him as clear as day. As day? It sounds distant, like a joke told, laughed at, long past, and replaced by more serious conversation. He walks passed me as they always do. He is a big man, probably the man in the picture on the mantle. He switches on the small table lamp, one that I'm sure is the least revolting at this time of the night. He turns, and there I am.

I am always curious as to what their expression might be. This one ... his mouth hangs open and he sucks in air, like he has been holding his breath. He does not have the mustache like in the picture—is it no longer the Seventies? His small sandwich plate drops to the floor, the triangle-shaped wedges of white bread separate and the cheese falls out. I don't know whether to laugh or help him pick it up. He keeps hold of his glass of milk.

He looks less terrified, and more like a boy who was caught masturbating while looking at his father's dirty magazines. His mouth starts to move, but rather than words he releases a yowl. It is odd coming from such a large man. He now looks like an oversized boy, standing there in his striped pajamas, glass of milk in hand. I rise. His expression changes.

This is the part I enjoy the least. I call it the frenzies. Like two magnets being drawn together, I am pulled toward this man. My body, no longer mine, moves by unseen puppet strings, driven by an unseen puppeteer. He throws his glass of milk at me, but it misses, flying by my right arm, bouncing off the ugly-ass couch and finally shattering on the hardwood floor.

He stands ready to fight, cocking back his right arm. At one point, I might have admired his determination to protect his home, family and maybe his own life—if he so considered it. Before he can throw his punch, we are together, like both sides of a heart, one pumping blood into the other. The only problem—nothing or no one—is pumping blood into him. Our embrace, which can last up to an hour, always feels like minutes. Each time it seems like a dream, like when I was a man ... a man? Oh yes, a man, those moments enjoying sex, one and then done. I never understood why such intense moments, so clear, became so clouded, then faded just as fast as they arrived. Each time I think of this, it reminds me of old British dramas, where a gentleman says, "Sorry old chap, I won't be staying long."

Around this time, I hear a few thuds on the wooden treads of the stairs, then quiet controlled footfalls, betrayed by creaky wood. Someone is coming down to have a look-see. She appears half behind the wall. This must be the Seventies guy's wife. After seeing his body at my feet—my feet? Is that what is dangling below my vision? I see limbs and a body as I look down, but I feel as attached to the Earth as a balloon held down by a street vendor, or a child. She sees that I see her, and disappears behind the wall, like a gopher that has spotted a hawk.

If I was given enough time with the man, the frenzies would have stayed away, but unfortunately I was denied. My misfortunate is passed onto her. She is only two steps on her way up the stairway to heaven, or rather safety, when I have her—dragging her down to my hell—thud, thud. She cries out like an animal in a trap, as her knees bludgeon the wooden stair treads. I have her by both ankles, legs open, like a human wheelbarrow. Just like a wheelbarrow in fact, she's damn hard to steer. We would not make a good team in a race, where one person has to run on their hands, while the other holds up their legs. I walk her backward into the adjacent dining room, and flip her up on the table, like a fishmonger at the market, trying to wrangle a large tuna. She kicks me in the face and chest, but I feel nothing, like watching someone boxing the camera on television. She looks passed me, mouth open, finding a greater terror. A young boy stands at the foot of the stairs. He must be her son. The son of Seventies? Sam? Is that his old man's name?

I kiss her neck and she becomes quiet. Crimson lines run from my lips down to her shoulder, disappearing under the folds of her night gown. Her body twitches, like she is having a bad dream.

"Are you having a bad dream, Dear?" I think to ask her.

Of course it is just a thought; I'm too busy to vocalize, or even care when the frenzies have a hold of me. These thoughts that enter seem like someone speaking to me, but often they are difficult to hear, or maybe I'm just being a bad student and not paying attention? The only thing that does make it to my desk is the sound of the boy's voice coming from the other room. His voice is sharp and erratic. He is speaking to someone, but who? There were only three … man, woman, then boy.

I finish. Her body is limp; even her bones seem to sag within my arms. She is now part of me, or part of her is inside me? Put whatever philosophical spin on it as you see fit. With the frenzies passed, I step into the living room. The young boy stands in the doorway at the opposite side of the room, a phone receiver in one hand. It has a cord, so he's tethered to the room, like an astronaut tethered to a spacecraft. He tries to fill the frame with his small body. I doubt he is trying to be heroic. Should I spare him?

Ah … decisions, decisions? Before I can make one, I hear the front door lock surrender, and the door swings wide and fast. Several probing beams of light float about the room. There is shouting behind me, which propels me forward. I hear thunder and several intense concentrated blows impact my back. I suppose the projectiles penetrated, but they feel dull, like when my cousin Tamara used to poke me with a wooden kitchen spoon. She hated me. I wish I could see her now—rip the long golden hair from her head—then she could join her Barbie dolls on the shelf. I am sure she is old now; time has most likely claimed that opportunity. Like all my thoughts, regardless of past emotions, they slip through my mind like passing clouds.

I charge the boy, and push him aside like he's a cardboard standup. His expression makes me smile. As I crash through the back door, I yell back at him in song, "It's a hard knock life for you! It's a hard knock life for you! …" Poor little orphan Andy, or whatever the kid's name is. I wonder if this is what it feels like to be a deadbeat dad. Feels like? One of those guys who walk out on their wife and kid, sucking the life out of those who remain. The thought leaves as quickly as it entered, zero calories, zero regrets. The bouncing beams of lights that follow me soon disappear, as I am lifted and embraced by the night, like billowing leaves caught in a whirlwind. I hum the good-night ditty from the Lawrence Welk show. I can almost hear the orchestra, almost … "Good night … good night … until we meet a—gain … ".

GROUND WAR

Recon Assault Elements, Third Generation Bryce Landers and Seventh Generation Christopher Telfer hid within the trees. As they looked out beyond the vast landscape of open green plains, the enemy's colossal war machine lumbered off in the distance, distorted by the mirage of heat waves. It would be at the colony's doorstep by the day's end.

Both soldiers shifted within the shadows of the trees. Their dark-armored, full-body exoskeletons held a rich sheen and glimmered like black oil. Their specialized lenses increased their field of vision to almost two hundred and forty degrees.

"Have you been to this colony before?" Landers asked.

"No, but it looks like any other small colony. Just another one created to extend the reach of the empire, from what I understand," Telfer responded with a tone of resentment.

"That's right, about three-hundred-plus gatherers with only a small defensive detail," Landers said.

"Hardly enough numbers for this suicide mission; we have taken much greater losses in other regions. Wouldn't you agree?"

Landers did not return Telfer's gaze but kept his eyes on the lumbering giant, its silhouette blending in with the farthest reaches of the horizon.

"You know our fighting creed is to never back down from a battle, no matter how bleak or senseless. I have lived countless sunrises and I'm doubtful that this mission will be the sunset of my existence, so steel yourself Telfer. We can not fail this colony, no matter how small."

Telfer returned his sights on the horizon and said nothing further. Landers imposed his will on Telfer mainly for the sake of his military position as his commanding officer. Regardless of the difference in rank or seniority, Telfer was Landers equal as a warrior. Both would fight to the end and greet death with joy.

After monitoring the distant movements of the enemy, Landers pointed to a dense area of vegetation and grouping of trees where they could engage the titan. Getting there would take a few hours and they had to make sure that their calculations would put them in precise proximity to make that connection. Information gathered from the ground was limited, so they needed to search the actual beast for weaknesses they could exploit.

Both had hoped for more support to handle this mission, but the empire's main stronghold was attacked just weeks ago and all personnel was stretched well beyond their individual capabilities. Sentry duty or escorting a food-gathering team held less appeal; here they at least had a clear fight.

A thunderous wave carried across the tops of the dense jungle. Telfer and Landers wove in and around outcroppings of mixed rock formations and thick vegetation, arriving at the waypoint ahead of schedule. They only had moments to further evaluate the situation. The ground vibrated and the sky darkened as the giant approached. Its shadow, similar to that cast by thick cloud cover, created a dark band over the grassy plain and subtle rolling landscape.

"There, check out the topmost section of the biological mass," Landers pointed and added, "see those two satellite-shaped forms on either side? I would wager they are helping to guide the cyborg beast; perhaps that whole section is some sort of command center."

"I hope you're right; if the whole thing isn't being controlled by that section and instead within the mechanical forward section, then we could be in trouble," Telfer said.

Landers stood for a moment in agreeable silence, then spoke. "Regardless, we need to do the most damage we can. I tried to convince the members of the new colony to evacuate if that thing reached a certain point, but they refused. Their grand plan is to take shelter within the deepest reaches of the caverns. Fools."

Telfer nodded in acknowledgment. They prepared themselves for first contact. Watching the mountainous cyborg's approach was like witnessing a tsunami make landfall.

The hurricane turbulence that came from the forward war-wrought machinery was deafening. Its metal-shelled shroud hovered over the landscape devouring all vegetation. If they were to survive a direct encounter, they would be left exposed, spotted, and dealt with. They were confounded by the technology that powered the destructive mechanism; a direct assault would be suicide.

"We need a good entry point," Landers shouted, pausing for suggestions.

"There." Telfer pointed. "There's an opening at the base of one of the two support legs or stanchions."

Landers agreed as they had no time to waste; the initial assault would hopefully buy them more time and give them more insight as to what they were dealing with. They positioned themselves to be in line with one of the biological stanchions before the thing made its pass. The sky darkened, as the shadow of the behemoth fell over them.

"Now," Landers shouted.

Both ascended the stanchion. A dark corridor led upward; they climbed with deliberation. The surface flexed beneath their feet; they surmised that the whole section was made of biological materials.

The soft, porous floor exuded sporadic streams of moisture, perhaps to cool the interior or overall workings. Fibrous, whip-like tentacles grew from the floor in random places.

Telfer called out in the darkness, "Maybe this is some sort of cooling tower?"

Landers pointed and replied, "Careful of those—they might be deadly or perhaps some sort of alarm system. So far I don't think we've been detected."

They agreed that they needed a more sensitive location to attack, one that would yield the most damage. Without further discussion they continued to climb the irregular corridor, weaving between the wiry tentacles. Both noticed the shifting ceiling height, which seemed to have no practical function, or at least none that they could discern. An archway opened ahead;

the intense light temporarily blinded them and slowed their approach. They cautiously peered outward. There was a gap that opened to the sky, then a wide entrance to another corridor. Once out in the open, they realized that they were halfway to the top. They raced to the upper corridor entrance trading stealth for speed.

A large probing device with five sensors swept the open space where they had just been. Connected to a large crane or structural appendage, it withdrew from view.

"Telfer, I think we should try to make it to the two satellite arrays. If we can take out one or both, that might be our best hope to slow or stop this thing," Landers said.

Telfer nodded in agreement and they both continued their ascent into the passages of the upper region. There they found no wiry tripwires or tentacles, but a greater amount of coolant ran down a central trench, almost in a waterfall. The floor was shiny and slick, slowing their progress.

"We're almost there—I can see an opening ahead," Landers said.

He turned but Telfer had disappeared. Peering down the passage, what now looked like a sheer drop down a narrow crevasse, he searched for Telfer. There was no sign of him. Landers controlled his urge to cry out for Telfer, for fear of compromising the mission and giving away his position. Telfer knew what was at stake and Landers had no time to search for him, he had to keep moving, so he continued his ascent toward the light. He hoped that Telfer survived the fall. All Recon Assault team members dreamt of dying in battle; losing one's life outside of combat was unthinkable.

* * *

The upper corridor opened to the sky; one of the lateral satellite arrays came into view. At this height of the biological mass, the floor vibrations were much more intense. Landers was mystified as to how the giant remained upright with such structural instability. The incredible struts that connected the biological to the mechanical were perhaps the key. Without any clear ideas of how to destroy the link between the two, he opted for an initial strike on the satellite array.

Landers made a quick, direct line from the cover of the upper corridor opening to the base of the array. More fluids coated the floor, making it difficult to move with any great speed. He cared little about being stealthy, especially out in the open; getting to safe cover was paramount.

The array, composed of living materials, was a bizarre funnel-shaped growth with a small shaft running down the lower portion. It descended into unknown darkness. From their ground-level analysis, their best guess was that both lateral arrays were for communications and possibly radar, but now he had doubts.

He had made it to the base of the array just as the sweeping probe returned to make a pass across the opening. Pressing his body flat against the wet surface, he held fast for fear of slipping into the probe's path. Unsure what might happen, being taken prisoner or maybe even instant death entered his thoughts. The probe passed without incident; time was running short, so he risked placing his clamp at the base of the array. The sharp, serrated blades attached to his headgear bit into the fleshy mass then the destructive chemicals were injected.

The entire beast came to a halt; the upper region swiveled wildly. He kept the clamp in place, trying to deliver as much of the toxins as possible. Suddenly his body was hammered by the probe, pain was everywhere, his lower left leg was crushed, possibly broken. Before the probe could strike him again, he released the clamp and leapt for the upper corridor entrance. Using the slippery surface as well as the heavy swaying motion of the beast, he was thrown into the opening. He landed directly on Telfer, who had been trying desperately to make his way back up.

"You beautiful son-of-a-bitch, you're alive," Landers said as they both steadied themselves.

"Can't let you have all the fun. On my tumble down, I think I found a good spot to place my ordnance. I got thinking about the coolant streams coming from the surface. That might help to distribute the chemicals. Not exactly a bloodstream, but might have a similar effect," Telfer said.

"I'm out, so that works for me, let's do it," Landers said.

They descended the center corridor in haste, almost half falling, disregarding their safety for another attack. After they reached a position where liquid was streaming heavily, Telfer injected his chemicals into the slimy biological surface. The floor shook even greater than before, knocking both soldiers from their feet.

Before they could stand, the probe had ahold of them; it had made its way from the bottom passage upward to their position, undetected. As they were drawn out into the sunlight, the white light blinded them. Expecting to be crushed and quickly disposed of, instead they were released into the air, bodies tumbling and falling. The cyborg's heavy machinery had already taken most of the green plant life and left them with a barren dirt floor to greet them. Only the blunt stumps of vegetation remained. As his vision faded, Landers could see the giant stagger and move erratically.

The ground shook, dust rose, and the sky went dark. Before they could know the effectiveness of their attack, they were pinned to the earth by a sudden, overwhelming force. Telfer thought his armor should hold, at least for a while. Landers's fate was unknown and communication was down.

Light slowly filtered in around the dark mass. He crawled within the newly created trench, among symbolic ruins, to find Landers held within a star shaped pit, his body crushed. There was no movement, sound or breath—Landers was dead.

The sky darkened once more, and he feared his movement had caused unwanted attention. As he glanced toward the sky, the shadowy mass descended. He could see the star-shaped weapon and knew he could not defeat it. A final acknowledgement, a piece of intel he would never be able to impart, below the star-shaped hammer were symbols, characters in an unknown language ... *Converse All Star*, but to him no translation was needed; it simply meant doom.

Tommy Sanders lifted his shoe to examine the two large ants he had crushed, imagining them as two bullies from school, Chris Telfer and Bryce Landers. At the edge of the lawn, his father's mower made a dull thumping noise. The sound of blades being bogged down by dirt and debris. He saw a large anthill that his father had mowed over, the upper two-thirds decapitated. The flat surface was animated with a flurry of dark specs, ants fleeing in every direction.

KING OF THE ROAD

I-75 was murder as usual, another beautiful sun drenched standstill, miles of four-lane parking lot. Entrances and exits flowed to and from the expressway like veins to an artery. Its bloodstream gorged with frustration, impatience, and high-pressure rage. Jerry McIntyre's Toyota Prius was just another blood cell within the system. Today's clot was caused by the fantastic phenomena known as rubbernecking, an irritation resulting from a red Ford F150 that smacked the behind of a gold Chevy Impala. The Chevy's trunk was completely crushed and pushed halfway into the back seat.

It's my God given right to stop my car and check out the carnage. Hey, got to see if mom or dad, or even baby sis, are in that twisted mess. Jerry thought of what absurd reasons one must have to justify having a look. His face was held tight, if someone were to slug him, his head would undoubtably shatter like glass.

"Come the fuck on," he muttered to himself.

Jerry ignored the wrecked cars on the shoulder and instead craned his neck to the side, as if he had the means to see ahead and give whoever was driving slow the evil eye. *And people wonder why they get shot at for their nonsense. There's always a cause and effect people! Live it, learn it!*

The wreck was absorbed in his rearview mirror by the reflection of the tightly packed parade of commuters. He was getting closer to the office, only three more exits. The only thing that held him up were the cars trying to exit on Fourteen Mile. *The nerve of some of these bastards, trying to cut in from the far left lane, to exit at the last minute.* Jerry kept his Prius close to the Civic in front of him. *Like hell, if I'm going to let you in. I bet they are the same folks that camp out in the post office the night before, sitting on the floor trying to fill in their tax forms before midnight. If I ran the post office they would close at the normal business hours. Live it, learn it!*

Turning into the parking lot, the struggle for life or death, the coliseum, the lions, the gladiators, were all behind him, at least until evening rush hour. *Martin Webber, that prick, was standing outside smoking as usual. What's wrong with having a cup of morning coffee like the rest of us?* Jerry often had the pleasure of walking through Martin's toxic cloud, just another one of his daily gauntlets. *Never mind my health, as long as you're happily pumping out more smoke than a factory.*

"Morning Martin," he said before reaching him, with hopes that he would put out that tumor stick before he got closer.

"Hey, morning Jerry. Think you'll have those sales jackets ready for this afternoon's meeting?"

"Sure, anything for you," Jerry said, offering a brief smile and quickly slipping into the building, Martin's cloud followed him in.

Although it was a slow intravenous drip getting there, he was early by twenty minutes. Coming in late was not an option, especially since he was the Director of Print Operations. A hard earned title, but one which garnered little respect; Director of Clown Operations would have been more accurate. Jack Tanner,

CEO, always said, "It's the presentation people. Get it right." As far as Jerry was concerned, his department was an integral part of the company's success. Print Operations handled design, printing and assembly of all presentation materials from marketing and sales to even the company's annual report. *Booyah! Our shit don't stink, right?*

He walked past the two large utility tables, the four large format color printers, the three design stations and into his small office. It was only a ten-by-ten foot square room with florescent lights, but it did have a door where he could shut out the insanity, unless it came over the phone. He was in good with the building manager, Dan Myers, who outfitted his department with daylight spectrum bulbs that were very easy on the eyes and allowed for the best color control. *It's who you know, not who you blow, get it with respect and don't be a reject.*

Sitting his messenger bag on top of the cabinet, he plopped into his Herman Miller Areon chair, another perk from building management. They had an extra ten chairs in storage with no warm asses to fill them. Only the boardroom and the exec's got them. *As long as Erika Werner kept her stupid cackling wormhole shut, they wouldn't take it away from him.*

Every Monday morning was a review of Friday's all so urgent requests. His phone's voicemail light pulsed like a heart monitor, a virtual waiting line. Sales and marketing always phoned in their requests, as if their verbal demands would rank any higher than an email marked high priority. Then again, high priority emails were all too common, and he had to prioritize them as well. Working closely with those who really mattered made it easier to turn away and filter out the bullshit. *Voicemail and email alike, a squire's cry would never be louder than a king's whisper. Remember that Tony Kahn, we don't print your kid's birthday shit here.*

Martin's voicemail from Friday, "Hey buddy, remember to bang out those sales jackets for Monday. I'll check again with you on Monday morning, have a great weekend." *Baby sitting motherfucker. Why do some people feel they have to micro-manage everyone else? Trust me to be a professional, and maybe, just maybe, I'll trust you to do the same.* Jerry pushes the phone's clear button with a smile, deleting Martin's message, "yeah maybe, or maybe not."

Gun-Woo Kim pushed through the door with his arms full, "Morning boss, yes boss, yes boss," he joked.

Pivoting his chair back, Jerry poked his head into view, "Hey Gundam, annyeong hashimnikka, my yellow brother." His personal nickname for Gun, based on the Japanese anime series and combined with the traditional Korean morning greeting, with a little hood flavor to boot.

"Morning Maguire, you complete me, or maybe it's Webber you complete," Gun said laughing.

"He stopped me to ask about the sales jackets. I told him to chill out, that number one fucky, Jerry McIntyre, had it under control." Their twisted affection for movie dialogue often sprinkled throughout their conversations. Today it was *Jerry Maguire* and *Full Metal Jacket*.

"You didn't really say that to Martin?" Jerry asked.

"Hell no, but I hope he can read my mind," and they both laughed.

"What's that?" Jerry asked, nodding his head at the stack of printouts Gun carried in.

"Another a-dumb-dumb to add to the sales jackets. I ran up to Nancy's office to get them," Gun said.

"Martin already has two addendums, anymore and he's going to ask us to print and assemble the batch over, what the hell is wrong with this guy?"

"Who knows, anyway I doubt it bro, he needs them just after lunch," Gun said with confidence. As Gun took the pile over to the production table, the rest of the department started filing in. The day pressed on. It was a long stiff neck sort of day, but everything got done in a timely manner and at the quality level that Jerry expected. Another triumph for the Print Operations department. Job done, case closed, who cared if Martin welched on buying them drinks or bringing in donuts, which was his typical modus operandi. Jerry often took his team out for pizza or sandwiches, which made up for any unfulfilled promises by the deadbeats that relied on his department. Feed the troops and they'll fight harder was his logic.

Jerry's Prius inched along on I-75. It was a typical evening rush hour, everyone just dying to get home: eat, shit, pray, sleep, (if you're lucky) fuck, and do it all before morning rush hour. A raised up, 20-inch chrome rimmed, Dodge Hemi, black pickup pushed its way into the right lane, Jerry's lane.

"Watch it asshole. Am I invisible? Think you're king shit with that big ass truck," Jerry's voice projected into the windshield.

He looked at the truck's license plate, as if that knowledge would bring any legal grounds to press charges. Then he saw it, bright as day, a huge chrome scrotum dangling from the truck's trailer hitch.

You have got to be kidding me, he thought. Wishing he could grab the truck by its shiny balls and make its obnoxious driver pay for his inconsiderate actions. Clenching his fist, he felt weight inside, like he was holding something, but it didn't seem to have any mass. He attempted to open his hand, but it held fast in an unyielding spasm. When he shook his fist, in attempts to relax his tendons and muscles, the truck ahead swerved violently. The driver struggled to hold the lane, and was forced off to the right shoulder. The tall imposing Dodge 4x4 still maintaining its speed, angled to slip back in front of Jerry's Prius.

"The least you could do is signal," Jerry grumbled under his breath.

He shook his fist again to the right and the truck again swung off the shoulder, this time rolling onto the grass and heading for the ditch. The driver quickly applied the brakes to control the vehicle.

After a moment, he looked in the rearview mirror, and saw that the truck was still sitting on the shoulder. Jerry's locked fist finally released—he expected something to fall out (perhaps he grabbed an object in the car during his fit of anger), but his palm was empty, the added weight was gone.

The traffic remained thick, and would stay that way even beyond Jerry's exit. More people were moving north, houses were cheaper, apartment rent was cheaper, life was cheaper, but the commute was a bitch; some folks sacrificed two hours or more each way. Jerry's was just over an hour and that was still too long for his taste. The only two things he could hope for were that the traffic flow remained constant, and that its speed was no lower than the posted minimum. Each passed exit was like aspirin that thinned the blood and improved the flow.

Arriving home, his door opened to a dark hall stretching to the living room, kitchen, then bedrooms. He flipped the hallway switch and dropped his car keys into the tray on the narrow table by the door. As he flipped through his mail he un-shouldered his messenger bag and placed it on the floor, next to one of the table legs.

He stood there for a moment holding his right forearm, working his fingers. The stiff tendons dragged through his hand like rusty springs that had lost their ability to stretch and bend. A hand cramp was very likely, he did after all pitch in with the assembly of the sales jackets for Martin.

Tired, he made his way through the condo, switching the lights on and heading to the kitchen to get dinner going. A late night frozen meal was all his remaining creativity could muster; that served up with a little TV, a quick shower and shuteye. At least he would get in the eat, sleep and prayer part. Maybe he would overcome his constipation and that in itself would get him lucky on Friday night.

That night he dreamt of being on the expressway, all traffic at a complete standstill. He raised his hands to his face, in a praying position, but instead of asking for God to forgive the sins of his fellow drivers, he quickly and forcibly opened his hands and pushed outward towards his sides.

With his arms held open like Moses parting the sea, the vehicles in front of him started to shake and move in a wavelike motion, bouncing on their shocks then lifting into the air, bobbing on an unseen surface like a child's bathtub toys. The invisible ripples grew larger, cars and trucks of all sizes were flowing, giving shape to ever growing tides. The panic stricken drivers were tossed and turned in their personal metal spaces, rising higher within the air.

The tidal waves that held all the vehicles in front of Jerry's Prius washed violently to both sides of the expressway, metal crashed, and cars rolled like heavy stones tossed upon one another. Jerry's car crept forward. He slipped through the wreckage and soon got to the minimum posted speed. He had little sympathy for anyone injured or deceased, for they were the enemy. They held no compassion for one another; they were mankind without the kind.

The new day brought lots of sunshine, which reflected harshly off the windows of the infinite rows of cars that preceded Jerry's Prius. They inched forward like a celebrity's funeral procession. A news helicopter hovered and no doubt made the correct traffic diagnosis of a clogged artery and soon to be heart attack victim. Their statement, much like a real physician's would be delivered in a solemn, emotionless tone, except to a wider audience tuned into the various AM stations. Jerry avoided listening to the morning news on his rush hour commutes. He was already committed to his route, hearing the traffic report made no sense to him, as it would only serve to raise his stress level.

It always seemed to Jerry that the politicians running the state held little, or no, interest in upgrading the roads to accommodate the ever growing volume of traffic. *Have them drive this stretch of road for a month during rush hour, and perhaps that would put things into perspective.* Being of the conservative persuasion, he felt that the people holding jobs and the businesses that employed them were the state's lifeblood. *Stopping the blood flow means stopping the heart, which would bring about a dead economy.* He hated all of the advertisement spending on tourism, as if the state were a troubled theme park with no one to ride the rides.

A loud metallic gurgling mixed with a heavy pounding bass came from two cars behind him. In his rearview mirror he could see a lightning blue Honda Civic zipping back and forth between both lanes, jockeying for a way through. It was a hatchback model; the owner had it lowered to accommodate thin walled performance tires and equipped it with an oversized, performance muffler. A once practical car, the hatchback space was now filled by an oversized bass speaker. All Jerry could hear was the loud thumping, until the gas was applied. *Was that supposed to be music?* With no melodic rhythm or rhyme, the sonic attack only imparted thunderous vibrations, which was testing his sanity, as well as the shatter resistance of the Prius's windows.

The intense cacophony grew overwhelming as the Honda slipped behind Jerry's Prius. A man close to Jerry's age was behind the wheel. *You should be old enough to know better.* He was sad and embarrassed to see someone his age acting like a fool. The driver seemed to relish the thought of being a punk, a bad boy, a rebel without a clue. Jerry thought that this guy's age appropriate compass was definitely broken. *You, my friend, have become the old guy that buys the beer for the under-aged partygoers, only to be laughed at behind your back, or worse pitied?*

The Honda's oversized muffler boomed a grating metallic gurgle. Jerry only saw a lightning blue blur in his rear view mirror, as the car zipped into the left lane, and pulled up along side of him. His windows vibrated violently, he was surprised they were able to sustain the sonic attack. Another sudden blast of the Honda's muffler followed as the Honda almost rear-ended the minivan in front of him, barely slipping into the narrow space in front of Jerry. Now at the business end of the Honda's muffler, a loud churning of angry bees seemed to be emanating from the chrome tipped exhaust pipe. *This guy is going to hurt someone, or at the very least wreck someone's car and hold everyone up.*

The driver decided to make a break for an open space three car lengths ahead. The Honda bolted onto the shoulder and launched forward as the space was closing from two car lengths down to one, and if he didn't make it he would either have to keep riding the shoulder, or stop and accept that he was a jerk and allow everyone to jeer, shaking clenched fists at him. *No, this guy was going to avoid responsibility, and probably just didn't give a shit.* He zipped ahead and barely made the cut which forced the cars that followed to brake hard to avoid hitting him. That gave him confidence to try it again and see how much more ground he could cover. The Honda moved from side to side within the lane, as the anxious driver prepared another jump ahead. An overpass was approaching, so it was now or never.

Jerry could see the blue Honda zip out onto the shoulder, as his eyebrows furrowed and his jaw tightened at the driver's utter audacity. His fist shook, his forearm muscles and tendons tightened, and his bicep flexed to hold up an unseen weight. The lightning blue Honda's speed increased exponentially. It swerved trying to make the opening, but missed. The car veered away, speed still increasing, as Jerry's hand continued to convulse. The Honda's brake lights flashed as the driver stomped the break pedal. It was like watching a movie without the sound, no *Wilhelm Scream*, just the vision of the car plowing forward into the guardrail abutment. The back end of the car lifted off the ground, still trying to continue forward, unaware that the front had stopped.

Jerry's hand finally relaxed, this time obeying his mind's command. His palm felt as if he had been holding something warm, like a hot coffee cup, and the tendons were unbelievably strained. Moving his fingers took some effort.

A man in a Wilson's Carpet van pulled behind the wreck. He was at the Honda's driver's side window, hunched down like a hear-no-evil monkey, one hand covering one ear, the other hand cupping a cellphone to the other ear. Traffic slowed to accommodate the blood lust, which proved to disappoint those eager to witness a life or death human experience. No external injuries to the driver were visible, but the damages to the vehicle lead one to believe there were certainly internal ones. Jerry's rule about rubbernecking still held; he didn't bother looking at the wrecked Honda, but rather minded the road in front of him for any shattered glass that might have spilled out across the lane. His only acknowledgement as he passed was his mantra quietly slipping through his thoughts, *Live It, Learn It.*

During the rest of the drive to the office, he kept looking at his hand, at the very least wondering if it would be functional to make it through the work day.

Jerry had Gun run the department while he stayed in his office with the door closed. As he returned a few calls and read some of his email, he examined his hand. Part of him thought he was crazy to believe that he caused the morning accident. *That guy was totally out of control, putting people's lives at risk by darting in and out of the lane and riding on the shoulder. People like that deserve what they get.* His love for science fiction made him want to believe that he was given some gift to right the wrongs of the world. *Was that just wishful bullshit? Isn't that why they tack on the word 'fiction'?*

Today was a slow workday, so Gun and Jerry took a leisurely lunch at the local diner.

"Do you believe in ESP, telekinesis, and all that stuff?" Jerry asked Gun.

"I've seen police departments use psychics before, and with some success, so yeah I guess so, but just ESP," Gun answered and added, "are you talking about shit like Stephen King's *Firestarter?*"

"No, hell no. Well, maybe a little, something smaller scale. Do you think you have to be born with something like that, or can it be developed somehow?"

"Dude, I think you have to be born with it, so sorry man, you're not going to rise up like *Magneto* and start tossing heavy objects around."

Gun had been looking out the window. He expected a smart-ass reply, but instead he noticed Jerry staring at him in deep contemplation.

"Hey, are you in there? Why are you asking about that stuff anyway?" Gun asked.

"I don't know. There was this accident this morning and … I felt like I had something to do with it."

"Are you kidding me? You with your Earth friendly Prius, tagged with a collage of peace symbols, tree hugging, and save the wildlife crap."

Jerry laughed awkwardly, a little embarrassed that he brought up the subject. The food arrived and they switched the topic.

That evening while he drove home, he kept looking at his hand. Although he could grip the wheel, his tendons still felt like piano wires stretched to the point of their tensile limits. Any further stress might easily snap them, sending them whiplashing in both directions. He imagined his tendons and forearm muscles were strung like a tripwire set to pull the pin on a grenade. The mechanism seemed unstable and rigged with uncertainty.

He approached a black Saab; it was Martin's car. He slowed to leave distance between both vehicles. He wanted to avoid being spotted and being obliged to put on any friendly office coworker airs. *That is, look, smile, and wave diplomatically at the disorganized, over paid bastard, who always needs his projects done the same day.* Jerry had a sudden urge to confirm the impossible. Clenching his already tight hand into a fist, he concentrated on the Saab. It began to slow, and he noticed that Martin turned on his hazard lights and rolled onto the shoulder. *Bingo.* He passed Martin's stalled out Saab with a warm smile and only looked in his rearview mirror after he had a little distance. Martin stayed in the car and was no doubt on his cellphone calling AAA for roadside assistance.

Jerry looked at his knotted up hand, his fist and fingers were unresponsive. It would take deeper concentration to get his hand to open. One thing he did recall from the few yoga classes he attended at Bally's, was that he needed to be more meditative, to slow and control his breathing, and then clear his mind. *Namaste.*

At home Jerry lay in a warm tub of water, with only his knees and head exposed. His lower right arm felt the warmth seeping into his muscles. The bath was unplanned, a treat he seldom indulged, he'd guessed that the last one was over two years ago.

As he relaxed, he allowed the warm bath to let his mind wander. He examined the few objects he had around the edge of the tub. Focusing on the bottle of Nivea body wash he attempted to move it with his thoughts. A car was huge by comparison, moving the bottle should be easy, but nothing happened. He should be able to at least make it stir. With his current level of concentration he expected it to shoot across the room or levitate in front of him. Still nothing. Maybe it needed to be metal, he thought. Looking around the room his eyes spotted his shaving razor; he had one with a metal handle that took double edge razor blades. The steaming bathroom was dead silent except for the subtle sound of him moving and clenching his fist under the water as he focused on the razor. After several attempts he gave up, the razor remained undisturbed on the narrow glass shelf below the vanity mirror.

Hump Day, Wednesday, halfway through the week, another bright sunny morning. The weather would have normally lifted his spirits some, but he was getting low on groceries and had nothing to eat for breakfast. He considered stopping somewhere closer to work for coffee and a donut, but stopping now might make him late; the traffic was too unpredictable to pick up something before hitting the expressway.

The commute from Wednesday through Friday was usually the worst. People were more aggressive knowing that the weekend was coming and somehow that translated into racing to some imaginary finish line. *That's right bitches, drive as fast as you like, but don't be surprised if you end up meeting Jesus, or if you're lucky, the police.* Jerry had doubts about the latter, and sometimes wished for the former. Wishes aside, he wanted to live to see the weekend, and refused to partake in the madness. *Idiots, don't you know, haste makes waste?*

A Mercedes was closing in fast from the on-ramp. *Good driving manners states that you should signal while entering or exiting the expressway. Sure, drivers already on the expressway knew that others would be joining them. However, it was a courtesy thing, a polite asking if someone might slow to allow them on.* No signal came from the Mercedes; instead, it just pushed its way into traffic. *One more friendly token of civilized man flicked down the well of selfishness.*

Jerry's fingers twitched and curled, and the Mercedes lurched forward connecting with the blue Suburban in front of it. Both vehicles moved onto the shoulder. As he passed the accident he did glance just briefly, noticing the Mercedes's hood and front end were crumpled pretty good, as it sat lower than the larger Chevy Suburban. From his rearview mirror he saw the driver of the Mercedes was a stumpy round man in a dark charcoal suit. The man was well animated, yelling and pointing his finger at the younger man who was driving the Suburban, as if it was his fault. *Perhaps he should sue the city for building the sidewalk too close to his ass.* Jerry wondered why most drivers of expensive cars acted like assholes. They were society's self privileged, self important, and self absorbed. They would use their money and power to dodge responsibility, he thought, shaking his head. Those kind of people never learn, unless they get caught and end up in jail for insider trading, company embezzlement, consumer fraud, or whatever they happen to stub their toes on.

The arthritic tension in Jerry's hand kept his fingers curled like a dead spider's legs. With his fingers gnarled back, he rested his palm on the car's shift lever to take the weight off his arm and give his hand some relief.

Almost half way to work his hunger combined with the aggressive driving of his fellow commuters made him feel even more desperate and angry. His limits were reached when a young woman in an older drab green Hyundai Accent almost side-swiped him.

"Yeah behotch, the lane's occupied," he said as he gave her a stern look.

Unable to hear his comment, still to his surprise she called his gaze, and raised the ante with her middle finger.

"What? So I'm in the wrong for being in your way?"

His fingers held like an eagle's claw. The previous pain had become a strangely welcoming sensation.

Jerry was pushed to the edge of morality's precipice. He already knew what was down there, at least to a certain depth. Those occupying the depths must be ripe with evil, and filthy with dark secrets. A sacrifice they seemed willing to make. *Play in this world, pay in the next.* Peering over the edge was an act of willpower; it would be too easy to be seduced into tumbling off, plunging into lawlessness. His desire for righteousness was his vanity. Now with this new power, this gift, he felt it was his duty to become the referee of the road, to make sure everyone was playing by the "same" rules. All it took was a second subtle glance over the edge. Those who desired power and were able to touch it, to know it, were forever changed. Now that he had touched it, it was easier to slip off the ledge.

His eyes became wild with the knowledge that he could change the world around him, an opportunity to play a bigger part. *For the good of all mankind.* His forearm muscles knotted, tendons pulled taut to a degree that they felt half their length, and his fist balled solid. Jerry's arm and hand no longer felt like his, but rather like a stone appendage, with weight to match. With every attempt to open his hand and shake the tension from his lower arm, cars rose into the sky, as if attached to invisible puppet strings. First the obnoxious girl in the green Hyundai, then others, all moved in a violent wave. Every vehicle dipped and tossed, coming mere inches from colliding. His arm became a musical conductor's baton in a symphony of devastation and destruction. All vehicles poised like instruments ready to create beautiful music full of fire, flesh, and twisted metal. His dream was a nightmare for those within the vehicles that peppered the sky. They all awaited the first movement of the symphony to begin.

Both of his arms were open just like in his dream. Although his hands were no longer on the steering wheel, even his Prius was under his mental control. It glided forward slowly, three feet off the ground. His facial muscles tightened into a mask of vengeance and hatred, his eyes electrified.

The vehicles in the sky churned like snowflakes inside a child's Christmas snow globe. They only stayed suspended briefly then started to drop to the earth, a few at a time like sprinkles from a salt-shaker. Each car tumbled and rolled to such a degree that Jerry could not see the drivers clearly, could not relish in their horror before they hit the ground. Some crashed headlong like tent spikes being driven into the ground, while others landed on their sides, or corners, then rolled.

A few horns blared among the steel scattered heaps, and several fires lined both sides of the expressway. The dull flutter of two helicopters filled the sky. With a simple glance at each one, their engines cut out and they dropped, joining the wreckage and adding to the carnage.

Surveying the landscape, Jerry never knew such power could exist, even beyond the scope of the richest or most influential men. His Toyota still hovered over the road at ground zero. The destruction was more than a mile in both directions. Traffic beyond that was halted and paralyzed in great awe.

Jerry brought his hands down and held the steering wheel. The car lowered to meet the road. In a dream-like daze he looked straight ahead and drove on, just minding his lane as the road was clear of any obstructions. He paid no attention to the wrecked vehicles; they might as well have been rock formations on the side of the road.

He arrived at the company parking lot almost an hour early, grabbed his things from the back seat and headed to the building. No wall of smoke to pass through. No Martin waiting near the door to greet him. Must be on vacation, Jerry thought.

Jack Tanner was at the main entrance reception desk, talking quickly, deep concern across his face. He was asking Myra Brandt to inform him right away when specific employees arrived.

"Morning Jack… Myra," Jerry said, wondering if they noticed him.

"Oh—hey Jerry. Don't you live north, and take I-75 in?" Jack asked.

Before Jerry could reply, Myra cut in, "Yes Mr. Tanner, Jerry McIntyre is on the list."

"Good, good," Jack said and added, "keep me informed about the rest."

"Yes sir," Myra replied and crossed Jerry's name off the list.

"Jack, what's going on?" Jerry asked. Jack just motioned for Jerry to follow, and they both took the elevator up to the top floor where Jack had his office. When they got there, Jack walked quickly to the boardroom and Jerry hurried behind him. Most of the other executives were gathered around the large flat screen watching a live news broadcast.

No one responded to them entering the room. Groans, gasps, and shaken silence came from those watching the screen. The traffic catastrophe played over and over with brief shots of the news anchor rehashing the event, adding any new tidbits as they became available.

Nancy looked up, "Nothing new Jack. Oh thank God, Jerry you made it. Did Martin get in yet?"

"Martin's not in yet, I just checked with Myra," Jack said.

"I know he always comes in early, and I don't think he took today off, God I hope he did," Nancy replied nervously rubbing the small crucifix around her neck.

Nancy Yates was one of the more outwardly religious employees, not the "have you accepted Jesus into your heart" type, but the, "I'll say a prayer for you this Sunday," type.

She returned to watching the breaking news report.

"Jack, if you don't mind, I'm going to head to my office," Jerry said.

Jack just nodded and waved at him, then moved to the other end of the table to join everyone watching the report.

Jerry turned on the lights to the main production room, then headed straight for his office, closed the door and sat in the dark. The light on his phone pulsed with the day's voicemail requests. His computer remained off, and he just stared at the empty powered down screen. It might as well have been an empty cardboard box, the vacant space drawing him in. The phone rang, jolting him from his thoughts. It was Myra calling to inform him that the office would be closing for the day due to the traffic catastrophe. He waited for fifteen minutes, figuring that Myra was able to reach everyone, then turned off the lights and headed to the parking lot.

His Prius was the only vehicle left in the lot. He sat there for half an hour watching the traffic go by on the nearby expressway. Everything prior to arriving at the office seemed like a dream. No feelings of joy or sadness entered his mind. He just existed for the time, neutral. If he held any feeling, it was one of complete balance.

Morning rush hour had long passed, and it was still too early for any lunch hour traffic. The drive home was pleasurable and the traffic sparse, even though he was detoured to local roads around the accident site. He drove straight to his condo, avoiding any previous thoughts of stopping at the grocery store. It had been a long time since he was at home at such an hour, and it seemed strangely quiet and alien with the sun highlighting the space. The mornings and evenings were his only frame of reference. He never entertained any guests there, so it struck him funny that his condo felt more like a simple storage place for his things and somewhere to sleep.

Yesterday was distant, like some forgotten date months in the past. He looked out at the crawling traffic before him. Tension built to the point of a headache. Now with the means to his desired end, he imagined a rippled space between both lanes. Without thought he pushed heavy on the accelerator, and since the car to his left had passed, he moved to straddle the dividing line. Before his Toyota could slam into the back of the two vehicles ahead, both swerved on to their adjacent shoulders and opened a space for him to drive through. With his speed increasing, each preceding vehicle moved to the side and returned to their lanes after his Toyota passed. From the sky, the Prius would have looked like a slider on a zipper, with both lanes of traffic meshing together as he made his way through.

His lips curled into a sinister smile. *That's right, who's the king? Ding—ding—ding … me. Live it, learn it … then again, who the hell cares, I'll just deposit your car in the ditch.* He arrived at his exit almost an hour early. *I guess I do have time for breakfast after all.*

Sitting in a nearby Denny's, he ordered a large breakfast. From under the table he felt his hand was locked into a fist. Trying to pry it open with his other hand was useless. This power had claimed his right hand and forearm. *Everything has its price. A small sacrifice for justice.*

Another dull work day; everyone only wanted to talk about the major traffic accident that happened on Wednesday. Traffic investigators and scientists were at a loss, but to keep sanity and order among the common folk, they suggested several natural occurring events. The news had speculated that it was due to an earthquake, or weather phenomena, as there was no evidence of any type of explosion. People could pick one that best suited their comfort level and then get on with their lives. Eager to get away from it all, Jerry left right at five, leaving his trusted crew to finish the assembly of tomorrow's marketing materials. He opened up the traffic as he did earlier and sped home. *The pleasure that cops and firemen must feel, flashing lights, blazing sirens, the sea of traffic parting before them.*

Friday morning he left for work an hour later. Why rush? Have a nice leisurely cup of coffee, maybe some eggs and toast, a read of the paper, he had it covered. Like the day before, he sailed through traffic. His addiction had now taken his right arm. Movement was limited at the shoulder, which he could only raise and lower. It became a mannequin's arm, an alien prosthetic.

As he crossed back into the right lane for his exit, he cut hard in front of a little old lady driving a Subaru hatchback. He just laughed at her and watched her shaking her fist in his rearview mirror. With a second glance he thought he saw a flash from her eyes and did a double take, but saw nothing. He quickly brought his eyes back on the road, and struggled with the steering wheel. He overshot his exit and the car launched forward, heading toward the concrete abutment. He mashed the break pedal, but the car just went faster, the steering wheel unresponsive. Before he could take further action, the Prius plowed head first into the thick walled concrete base, completely mashing the front wheel well into the cabin.

* * *

Several police cars surrounded the wreck. Two state troopers directed the parade of rubberneckers around the scene. Two troopers checked on the victim.

"What do you got Mike?"

"Hey Joe, looks like another speeder. Young guy, probably tried to cut from the far lane to exit the expressway at the last minute. Obviously missed."

It would be a while before the other emergency service vehicles could make it through the thick traffic. The rubbernecking drivers passed by slowly, looking upon Jerry like funeral attendees paying their respects.

He was bloody and battered, the engine block pinning him inside the cabin. The fire department cut Jerry out of the vehicle, placed him in an ambulance, and got him to the hospital where he was officially pronounced dead. It was procedure, even though all involved knew his fate. *Live it, learn it.*

SNOWBALL'S CHANCE

The old timber cabin on the hill disappeared as she scampered over the ridge. With the sure footing of a cat, an all-white Siberian to be more specific, she negotiated the rocky sharp outcroppings, traversing diagonally to control her descent. She had gone down the steep hill only once before. The lush valley below was full of earthy aromas; its rich dark soil fed the ferns to the honey-locus and towering spruces. There too was a brook, which danced its way through the trees with a delicate musical gurgle. It seemed to greet every tree and stone it approached with grace, like a beautiful young debutante at her first cotillion. Among these proud trappings fluttered winged insects dominating the air, while lazy soft-bodied newts and frogs lie at the brook's edge.

Today she would risk another difficult climb down the steep hillside. Her human companions, with their notion of cats having nine lives, were charming but laughable; she knew she only had one life, but would chance everything to enjoy and explore the world around her. She knew that she was clever and agile, which had allowed her to tempt fate and avoid death's noose.

Just beyond the base of the hill, she bounded through the tall grass chasing a dragonfly. Its body was electric blue with brief rings of dark bronze. It floated on the breeze then flicked its wings only a couple of times and was carried off yards away, landing momentarily before taking flight again. All attempts to capture it were in vain, but she still enjoyed the chase.

When she arrived at the brook, she heard several plops followed by splashes. Before the next one, she saw a small leopard frog leap for the water and dive. It made an unceremonious belly-flopping splash as it broke the silvery surface. She watched as it kicked its legs until it vanished within the murk of the sandy bottom. She dallied along side the water's edge, her paws sinking into the soft moist earth. While trying to creep up on another frog that was sitting along the bank, she heard a faint but shrill cry that penetrated the tiny forest. With both ears pointed up and turned in the direction of the noise, curiosity took hold and she scurried to have a look.

The white cat wound through the underbrush and stood on top of an exposed root of a large maple. From there, she saw the rusted steel roofing of an abandoned sawmill. She sniffed the air for signs of warning and turned her ears in all directions, but the only thing that caught her attention was a small cloud of gnats attracted by her breath. The muffled sound of faint sobbing put her again in motion.

The loading dock of the weathered wooden McKinney Mill sagged heavily on crooked posts, like an old man's legs, ready to sit down at any moment. In its heyday trucks would drive under the port to pick up their loads. The last truck to pull through was in September of 1963.

Arriving at the side of a partially overgrown dirt road that ran alongside the mill, she paused to check for danger. Although the moaning had stopped, there were sounds of movement coming from the belly of the old wooden structure. She darted across the road, using the random patches of overgrown grass for cover and slipped behind the footing of one of the dock's support posts. Next to the heavy concrete footer, she lowered her body to the ground and waited—listening.

A shadow flashed in the open spaces between the wall boards, and a man came into half view at the corner of the building. His enormous size was unnatural compared to any other person she had ever encountered. Then he moved and the building blocked her view. All she heard was his heavy boots shuffling over stone and dirt, then invisible metal creaking followed by the slamming of a metal door from around the building.

Still crouched and hidden behind the base of the large wooden post, her body tensed at the sound of a vehicle's engine coming to life and the crunching weight of its tires over the stone and dirt road. Her tension eased at the diminishing sounds of the vehicle leaving the old mill.

When the surrounding sounds of nature reclaimed the area, she slipped from her hiding spot and crept alongside the sun-bleached wooden walls.

"Damn crafty women. I know momma, it's hard to find a good Christian woman. Like you said, I ruin them before marriage, can't keep my hands off their titties, among other things," Lance said aloud.

He wore a smug smile of embarrassment and satisfaction. Embarrassment that his mother would not approve of the women he had been picking up, coupled with the satisfaction he got from stealing the warm cookies his mother laid out.

Lance walked with heavy footsteps and squinted at the bright sun as he exited the dark sawmill, dipping his bloody hands in the rain barrel just outside the doorway. He dried them on the work rag half tucked in his front pocket, then lumbered to the old Dodge pickup his neighbor, Bob Warren had lent him. He had been just a teenager when his father died. Mr. Warren stepped in to look after him and his mother. Mr. Warren was a nice enough fellow, but he tended to stay up late with his momma, which made Lance mad. She would tell Lance not to worry, that her and Mr. Warren had lots of praying to be done, and they were not to be disturbed when communicating with the Lord, especially when she was crying out to God and Jesus.

Lance sucked his spit through his front teeth, then got in the white pickup and slammed the door. A trip to town was in order, and it had to be today, as tomorrow was Sunday and there was to be no work done on Sunday, nor any fornicating either.

He smiled as he drove down the hill away from the old sawmill, thinking about his new honey, crawling around on all fours in the dust and dirt. Her pasty white ass trembling with the big red hand marks on them. Looking like two beautiful loaves of sourdough, which he loved squeezing.

The truck's suspension rattled going over the bumpy dirt road that nature had almost reclaimed. As the tires rolled over the rain-washed ruts, the big man bounced around in the cabin and his heavy boots thumped the floorboards. It was a beautiful day.

He whistled until he came to the main road, where worn truck tires met a more civilized surface.

The young woman lay face down on the dirt floor of the McKinney Mill, motionless. Her shallow breathing did little to disturb the dust on the floor. Her cheek, covered in blood, was now pressed into the dirt. Cream and peach colored panties were down around her ankles, almost hiding the handcuffs that were attached to one of her legs. The other end of the handcuffs was attached to a heavy rusty chain that was wrapped around the center post in the room.

The girl's yellow tank top was pulled up, exposing her breasts and belly to the dirt floor. Her pale white buttocks bore red hand marks.

When the world came back to her, she coughed, choking on dust and stale air. She lifted her head. An encrusted mixture of blood and dirt stuck to the side of her face. She coughed again, rolled on her side, and struggled to pull her top down to cover herself. Rotating on her back she put her hand between her legs, cupping herself. It was a natural reaction that did little to comfort her or take away the pain.

She sat up. The chain holding her made dull sounds as she moved, dragging it over the dirt and wooden floor. When she got her panties back in place, she scanned the room for her skirt, but it was out of reach on the ground. The blue denim mini, which her mother often warned her against wearing, was almost unseen in the shadows.

She doubled over sideways when a sudden sharp pain shot through her stomach. She grunted and almost closed her eyes. She thought she saw a silhouette along the upper edge of the wall that cast shadows through the sliver-sized spaces between the wall boards.

"Hah, hey. Hell—lo," she cried out. Her throat was dry and sore from her earlier screams. The shadow disappeared. Tears filled her eyes as she thought her cries were too weak to reach beyond her wooden prison.

"Hello," she called again as loud as she was able. The word came out dull and boxy. Her head fell back and her body shook with desperation.

She crumpled forward into a fetal position, but moaned at the pain in her ribs from the earlier assault. Her thighs also burned from kicking her legs. They had failed her in all attempts to stop or escape her attacker. Tears moistened and cooled her cheeks; her mouth hung open and ribbons of drool created a tiny design in front of her knees.

"Merrrrow," came from her left side.

She tilted her head and glanced upward through heavy wet eyes, blinking several times to clarify what she was seeing. A white cat's head seemed to float in the middle of the wall.

She closed her eyes for a few seconds. When she opened them again, she confirmed that there was indeed a white cat outside, poking its head through a small hole in the wall.

"Merrrrow," the floating cat's head spoke to her again.

"Ever seen this girl?" a man in plain clothes asked.

He presented a wallet size photo to the girl working the counter of the Mobil station. The sandy blonde haired girl in the picture was wearing braces, which had come off a month after the photo was taken.

"You a cop?" the girl working the counter asked suspiciously. She arched one eyebrow as she addressed the man on the other side of the counter.

"No, no, I'm the girl's father. Her name is Coleen."

He opened his wallet to show her his driver's license.

"Mr. Pie—, Piejak? I think I've seen her gas up here a few times. Did she go to Lincoln High?"

"Yes, this is her high school picture. Its over a year old, but she hasn't changed much. When did you see her? Was it last night?"

"No—," she said. Her reply was slow.

She paused, staring at the counter as if the answer was somewhere there in fine print.

"Um, I might have seen her maybe a week or two ago."

Uncertain if this man was an abusive father—something she was all too familiar with—she was uncomfortable passing on any detailed information. Two days later, when a deputy from the East Waterford Sheriff's Department would come by asking questions, she would tell the officer that the girl got into an old white pickup truck ... make, unknown ... driver, unseen.

The cat slipped along the outer wall of the old sawmill. Her bright white fur contrasted sharply against the washed out, dull greenish-gray structure. She stopped ever so often to smell the mossy wood; the only thing that kept her moving was the voice of the girl calling to her from inside. The other half of the building descended down a slope. In its early days the mill had a stream running under half of it. Cut trees were channeled from the nearby river down the stream and eventually made their way to the mill where they were processed.

The slope was now a dried out trench of sand and stone, with a few patches of weeds and grass. Her paws sunk in the sandy parts where the shade retained the ground's moisture. Jumping and stretching her body in long strides, she reached the deepest part of the dried up stream bed.

She could still hear the girl, whose cries were now heard by only privileged ears. The underside of the mill, where floating logs were hulled up from the stream, was now boxed in and boarded up. A rough hung door lay half open on its makeshift frame, uninviting and impending, like the raised blade of a guillotine. Although her eyes were well adapted to penetrate the shadowy gloom, she dialed both of her ears forward and listened. With no signs of danger, she stepped forward cautiously, looking through the narrow opening and into the darkness. The air within was thick and stagnant.

She entered with stealth, using the silent footfalls she usually saved for hunting mice. The length of the corridor and the height of the ceiling made her nervous. With neither side offering much concealment, she hurried alongside the nearest wall, which tapered into darkness. She reached the corner, which rounded into a blackened storage space. It was cluttered with raw pieces of wood only fit for a fire. A shovel and pick lay on the floor near the feet of another girl.

Unlike the girl that called to her, this one lay in stillness only reserved for one purpose. The girl was lying on her stomach with her face to one side. Her long dark brown hair cast over her like a veil, and obscured her face. A coating of dirt powdered most of her pale naked body. The cat sniffed at the girl's feet, which were surprisingly clean, as if she had worn invisible shoes. There were bruises around her left ankle and wrists, along with random markings on her thighs and buttocks.

"Merrrrow," the cat announced itself, then walked the length of the body and sniffed at the girl's hair.

"Help. Hey, you dumb cat, where did you go? Here kitty, kitty," a cry came from the above adjacent floor, followed by the sound of someone choking on their tears.

The cat froze briefly. Its muscles tensed at the girl's voice, then it looked toward the ceiling for a way up.

A stocky balding man in jeans and a gray button up work shirt was gathering the last of his grocery bags from the trunk of his Chevy Impala. He paused as he watched a police cruiser come up the driveway, and waited for the officer to step out of his car.

"Good afternoon. You Robert Warren?" the police officer asked.

The deputy appeared to be a junior officer. To Bob, he looked fresh out of high school, but he thought it absurd that the police would hire someone so young, so he had to be older.

"Yes sir, that's right, I'm Bob Warren," Bob replied with a puzzled look of concern.

"I'm Deputy Phillips of the East Waterford Sheriff's Department. Mind if I ask you a few questions?"

The deputy kept a safe distance at the front corner of the cruiser. He stood confidently with his hands on his utility belt, palm firm against the butt of his holstered .357 revolver.

"Sorry, what's this—all about?" The words tumbled out of Bob's mouth; he was unsure of what to make of the situation.

"I'm following up on a possible hit-and-run. Do you own a white Dodge pickup truck?"

"Well—well, it's not here. I let a neighbor use it. I haven't driven that truck for years," Bob said.

Bob was uncomfortable with the deputy's accusatory tone.

"Who's your neighbor?"

"His name is Lance Berry, but I can assure you that he wouldn't have driven off. That's not like Lance. Did anyone get hurt?"

Deputy Phillips assured Bob that no one was hurt in the accident. He took Lance's description and the address that Bob provided, then drove off.

A small bell gave a crisp ring as the spring latch was triggered above the door to Miller's Hardware. Terry Miller glanced up from her newspaper and offered a brief smile.

"Hi," Samuel Piejak said. His voice was low, as if he were speaking to someone in a library.

"Can I help you find something?" Terry asked.

"Can you tell me if you've seen this girl around? She's my daughter, Coleen. I'm Samuel Piejak," he said, stepping forward to hand her the photograph of Coleen.

Their voices carried down the isles of the store, past the bins of numbers and letters for making one's own house address sign, or personalizing one's mailbox, to the end of the row where an array of small drawers that contained an assortment of nuts, bolts and screws. Lance Berry stood in front of the tiny open drawer to some eye screws. His poked his hulking fingers about the drawer feeling the sharp points of the screws. They reminded him of when he was a child and he had found four abandoned ducklings. They would nibble at his hands when he fed them. Their mother had been most likely a victim of duck season. Although his father refused to let him keep and care for them, Lance hid them in the barn, hoping they would remain quiet when his father took out the tractor. Two of them died before his father found them. In a rage he stomped the other two in front of Lance. His father said that he was giving them back to Jesus. Lance was only six.

His memories of the little ducklings vanished when he heard the name *Coleen*. Someone in the front of the store had said her name. His new girlfriend's name was Coleen. He recalled her wide smile as she jumped into his pickup. She was eager for them to hit the road; she told him that she had been waiting for a ride at the Mobil station for almost two hours. He pinched a palm's worth of eye screws. His lips tightened in frustration at her refusal to smile any more for him. That was small compared to her trying to run away. Momma would have told him that she was just another one of those fast and easy types.

"There you go again, pick'n the wrong one. She aint gonna marry you boy. She just wants to use you up and spitcha out," momma would say.

"I'm big, momma, no man can beat me, and certainly no woman," he would say.

"Don't matter the size of the gal. If she's got her claws into ya, you'll be doin everything she wants ya to."

Usually at that point in the conversation, he would remain quiet in hopes that she would get tired of hearing herself and just shut up. He knew women loved to talk, but he had his ways to make them quiet, even his momma.

Lance stepped heel to toe half way up the aisle. He could see his white pickup in the lot through the store's front window. After hearing much of the conversation by the cash register, he knew they were talking about a missing girl. He waited while they chattered. The conversation seemed to never end. Wanting to appear inconspicuous, he turned to the drawers of numbers and letters, opening and closing them at random. When he pulled the drawer marked 'P', he paused and decided to take one of the large stickers. It was a shiny silver 'P' on a black background. He remembered seeing CRP somewhere, so with a strange delight, he pulled an 'R' from one drawer and a 'C' from another. Holding the letters he felt a strange satisfaction and a feeling of ease. He headed up the aisle.

"Sorry, Mr. Piejak," Terry Miller said, looking toward the large man approaching the checkout.

Samuel Piejak stepped aside and out of the way as Lance placed his things on the counter. His purchase consisted of a handful of eye screws, a spool of medium gauge electrical wire with a green plastic insulation, and three large peel-n-stick address letters.

"Hi, Did you find everything that you needed?" Terry asked Lance.

"Yup," Lance said, looking down at the counter as he fished for his wallet.

Samuel just watched the two, waiting to continue his conversation with Terry. As a man who enjoyed working with his hands, Samuel was often curious as to what projects other guys were working on. He thought little of the things Lance placed on the counter, but it did strike him odd that someone would only purchase 3 letters for a sign they were making. Maybe he lost a few, he imagined. He tried to imagine what word the man was repairing with the letters 'R', 'C', and 'P', as they were arranged on the counter. Only after Terry scooped everything into a brown paper bag, did Samuel feel like he just awoke from a dream.

"That'll be fourteen fifty-six," Terry said.

She gave Lance his change and looked at Samuel, who looked like he was trying to solve a math equation.

"Like I said Ms. Miller, I mean Terry … the police seem to be moving slow, and I can't sit around doing nothing," he said.

She nodded and told him that he could place one of his bulletins in the window.

The chain holding Coleen made a dull heavy melody as she rolled on to her side on the dirt floor. Her chest heaved as her body competed between sobbing and breathing. With the left side of her face to the floor, she stared out across the room. A white dot at the base of the wall caught her eye. She blinked. It was the white cat she had seen earlier. Half of its head seem to be rising from the floor, but only ears, eyes and nose were visible. Coleen tilted her head, trying to make sense of the illusion.

The white cat fought to remain balanced on the woodpile. It dug its sharp claws into the wobbling wood beneath its paws; it was time to decide, either go up or down. The cat cocked and thrust its hind legs and gracefully leapt through the hole to the upper floor. The girl could now adore the animal in all its feline glory.

"Here kitty, kitty," Coleen said, trying to sound inviting.

The white cat sat where it landed, looking at Coleen as if she were a mouse in a trap that offered nothing to chase and little to play with. They both stared at each other in silence, for what seemed like an eternity.

"Here kitty kitty … aren't you pretty?" Coleen said, stretching an open hand toward the cat, but wincing from the pain in her ribs.

The cat looked at her for a brief moment then began grooming itself. Coleen dropped her hand to the ground and sobbed with her face down. Her tears wet the dirt floor, creating tiny craters on the patches of dirt and sand. When she looked up, the cat was right in front of her. She moved slow and deliberate, finally touching it. Its white fur was in contrast to Coleen's dirt encrusted hands. She smiled when it paced back and forth, allowing her to pet both sides.

Eventually the cat came close enough and allowed Coleen to scoop it up. She crossed her legs and placed the cat in her lap. It purred and sniffed at her hand, then climbed her chest to smell her face. Coleen gave the cat a big hug, but then a glint of silver caught her eye. She leaned over and stretched to the leg of the beat up work table. It was her necklace, a silver locket her dad had given her for Christmas several years ago. Her eyes blurred with tears as she wished her dad was there to take her home. This time she would let him cash in on all her promises to be a good girl. She watched the cat as it swatted at the dangling chain.

"You like that, huh?" she said to the cat.

While massaging the cat's neck, she noticed it had a collar. The small silver medallion attached to the collar made a faint jingle.

"Snowball. So that's your name," she said.

Before she could read the address, the familiar sound of a truck's engine startled her. Soon she would hear the sound of its tires negotiating the deep ruts and stones. Coleen felt the animal's muscles tense and tried to soothe it. Her body trembled and she thought, what can I do?

The brakes on the old Dodge pickup made a dry squeal as Lance pulled up to the side door of the old McKinney sawmill. He stepped out and fished behind the seat, pulling out a denim knapsack. It held the girl's hairdryer and makeup, his supplies from the hardware store, and a Coke and ham sandwich he picked up at a Wawa on the way out of town. On the front of the knapsack was stitched in big puffy letters, 'CRP'. It was one of the two bags the girl had with her when he picked her up. The other bag was larger, pink, and held her clothes. He liked looking through her things, especially her underwear. It was one thing to see it in the stores on the rack, and another filled with the fleshy curves of a girl's body. He was enchanted by the thin fabric and lacy edges and surprised at the design of a few of them, which at best would only cover the front. The corners of his mouth curled up in an awkward smile as he thought of his mother's disapproval for such things. He could imagine her spiteful comments, her loath for his malevolent glee and deliberate disobedience.

He grabbed the knapsack and headed for the mill. His work boots crunched over patches of gravel and twigs creating a hollow sound, as if he were walking atop a pile of dry bones.

Coleen sat up, cradling Snowball who was squirming in the girl's arms. The cat could sense her fear and wanted to be free of any restraints, even the trusting hands of its new-found friend. Coleen stroked the cat's fur, trying to calm the animal.

When the old floorboards above them creaked from the weight of the man's steps the cat attempted to get away, but Coleen held it fast within her arms. A familiar knapsack fell though the opening in the ceiling, where an old wooden barn style ladder was fixed against the wall. The bag made a dusty thud when it hit the floor. Its contents were light enough, and of little value, as not to be of any concern.

The big man's legs appeared as he descended the ladder. The cat jerked within Coleen's arms. She cradled the animal and began winding her necklace around Snowball's collar. The cat's hind legs pressed into Coleen's thigh until it finally dug its nails into her flesh and broke free. It bounded off of her forearm and landed on top of the work table, then turned its attention to the big man who now shared the room.

Coleen noticed Lance had brought her knapsack, but said nothing. Her eyes were fixed on him, like someone who was watching a hungry tiger approach. She knew he enjoyed hurting her, which had been the norm of her past relationships or encounters with men. She had even been cuffed to a bed before, but under friendly and playful circumstances. Being held captive was a first for her.

"Honey, looks like you found yourself a friend. Didn't I tell you not to bring home any stray animals? A dog would have been bad enough, but a cat?" he said. His face contorted as he struggled to form a smile.

Coleen drew up her knees and hugged herself into a ball, hoping that she could make herself so small, that she would disappear from his view. Lance smiled as he watched the girl cower, but his interest shifted to the white cat. He lowered the knapsack to the floor and advanced with slow steps, trying not to spook the animal. He held his arms out with his hands ready to capture his new play thing. It remained on all fours, shoulders tense, trying to judge the man's intentions. Friend or foe?

Lance could see its claws. If it had an owner, he imagined their furniture must look like hell. The corner of his mouth tightened and turned down at his memory of the last cat he handled. He was seventeen. It was a stray with a marbled coat that would come around his mother's house. She would sometimes put out milk for it. He thought of cats the same way he thought of the women that turned their noses up at him, pompous and thankless. He had only allowed the marbled cat one shot at him. It had attached itself around his thigh, claws sinking deep into his flesh, mouth open trying to bite his nuts off. The searing pain in his leg only registered after he twisted its neck and its body lay limp across his shoe. He remembered punting the cat's body against the side of the house. His only regret was that he had to clean the blood off the wood siding under the kitchen window.

This white cat looked more docile, giving him the confidence that he could crush it easily within his grasp. He felt that he had a gift, where he could look inside a living thing and see its life force. Sometimes it burned bright like stadium lights, or dim like a single birthday candle. Even when he was a young boy, he could see inside people. When Mr. Warren's wife, Carol, was ill, he could see her light. It was a single candle, flickering against internal winds. Although this cat seemed to have a gentle nature, its light was bright. How dim would that light have to become before the animal would fight him? he wondered. He cast a brief look at the girl. He enjoyed her expression of concentrated anticipation and anxiety. The corner of his mouth twisted into a challenging smirk. Three slow steps brought him within striking distance. He lunged at the table and managed to grasp one of the cat's hind legs. His hold was weak, with only the animal's foot between his thumb and fingers.

With amazing speed, the cat raked its claws across the top of Lance's hand, trying to cut deep, but failing to reach the veins and tendons. Lance pinched its foot between his thumb and forefinger, trying to hold on. Its body jerked wild and frantic almost tearing its leg muscles in order to get free. Summersaulting across the table and over the far edge, the cat made a rough landing, albeit on all fours, and dashed to the hole in the floor. Lance tripped over Coleen in his attempt to chase the animal, but ended up lying on his side laughing as the cat disappeared down the hole.

"I never did see a cat run into a hole like a mouse," he said laughing.

His jovial mood lasted only seconds before he jumped to his feet and raced toward the loading area, where he could climb down to the dried up stream bed and the space under the mill. If he could get below quick enough, he could block the cat's escape. He fantasized about placing the cat's body in the arms of the dead girl and burying them both down there. It would be a gift ... a pet to take with her to see Jesus ... just like how Dorothy took Toto with her to see the Wizard, he thought.

Snowball dove into the hole in the floor from which she emerged earlier. Her front paws managed to land on the uppermost pieces of the wood pile, closest to the ceiling of the floor below. The rest of her body had tumbled out and slapped off the wall. Her front claws dug into the broken pieces of wood and helped launch her down the woodpile and onto the floor. She almost landed on the deceased girl's body.

Dust and sand rained down through the floorboards above. The big man was in a rage, stomping his feet. Although she escaped his capture, she felt like she had landed in a grave. The still girl's body seemed to be telling her, "Either get out now or join me forever." She considered the man waiting for her in the hole above, which left only one way to escape.

Snowball peered around the corner, penetrating the gray soup of shadows with her keen eyes. She cocked her ears forward, collecting any sounds that might be coming from the corridor. She could still hear the man's steps above her, the grinding grit of a sand covered floor under his boots. His movements slowed to a predatorial pace.

She slipped around the darkened corner, again trying to decide which wall felt the safest to have at her side. Her shoulder muscles were tight like a coiled spring, loaded and ready to launch her to top speed. She had moved only a few feet down the wall when a series of dark shapes fell before her, and she jumped back. Chunks of old wooden beams and joists came crashing down. Sand and dust rose from the floor. From a safe distance, she heard noises above her. Here the level above was open to the rafters; when she looked up, she spotted the big man who was lying in wait. He had freed a small pile of materials that was stored there and was now attempting to crush her or block her escape.

With ample room to the side of the dusty debris, she decided to make a break for it. The triangular wedge of light from the door at the end of the corridor seemed within reach. The big man overextended his reach to dislodge the stored pieces of wood and lost his balance. His body fell in almost silence like a giant spider descending towards its prey. She felt a heavy thunderous weight impact behind her, and her body compacted like a spring then stretched with each stride to reach the doorway.

She leaped again, but before her muscles could stretch the full length of her stride, her bones locked and she was snapped back. Her body jerked backwards, like a rabbit caught in a snare. She tried leaping again, but was pulled back. This time her body twisted, and she was face to face with her captor. His large hand held the entire length of her lower leg with a grip that seemed to tighten the more she struggled. His eyes and mouth expressed different sentiments ... one dead, the other glee.

The big man had landed on his stomach, with one arm trapped underneath his massive body. He seemed to have lost his breath from the fall, which slowed his recovery. It would only be a moment until he was back on his feet. Like all trapped or cornered animals, she attacked. With her free legs, she dug her hind claws deep into the flesh on his forearm, while her front paws went for his face. She managed to dig into his right ear and left cheek. This evil made of flesh even had its soft spots. The man cried out, but continued to hold her leg as he struggled to get his free arm from under his body. Her assault continued. She scratched at his forehead, and again carved more grooves into his cheek, while her left claws remained buried in the flesh of his ear, trying to tear it from his head.

The searing pain spread across his face, like lit gasoline. Blood from his forehead blinded his left eye. He held the cat's leg as firm as he could, trying to keep it far enough away to avoid being bitten. He rolled onto his side and was able to free his other arm. When he tried to shield himself, the cat bit at his fingers and clawed at him, opening up the veins on the back of his hand. Blood painted both his hands crimson red. He let go.

The cat darted for the narrow opening in the crooked hung door, but as it slipped through, its side clipped the edge. The door's bottom hinge came loose and the bottom of the door swung shut, closing off any future escape.

Lance spit into the dirt, blinking his eyes, trying to clear them of dust and blood.

"Fucking cat," he said with a cough.

He propped himself up with the arm that hurt the least and tucked his knees under him. He pulled a shop rag from his back pocket and looked at his arms and hands, which made him think of the first time he changed the oil on a car. His hands were covered, and most of his forearms as well. It took more than a single shop rag to clean up that mess.

Every wound seemed raised and throbbed with pain, radiating from dull to biting, as if the animal was still attacking him. Watching it bolt out the small opening in the door reminded him of slaughtered chickens, with their bright white feathers in contrast to the bright rich red of their blood. The only problem was this furry chicken was wearing his blood.

He got to his feet and braced himself against the wall. He gave up on cleaning his hands and touched the rag to his face, but winced. The blood had already started to dry and was sticky. The rough fabric of the rag just added insult to injury. He stumbled to the door, his left knee drawing his attention away from the cuts on his face and arms. He knew that he had fallen hard and imagined his knee had lead the impact.

No kitty—let alone a four legged one—is gonna get the best of me, he thought. Besides, he was still charmed with the idea of placing the dead cat in the girl's arms and burying them both. Before he kicked the door off its makeshift hinges, he smiled at the vision of the girl holding the cat. She was smiling and standing next to Jesus, with a rainbow behind them … no unicorns, maybe next time.

Samuel Piejak left two printouts describing his missing daughter at Mason's dry cleaners. He was heading north on I-15, when his shoulders tightened and he could hear his daughter, Coleen's voice in his head … "Where are you Daddy?" He jerked the wheel and pulled the car onto the shoulder. The brakes locked and tires skidded hard over the asphalt and loose stones.

He thought of the large mailbox letters again, RCP, which now rearranged in his mind … CRP. Was it fate, or the ghost of his daughter crying out to him? Tears washed over his eyes, blurring the passing traffic and road in front of him. His body felt heavy; he just wanted to curl up over the steering wheel or on the front seat. He thought, What can I do? … What can I do? Through his blurred vision, he could make out a white car with light bars on top approaching in the opposite direction. He blinked hard to clear his eyes, and as the car passed, the officer nodded at him as if to say, "Help is right here." Samuel dried his eyes on his shirtsleeve, waited for both lanes to clear, then made a hard U-turn, determined to catch up with the patrol car.

With the old mill to her back, and its rusted steel clad roof almost out of sight, Snowball slowed her pace. Even the faint cries of the girl at the mill had subsided. The underbrush and tall grass gave her some comfort and concealment, but was also disorienting. Her ears pointed skyward and rotated; she was listening intently for the sounds of the stream and its welcoming voice. The only sound she heard was the buzzing of a horsefly that let her know that she was lost. As she kept moving forward and away from the old mill, the terrain rose in a steep incline. Towering spruces stood imposing as she made her way up the hillside.

As she looped her way around the thick tree trunks and over their exposed roots, the pine needle beds felt soft under her paws. The sunlight warmed the surrounding earth and ignited a rich aroma under the cool shade of the pines. An unseen bird's song filtered downward to her. She then heard a second bird above her, increasing her excitement. She dug her claws into the soft bark and began to climb as stealthy as she could.

Halfway up the tree, she spotted the singing bluejay. She dug her claws into the tree's bark in preparation for a slow approach. At this height, there were more supporting branches to aid in her climb. She would move then pause, eyes always on her prey. When she reached the branch just below her singing feast, she became like stone. Only her eyes glided in subtle movements as she watched the bluejay with frozen intensity.

The tree swayed with the gentle breeze. Fresh pine sap clung to Snowball's paws. She wanted to groom herself, but the distraction was too little to take her concentration off of the bluejay. The bird continued to sing and looked about, as if trying to locate its mate. When the wind picked up, she was sure that the bird would fly off, but it stayed.

A second bluejay landed on a perch just above her. The first bird was now forgotten, for her new prey was within easy reach. She launched upward, paws open, claws exposed. As fast as she could imagine her prey within her grasp and finally between her teeth, she felt the same crushing jaws on her. There were no sharp penetrating teeth at her back, but a heavy crushing grip dug into her fur, stopping her short of reaching and capturing the bird.

"Gotcha kitty."

The big man held her behind her shoulders in a painful grasp, pulling her fur tight, making no allowances for movement. Her legs stretched outward, giving her the appearance of a stuffed animal. She was unable to face him. All she could do was squirm and try to claw for an open branch. His long arm swung and beat her against the tree's branches like someone beating the dust out of an old rug.

"Rrrreeeeeeew," she screeched over and over. Her body was now animated, limbs flailing, claws outstretched attempting to capture anything.

Lance smiled. Although he preferred the cries of his lady friends, he enjoyed listening to this beast in distress. There was no way in his Mother's Hell that he was going to let this one go, not this time. Each time he swung the cat, the fond memory of his mother taking him to Randle's Apple Orchard came to mind. He loved thrashing the tree limbs with a long crooked stick and watching the fruit fall, without a care of how many got bruised.

Trails of blood wove their way down his arm. The previous cuts on his hands and arms were raging again. They burned as if the animal was once again trying to burrow into his skin.

His smile straightened to a line of concentrated indifference. No human or animal qualities existed; he was pure machine. He stared at the white cat in his grasp, eager to watch its body bludgeoned and bloodied against the tree. He arced his arm wide to deliver a final crushing blow. He could see the light within the snowy white cat glowing ever brighter, like a lightbulb at the end of its lifespan. Lance's arm shot upward with the speed meant to drive nail heads below the surface. Before the animal crashed into the side of the tree, it clawed at whatever branches were within reach, but that only slowed its impact by a small fraction.

Lance's emotions flooded back into his body. He hoped he had crushed the cat into dust, which was the only way he could explain his now-empty hand. The snowy white cat had vanished. Had he dropped it? He knew he felt its bones crunch as he bashed it into the side of the tree. He searched around, but found the animal neither above nor below him.

In an empty lot that used to be a 76 gas station, Deputy Douglas Phillips and Samuel Piejak were parked alongside one another. After hearing Samuel's story, Deputy Phillips called Deputy Robbie Dodson on his cellphone.

"Hey Robbie … yeah listen … I have a gentleman here whose daughter has been missing. He described a possible suspect, who matches the one driving the white truck. Yeah, the truck I checked on earlier. The owner told me that a neighbor by the name of Lance Berry had been using it. Anyway, this gentleman describes seeing Lance Berry at Miller's Hardware, and some of the items he was purchasing sounded suspicious, like three mailbox letters … yeah the stick-on kind, they were the same initials of Mr. Piejak's daughter. Yeah, okay, thanks," Deputy Phillips said, then flipped his phone closed.

"Mr. Piejak, we're going to look into it."

"I want to come with you," Samuel Piejak insisted.

"No, Mr. Piejak, we need you to go home. I got your contact information. We'll let you know if we find anything," the deputy said.

Deputy Phillips stared down Samuel, hoping for his cooperation, then waited and watched him drive off in disappointment and disgust. He got on the radio to let the station dispatcher know that he would be returning to the home of Lance Berry. After speaking to Bob Warren earlier, he had visited the Berry residence, but no one was home. He planned a quick stop at Miller's Hardware, before returning to the Berry residence.

Bob Warren sat at the counter of Gracie's Diner. He was wringing his ball cap in his hands while he waited for the waitress to turn around.

"Nancy," Bob drew out her name, as slow and soothing as he could.

The close-to-retirement-age waitress turned. She wore a pale yellow dress with white trim. The only smile she could bare to produce, on her time and work weathered face, disappeared the moment she laid eyes on Mr. Warren.

"Robert Warren, I thought we agreed that you would not come here," she said.

He held his hands up in a mock act of surrender.

"I know, I know, but the police came by, saying that your boy Lance was in a car accident. I told you that boy daydreams too much. Surprised he hasn't driven off a cliff. I've been looking all over for him. Figured he was here with you. He better not have destroyed my truck, or I'll take it out of his ass," Bob Warren said.

Nancy Berry crossed her arms and tilted her head, wondering if it was a waste of time to reply to Bob's feeble threat.

"Robert John Warren, you have a lot of nerve whining about that damn truck of yours. It's prednure twenty years old. Sides, you're lucky my boy only hates you a little. You best thank the Lord for it," she blurted out. Her voice trailed off, to avoid any attention from the other customers.

"I've done more for that boy than any man, and you know it. If he's been in an accident, he should at least come to one of us," Bob said, examining her face for any cracks of understanding.

"Well, I haven't seen 'em," she snapped under her breath.

Bob snatched his cap from the counter and stormed out the door.

"I'll find the son-of-a-bitch," he mumbled.

He looked back at the diner, expecting to see a pot of hot coffee flung out the door behind him. He hated that she no longer wanted to see him. She wanted to get married, if they were to carry on like they had been. Although his late wife was long deceased before he started coming around, he had no intention of marrying again. He'd kept his distance for seven years. He supposed he had seen more of Lance than Nancy, as Lance helped him on occasion. Now that Bob was older, he just wanted someone to talk to and chase away the loneliness. Funny, he thought, even that was living in sin to her.

Parked in the high grass on old Route 101, Deputy Douglas Phillips sat in his car. Before the new highway came along, and even within his two short years on the force, he would often catch speeders on the old road. His visit to Miller's Hardware only told him which direction Lance was traveling in the white truck. He had hoped that Lance was returning home, but when Deputy Phillips arrived he again found the home empty with no sign of Lance or the white truck. He looked up and stared down the road, deep in thought. His breathing was slow and heavy as his mind sifted through the information for any connections. Then he saw a speck of reflected light down the road.

Bob stared out at the empty road. Only on occasion he would take old Route 101, since the new highway Thirty-Three was faster for getting to and from town. The old road with its patches of farmland and wooded areas brought back fond memories. As he drove on, the shoulder disappeared and the trees became dense on one side of the road. They stood like sentries guarding the forest and its secrets. Bob's eyes scanned the passing trees, and he thought about the old McKinney Mill, where Lance liked to sneak off and spend time. He'd caught him there a few times when Lance was a teenager and young man in his twenties. Bob just figured the boy was hiding some men's magazines there, or perhaps some booze and cigarettes. The boy didn't have any friends, hell maybe he just wanted to be alone, Bob thought.

When he saw a break in the trees and the trail that lead to the mill, he brought the Impala to an abrupt stop. He shook his head at his lack of judgment, and then he looked in the rearview mirror to make sure no one was right behind him. No one seemed to be around; although the old road was recently paved, it seemed just as abandoned as the path to the mill. He turned up the dirt road to the mill and drove slow, hoping not to bottom out his car.

With the many deep ruts in the road, it was impossible to keep the Impala's tires from dropping in them. The underside of the car scraped several times, jostling him in his seatbelt.

"Dammit all," he grumbled as he brought the car to a stop. He thought that this adventure wasn't worth losing his car's muffler over. After half stumbling out of the car and onto the uneven path, he hoped to God to find Lance there, otherwise he could have been home watching television.

He walked up the road, staying to one side as to avoid a twisted ankle or an embarrassing fall. He'd worn brogues most of his life, refusing to wear those silly old man's athletic walking shoes. Now he wished he had on a pair. The incline in the road seemed to increase with every step. He looked back, wondering if he should abandon his search and just wait for Lance to turn up. He made his decision when he saw that the Impala was now out of sight. He figured that he was at least half way there, so he may as well carry on.

After trudging farther up the hill, Bob slowed to catch his breath. He noticed the top of a white pickup truck. He had already seen the top of the mill as he climbed the sloping road, but now he was relieved to find his old Dodge there.

"Dammit Lance," he grumbled under his breath.

He spit on the ground even though his mouth was dry and pasty; it was more a gesture of disgust than anything. First order of business was to see what damage Lance had done to his truck, and then he would decide whether or not to take it out of his hide.

When Bob made it to the truck, he walked around it.

"Hmmm … don't see no damage," Bob mumbled.

He stood there confused, trying to figure out why the sheriff's deputy told him that Lance was involved in a car accident. Since there appeared to be no damage to the truck's body, Bob wondered if Lance had run down someone. Dear God, he thought. The thought of his truck being used to hurt someone made him sick, accident or no accident.

Bob turned and looked at the weathered building. Well, boy, let's see what you're up to … couldn't be anything good if the police are looking for you, he thought. He stepped with care to the entrance. The nagging stiffness in his legs persisted, so he paused and braced himself within the doorway. The hall appeared darker in contrast to the intensity of the afternoon sunlight. He would have to be inside before his eyes would be accustomed. He caught himself before calling out to Lance; his curiosity kept him silent.

Coleen heard footfalls above her. They were softer, as if someone was sneaking about. She wondered if Lance was still hunting the white cat within the mill. When she'd heard the loud crash earlier, she prayed that the cat had escaped.

"Lance? You in here?" An older man's voice came from the floor above Coleen.

"Hello?" she said, her voice almost inaudible. Her fear turned the word to a mere breath.

"Hey … down here. I'm down here. Help," she yelled, louder than before.

There was a pause followed by momentary sounds of confused shuffling. A foot appeared on the makeshift ladder, then another, until Bob Warren stood on the basement floor.

"Dear God," he gasped.

Bob looked at this girl in her underwear, shackled, and dirty.

"What's going on here?" Bob choked, struggling to get the words out.

"Help me please. Get me out of here, before he comes back," Coleen pleaded.

Bob looked around the room, wondering what to make of all this. When he heard the girl start to cry, it was as if someone had slapped him in the face. As he hurried to her he saw the handcuff around her ankle, which connected her to a heavy chain. The chain was wrapped and secured around a thick wooden post. His eyes ran back and forth, from the post to the girl, confused at what to do next. It was difficult for him to look at the half-dressed girl.

"Here," she said, tugging at the handcuffs.

"Can you break this?" she asked.

Bob looked around the room for something to hit the handcuffs with, but found nothing.

"I'm gonna check that other room, or upstairs to see if I can find something," he said.

"Please don't leave me," she begged.

"I'll be quick. If I don't find anything, I have some tools in my car," he said, withholding how far his car was from the old mill.

* * *

As Bob approached the doorway to the next room, he noticed a hole in the floor. Its size might accommodate a small child, he thought. A putrid odor rose up from it. His shoulders tightened as fear crept up his spine. A pile of old wood was all he could see through the ragged portal.

"Hurry, please," the girl pleaded from behind him.

The second room opened up to a space three times the size of the first room. On one side of the room, the floor dropped off to a semi-finished space with a dirt floor and makeshift walls that appeared to have been added long after the mill was closed in 1963. Bob searched for something blunt to break the girl's handcuffs. He found nothing that he felt confident would work. He peered over the edge, where the floor ended abruptly. There was a pile of scrap wood scattered below, which looked like it had recently fallen from the rafters. He walked the length of the drop-off, estimating the shortest fall would be five or six feet. He breathed out heavy, wondering if his legs could withstand the fall.

He kept his knees bent and dropped down, hoping the dirt floor would cushion his fall. He landed on his feet, but his weak legs buckled, crushing his body into a fetal position. His knees jammed into his ribs before they hit the floor.

"Oh—son of a bitch," he groaned, as he lay on his side.

Down the one section, he noticed a door knocked off its hinges, allowing a rectangle of sunlight into the otherwise dark space. He sat up against the wall and looked up at the floor above him, thinking he should have dangled to make it less of a fall.

"Idiot," he grumbled.

When he got to his feet, he was surprised that neither of his legs were broken, but a sharp pain shot up his left leg from his ankle. He shifted his weight to his right leg and hobbled along the wall down the corridor, which he thought might take him to the room with the hole that he had peered down earlier. As he approached the corner his shoulders tightened as the putrid smell once again filled his nostrils. He paused and leaned against the wall, afraid to turn the corner.

After closing his eyes for a few seconds to steel himself, he glanced around the corner.

"Oh, dear God … no … no … no …" his voice trailed off to a whisper.

He moved slowly towards the naked body of the girl who lay on the dirt floor. His feet dragged heavy beneath him. The thick and pungent air that filled the room seemed to have a life of its own. As still as it was, it felt like the only other living thing in the room besides Bob Warren.

The girl's body was pasty white. The bruises and marks had become dark around her left ankle and wrists. Her face was turned away. He wanted to believe that perhaps she was just unconscious, but he was unable to bring himself to touch her.

"Mister? Don't leave me. Mister? Are you still there?" Coleen's cries came from the floor above.

Bob looked up and saw the hole in the ceiling where he had looked down earlier.

"Hang in there, young lady. Don't worry, I'm still here," he shouted facing the hole, as if it were some kind of telephone receiver.

He looked around, and was surprised to find a shovel and pickaxe near the girl's feet. How did he miss them? Was his focus on the deceased naked girl that intense, or did God just now put them there, he wondered. Glancing around as if he had just woken from sleep, he grabbed the pick and contemplated how he would get back to the upper floor. The thickness of the air that filled the room forced him toward the doorway and prevented him from looking back at the girl's body.

His left shoe felt like a half size too small. Realizing that his ankle must have swollen, he took greater care to avoid putting weight on it and shuffled his feet the best he could. When he reached the corner, he thought he saw brief shadows moving down the corridor. The combination of the swatch of sunlight coming through the doorway and the dusty air in the old mill made everything hazy and dreamlike. Out in the sun, sounds of cicadas called out to him from beyond the doorway. He felt like he was in the land of the dead looking out upon the land of the living.

Stumbling back to the drop-off, Bob found two empty wooden crates sitting in the shadows. He prayed that they were not dry rotted. They creaked but held his weight long enough for him to toss the pick to the ledge above and then pull himself up.

"Hey ... old man?" Coleen called out when she heard shuffling from the other room.

Bob appeared in the doorway with the pick, holding onto the frame to steady himself. She could see the pain on his face, and judging by the dirt on his clothes, she knew that he had fallen.

"Are you okay?" she asked.

Bob's chest heaved and he motioned to her that he needed a minute to catch his breath. Coleen watched as an odd shaped oval ring appeared above his head like a halo, hovered there for a moment, then dropped over his head and tightened around his neck. Bob dropped the pick and both of his hands went up, clawing at the wire noose. The wire was already cutting into his flesh. The plastic insulation coating kept the wire from sinking deeper and with greater ease. Knocked off his feet, Coleen watched helplessly as the old man was dragged backward into the dark room.

Sounds of a struggle were brief. The floorboards of the adjoining room creaked as they bore the weight of slow and heavy steps. Lance emerged in half shadow, appearing just beyond the doorway, where the shadows seemed to cling to him. He just stood there staring at her. Coleen's body shook and the chains that held her rattled with a dusty metallic sound. Although she wore a tank top and panties, she covered her chest as if to conceal her naked body.

The shadows crossed Lance's face revealing the smile he now wore. He licked his lips as he watched her cower on the floor, and he almost wished that she were unchained so that he could chase after her. Coleen kicked her feet and used her hands to help propel herself backward, away from him, but he was soon above her, taking her by her ankles and laughing.

"You naughty girl," he said, as he held her by both ankles in one hulking hand and swatted her behind with the other.

"No—no!" she cried, trying to kick her legs free.

He twisted her feet, forced her on her belly, and shoved her face down on the dirt-covered floor.

"Pffaaah," she spat out the dirt and dust that filled her mouth.

Before she could use her hands to crawl away, he had her panties down her thighs, and he knelt down on the backs of her calves, pinning her to the floor. His weight crushed her legs, and she felt paralyzed. She could hear him undoing his belt and unzipping his pants.

"No, no, please, no," she pleaded. Her chest heaved, and her breath pushed the dirt in gentle puffs in front of her.

"C'mon darling, give me some lov'n," he said. His tone let her know that he was no longer smiling.

Her sobbing turned inward; her lips trembled violently and her chest started to spasm. If she complied she would avoid being beaten unconscious again. He shifted his weight just enough for her to flip over on her back. She pounded on his chest as hard as she could. His face was too far away to try and claw out his eyes, besides it appeared that the white cat had already given it to him good. She hoped that her furry friend was still alive.

Lance snatched one of her flailing arm by the wrist.

"Aaaaaagh," she screamed, fighting and clawing at him.

Before he could secure her other hand, she managed to dig her nails into the wound on his forearm. His expression remained as stone-like as a store mannequin. His large hand now held both of her wrists, and he backhanded her across the face with the other. She quieted down, almost losing consciousness. He pulled up her tank top to reveal her breasts.

"No—don't—please—," she muttered.

After groping her, Lance worked his pants down his thighs, intending to keep it simple. He released her hands, hoping that she still had more fight left in her, but they just tumbled down to her sides. Among her groans, he heard the grinding of dirt between leather shoe bottoms from across the room.

His eyes moved to the corners of their sockets, to see a man wearing a uniform.

"Police. Don't move," Deputy Douglas Phillips barked at Lance. His arms extended out to drive forward a .357 revolver he was white-knuckle grasping with both hands. Lance lowered his head, hiding his smile, while pulling up his pants and securing his belt.

"I told you not to move. Do you understand me?" Deputy Phillips's voice was now louder and filled the space.

Lance turned toward the officer. Deputy Phillips saw the wounds on Lance's face, arms and hands, even in the low light of the dust-filled room. He had difficulty believing that the girl had done all that.

"Sheriff's Department," Deputy Phillips said, taking a step forward. His voice betrayed a slight tremble, as he fought to maintain a commanding tone.

"Put your hands on your head where I can see them," he ordered.

Lance stood with his arms at his sides and turned his open palms toward the officer. Now seeing Lance at his full height, Deputy Phillips wanted to call for backup, but was afraid to take his hands off his weapon or his sights off of the big man. After finding Bob Warren's car on the old dirt road leading up to the mill, he expected to find Bob here as well.

Deputy Phillips took a cursory glance of his surroundings. If Bob was waiting to ambush him, Deputy Phillips needed to prepare himself for that possibility. He side-stepped so that his back was to the corner of the room, where there was little chance that someone could sneak up behind him. He held the heavy revolver steady at Lance.

"Step away from the girl," Deputy Phillips commanded. He took his support hand off the gun and pointed in the direction he wanted Lance to go.

Lance took a step toward the officer with his hands still open.

"Dammit! Over there," Deputy Phillips said, pointing.

Lance advanced closer to the officer. Bands of light fell across his face. Deputy Phillips noticed smeared patches of blood on the big man's face. He knew that some of it had to be Lance's, as he could also see the dark red grooves on his face and his one ear sat a little odd. The deputy wondered if the girl had tried to tear at the man's ear, and how much blood belonged to the girl?

"Do not move. Do you understand what I'm saying to you? Do—not—move," Deputy Phillips shouted, each new demand sounding less assured. If he needed to take a shot, the girl was just beyond his target and he would be taking a risk at hitting her.

"On your knees, hands on your head," he ordered.

Bob lay on his side in a fetal position, unable to swallow or cough; his fingers touched the electrical wire that was wrapped around his neck. His mind faded back and forth from black to a hazy fog of consciousness. Only the tiniest amount of air entered his body. His fingertips found two ends of the wire, where they were twist-tied together. Even his small attempt to unravel the ends of the wire made him blackout again, but the shouting from the adjacent room kept him from losing all consciousness.

He tried to calm himself and focus. The constricting wire only allowed for a brief shallow breath. His face had transformed from red to blue. With careful and deliberate movements, he reached up to the wires and started to untwist them. His lips trembled and his eyes rolled back. He felt his body slipping into the blackness, and this time he was sure that he would give into it. Just then he felt the two wires separate. He loosened the wire from his neck just enough to allow for normal breathing. His chest heaved, and he gasped, trying to draw in as much air as he could. He touched where the wire had been. It had left a nasty deep groove, but thankfully the insulation kept the wire from actually cutting his flesh.

After taking in a few less labored breaths, he removed the wire from his neck and pushed himself up onto his knees. He heard more shouting from the other room. It was a commanding voice, one he recognized as the police. He stood, holding the wall. A dull pain still radiated from his ankle. He shuffled toward the doorway to see what was going on. He wondered if the police had arrested Lance, although he knew that they hadn't yet searched the building, since they hadn't found him. He took comfort in the thought that help had arrived, but even in his condition, Bob wanted to help the police and the girl. The pick he had dropped during Lance's assault was gone, but he managed to find an old piece of scrap wood. He needed something to defend himself.

Atop one of the many ridges was the paved two-lane stretch that wound around the mountain ascending and descending, challenging even the most skilled motorist. Deputy Robbie Dodson stood at the driver's side window of a Mustang he had pulled over for speeding. Both vehicles were pulled over on one of the few shoulders of the mountain pass.

After handing the ticket to the young woman, he waited for her to drive off safely. As she rounded the corner out of sight, he felt something brush against his pant leg. Startled, he stepped back and saw a white cat rubbing against his leg. He was astounded by its stealth in approaching him while he was writing up the driver of the Mustang. The fur on three of its paws and legs, as well as on its back near its front shoulder blades, was matted and stained with patches of gritty crimson. It moved favoring its right front leg, as if the left had been injured, maybe even broken.

"Did you get in a fight with another animal, or did someone hurt you?" Deputy Dodson asked.

The cat continued to rub its face and body, working in a slow movement against the officer's pant legs, purring heavily like the engine of a jet airliner. Deputy Dodson crouched down, allowing the cat to touch and smell his hand. He carried the animal back to his car, careful not to touch its front left leg and sat it on the hood of the cruiser to examine it.

After a quick inspection, he saw what looked like splattered blood on its underbelly and paws. The animal's body tensed as he tried to roll it onto its side for a closer look. Deputy Dodson rolled some of the crusted red fur between his finger and thumb and then smelled his fingers. There was no chemical paint smell, so he thought it had to be blood. "I don't see any open wounds. Doesn't appear to be you, then whose blood is this?" he wondered.

A small silver chain around the cat's neck caught his attention. It was wrapped around the cat's other two collars: a white flea collar and tan leather identification collar. Both seemed in new condition and were a clear sign of ownership. Someone must have put the necklace there. Deputy Robbie Dodson tilted the small silver ID tag near the band's buckle so that he could read it in sunlight. It read: *Snowball, 112 Conklin Road, East Waterford, PA.*

He untangled the thin chain, his fingers slid along the tiny links as he unraveled it from the other two collars. With the chain removed he saw that it was a woman's necklace with a small silver locket.

He inspected the locket closely. On the back it said, "Christmas '07 Love Dad." He pinched it open and found two small cutout photos pressed into the cavities of each half. Judging by the clothing and hairstyles of both the older man and younger girl, they were probably pictures taken in 2007, when the necklace was given as a Christmas gift. The girl looked like most young girls her age, but the older man stirred the deputy's memory.

"Wasn't that the guy whose daughter went missing?" he mumbled to himself.

"Snowball, where in hell did you get this?"

Lance took another step toward Deputy Phillips. He was now close enough that one large step would put the two in contact.

"Stop. Dammit, I told you not to move," Deputy Phillips shouted. His hands twitched from both his nerves and the weight of the gun. He knew that he would soon have to decide whether or not to shoot. With only two years in the department and the limited training at the academy, he was uncertain about the tough decision that now lay at his feet.

From the corner of the deputy's eye, he sensed movement within the shadows of the adjoining room. A figure was forming in the doorway, holding something. It held the object like a batter preparing to swing. As it filled the doorway, Deputy Phillips realized that it was Bob Warren. He swung his weapon to address the second threat. Before Deputy Phillips could issue any further commands, the floorboards creaked as Lance shifted his weight. Startled, Deputy Phillips fired. The air in the room seemed to vibrate, and the blast filled the deputy's ears to the point of deafening silence. He watched the image of Bob Warren fade back into the shadows of the room where he emerged.

Deputy Phillips turned and found himself eclipsed by Lance. Both of his hands, as well as part of his revolver, were engulfed by only one of Lance's. The deputy tried to shift his weight, but before he could even move, his teeth mashed together, and for a second, his feet left the ground. Even when he regained his vision, everything was blurry. A crushing hold surrounded his neck and cut off his air. He was unable to free his hands. Lance had the deputy's hands locked tight against the grip of the .357 revolver. The big man stepped forward and like a forklift, raised Deputy Phillips to where only the tips of his shoes touched the gritty rough floor. Before he could kick at Lance, he felt himself moving backward. Lance tightened his grip around the officer's neck. Deputy Phillips's eyes watered, and he opened his mouth in a strained attempt to cough, but nothing came. He fired several times into the ceiling, a last ditch attempt to try and break Lance's hold. All of the deputy's senses became heightened and dulled at the same time. His mind was shutting down, and the ringing in his ears blocked out any other sounds, if there were any. A bizarre form of sleep fell over him, and then he felt a punch in the right side of his back, followed by extreme pressure and a dull lurching pain. With the lack of air to fill his lungs, his mind faded to black. Lance finally released him, and his body went limp, but somehow he remained upright. When he finally squeezed out a cough, the pressure in his back blossomed into searing pain that projected forward between his ribs to his chest.

"Oh Jesus," he cried.

Deputy Phillips realized that he was impaled on something protruding from the wall. His chest shuttered and his lips trembled as he took in several shallow breaths before passing out.

Deputy Robbie Dodson placed the white cat in the backseat of his police-cruiser.

"We'll get you home Snowball, don't you worry," he said, closing the door. Snowball curled up on the backseat just as calm as if she was already home. After Deputy Dodson climbed in the front seat, he told the dispatcher that he was returning to the station. He wanted to log the necklace and samples of the blood found on the cat before returning it to its owner. The dispatcher informed him that Deputy Phillips was looking into a matter nearby, so Deputy Dodson said that he would make a quick stop to check in on him. He was familiar with the old McKinney Mill. He had chased college and high-school kids from the old run-down building plenty of times, even one off-the-grid survivalist, who amounted to nothing more than a homeless squatter in army fatigues.

Samuel Piejak finished filling his gas tank and headed to the station's cashier for his change. He waited in line behind a woman who was buying cigarettes and lottery scratchers. He was still shaken and frustrated that the police refused to let him tag along while they followed up on the tip regarding his missing daughter. *A tip that he provided.* He stared at the racks of various items behind the counter. His eyes caught the flashing red LEDs on a police scanner that was also behind the counter. Each of the eight red LEDs flashed in sequence, animating the red dot as it travelled from left to right then started again on the left. It then stopped on the second LED, and a voice came over the scanner's speaker.

Samuel was so focused on the scanner that he almost missed his turn in line.

"Pump number two," he mumbled. He kept his focus on the scanner while the girl behind the counter calculated his change. The chatter on the scanner mentioned a location out on Route 101.

"Do you know where they're talking about?" he asked the girl.

"Yeah, that's probably the old run-down lumber mill," she told him as she handed him his change.

Samuel stuffed the money in his pocket, thanked the girl, and rushed out the door.

Lance took the radio off of Deputy Phillips, whose body was still pinned to the wall. He shut off the radio and silenced the voices that were coming over it. He then heard whimpering sobs. The girl was on the floor crying. Her face was down, and her hair covered her head in a mop of dirt, snot and blood.

Coleen heard the big man's boots clomping on the wooden floor as he approached. Her eyes were filled with tears. When she looked up, everything appeared in soft abstract shapes of light and color. She heard him mutter something that sounded like an apology. The shapes of the man altered and a sudden pain exploded at the side of her head. She knew that he had hit her, and not with an open hand like before. She fought to take hold of her thoughts, but fell into unconsciousness.

Deputy Robbie Dodson drove up the battered dirt road, which should have been surrendered to nature years ago. Not too far up the road he came upon Deputy Douglas Phillips's patrol car. Ahead of it was a Chevy Impala, and beyond that a late model Dodge pickup truck.

"What in the hell is going on? Looks like a damn freedom festival," Deputy Dodson mumbled to himself.

Since the road was too narrow to drive any further, he stopped behind the other patrol car and informed the station of his location. He lowered the rear passenger windows so the cat would have access to fresh air.

"Back in a jiff. Don't you worry none," he said to the white cat. It continued to lounge on the back seat, licking its paws and paying the officer no mind.

"Now don't destroy all the evidence," he said.

Deputy Dodson took a cursory glance at the area before approaching the other officer's vehicle. Everything looked in order. He was a bit surprised to see the shotgun in Deputy Phillips's cruiser. Then again, he recalled that Doug Phillips held little fondness for long guns. He got in the driver's seat of Deputy Phillips's patrol car and used his department's key to unlock the Remington 870 from its dash-mounted frame. *Always come prepared son*, Robbie Dodson's late father used to say, and it was advice that he took to heart.

After inspecting the Chevy Impala, he moved on to the white Dodge pickup. Each vehicle was pointed toward the mill, except the truck. The hood felt warm, setting off alarms in Deputy Dodson's mind. He looked around and listened for any sounds of movement. The only sounds he heard were the soft thuds of acorns hitting the ground. Childhood memories of hunting squirrels with his dad seeped into his thoughts.

He pumped the shotgun in a single loud and forceful stroke, letting anyone in earshot know that he meant business. He was still unable to shake off the uneasy feeling, even with the security of the added firepower. He approached the passenger side and directed the barrel of the gun forward, but rested his finger on the receiver for safety. The last thing he needed was to be startled and to accidentally shoot some poor kid. It had been a while since Deputy Phillips had radioed in. He wondered if Deputy Phillips's radio battery was dead.

Deputy Dodson glanced in the passenger side window of the pickup. He was surprised to find a half-naked girl lying across the seat. She appeared to be sleeping, or at least he hoped she was. There were bruises and scrapes all over her body. He tried opening the door, but it was locked. He tapped on the window, but the girl remained motionless.

"Dammit," he muttered.

He walked around to the driver's side door, but before he could open it, he noticed movement out of the corner of his eye. His patrol car was backing down the hill, but there were no engine sounds.

"Stop! Halt!" he yelled.

Deputy Dodson ran past the Chevy Impala, then passed Deputy Phillips's patrol car. He saw a blur of color to his right, then he was airborne, his shotgun went tumbling into the bushes as his body landed hard onto the dirt road. He landed on some rocks the size of footballs, which sent shooting pain through his side and into his ribs. As he rolled onto his back, Lance towered over him. Even with the sun to Lance's back, the deputy could see the man's blood-covered face, hands and arms. He could only imagine who the blood belong to, but feared the owner might be Deputy Phillips. Deputy Dodson kicked at Lance, but the big man grabbed him by the ankle and dragged him like an insolent child.

Deputy Dodson fought to unholster his sidearm, but Lance turned the deputy's ankle and forced him onto his stomach. Lance then sat on the officer and pinned him to the ground. Before Deputy Dodson could protect himself, Lance was raining down blows that knocked the deputy's head in one direction then the other. Deputy Dodson gave up on his attempt to draw his sidearm and instead tried to protect his head. Lance landed a blow that hit the deputy in the back of the head, sending his face crashing into the dirt and stars cascading across his vision.

Lance tossed the unconscious deputy's radio, cellphone, and firearm into the woods. He then handcuffed and carried the officer's subdued body by the back of his belt, just as if he were carrying a set of clubs on a golf outing.

"Son of a bitch," was all Lance grumbled as he flipped the deputy's body into the bed of the white pickup. There were now too many people involved in his fun. No way in hell was he going to bury these men along side his girlfriends. No, they had to be buried somewhere behind the mill, he thought. He decided not to trouble himself with moving all of the cars that blocked the road; he would just have to take the other path. It was steep and probably overgrown, as even he almost never used it. His only concern was that the police might have chained or blocked off the exit to the main road. School kids liked to party in the nearby field, with their bonfires and beer, but with some luck, they might have cleared any old stumps or destroyed any chains that might impede him.

Samuel Piejak almost never drove down Route 101. He never needed to. Nothing much was down this stretch of road, except now he hoped to find his daughter, Coleen there. He drove slower than the posted fifty, as no one was driving behind him. After some time he started wondering if he had missed the road. The girl at the gas station did tell him that it was overgrown. It seemed like miles before he came across a few driveways or unmarked roads, but they were on the opposite side where he was told that he would find the mill. He tried not to let his anxiety get the best of him. Before another thought entered his mind, he saw a flash of white among all of the browns and greens of the wooded area. He slowed and made a U-turn. Now on the opposite side of the road, he saw the opening in the tree line and turned up the trail to the old mill.

Up ahead, Samuel saw a police car sitting halfway in the bushes. Since the road was narrow, he thought that perhaps the officer parked his car there to allow other vehicles to pass. He stopped and got out of his car. When he approached the police cruiser he noticed that the rear bumper was mashed against one of the larger pines. He hoped to find the deputy sitting in the car, but instead all he found was a white cat in the back seat. It had propped itself up on the armrest and was looking out at him. To Samuel the animal looked a bit distressed.

"Hey, there. What the heck are you doing in there? I've heard of police dogs, but not no damn police cat. Or are you one of the bad guys? Did you get arrested for pooping where you should'na been?" Samuel said. He opened the car door, hoping to pet and comfort the white cat.

"Hey come back here," he yelled, as the cat bolted from the patrol car and sprinted up the old dirt road toward the mill.

"Son of a bitch," Samuel said as he ran back to his car. Before he could catch up to the white cat, he saw another police car ahead. Beyond the patrol car, was another car, but there was no one in sight.

"Well, where the hell is everyone?" he said to himself.

Part of him wondered if he should just leave the police to their business, but his paternal instincts overruled. If his little girl was up there, then he was going to go get her and face whatever consequences came his way. He left his car behind the patrol car and noticed that the first vehicle's wheels were fairly deep in some ruts. As he walked up the rough road, he thought that maybe the car bottomed-out and that's why everyone was parked down here.

Samuel was startled as he heard some voices coming from the woods. He looked all around until he heard them again. The voices sounded similar to what had come over the police scanner at the gas station. It was definitely a police radio, so he thought that they must be close. As Samuel made his way through the thick brush, he could still hear the radio, but no officers were in sight. He kept moving toward the voices, following the terrain as it sloped downward, then he saw the radio tucked under some wild ferns. Maybe one of the officers dropped it, he thought. After retrieving the radio, he almost replied to the dispatcher, but thought better of it. Instead he turned the radio off and headed back to the road.

Lance pinched the back of Coleen's arm as she lay on the truck's seat. She remained still and silent. He wondered if he hit her too hard, like the others. The truck's door creaked as he got out. The deputy in the truck's bed remained still. Lance shook the deputy to see if he was still alive. The deputy let out a muffled cough. Lance swatted the officer's head. Deputy Dodson's head made a dull thud against the metal truck bed, and then he remained lifeless.

Lance dragged the officer to the side of the mill and rolled his body down the steep slope to the dried up creek bed. He watched as the deputy's body flopped and skidded until it reached the bottom and could go no further. The deputy's uniform was covered in dust and dirt. Even his shiny handcuffs appeared dull in the light filtered by the overhanging trees.

"Now to get your buddy and you two can hang out together. I'll even bring Mr. Warren. Your buddy shot him. That wasn't very nice," Lance said, talking more to himself than anyone else. He left the girl in the truck, no sense dragging her inside, only to have to drag her out again, he thought.

Samuel Piejak jogged up the hill towards the old mill. He had lost sight of the white cat that raced ahead of him. The top of the old mill finally appeared nestled among the trees. Any other time this could have been a pleasant hike to a weekend cabin. Samuel slowed to a walking pace until he saw a white pickup truck parked next to the building. He knew that the man who drove it was named Lance Berry and that he had stood only a few feet from him at the hardware store. Samuel's body trembled at the thought of possibly confronting this man, as well as the fear of finding his daughter, Coleen, dead. Where in the hell were the police, he thought.

Lance descended the make-shift ladder to the room where he had kept Coleen. Deputy Douglas Phillips was face down and motionless. Above the deputy's body was a metal shelving bracket that protruded from the wall. It was dark and sticky with Deputy Phillips's blood. Lance only glanced at the officer's body, then walked to the other room. He almost stepped on Bob Warren, who was lying just inside the doorway. The room was too dark to see if Bob had been shot. Lance kicked at the old man's feet and got no response. He then tilted his head back in an attempt to direct his voice into the other room.

"Like I said, Mr. Warren isn't going to be very happy that you shot him," Lance called out. He reached down in the dark until he found Bob Warren's arm then dragged him to the far end of the room where the floor opened up to the one below. Lance released him like a child letting go of a toy. Bob Warren's upper body flopped over the edge, then his legs followed. Lance heard him land on the scraps of wood below. He stood there for a moment before heading back to the other room to fetch the deputy.

* * *

After Snowball had put some distance between her and the strange man, she cocked her pointed ears back and heard him huffing and puffing as he ran up the road behind her. She dodged under some ferns and wove her way around a few pines before she felt comfortably concealed.

She sniffed and chewed at some of the lower twigs that brushed against her whiskers. They only held her attention for the moment. She was more curious to know where the big man had taken her new friend with the shiny badge on his chest. She bounded through the underbrush and followed the crest of an embankment. The slope descended to the dried up creek bed. Ahead she saw the big man entering the old musty building. She lowered her body and slipped under the thick bushes. She looked down the embankment and saw the officer. She froze, not moving a muscle as she focused all her attention on listening. She could hear him murmuring. She watched him for a while as he recomposed himself. He then crept toward the building and paused for a moment before entering, giving her the impression that he had his own mouse to catch.

Deputy Dodson choked and coughed on the dust that filled his mouth and lungs. He rolled onto his back and looked up at the sky. His head swam from Lance's earlier attack, his eyes hurt and he was almost blinded even from the few patches of light that filtered through the trees. He had only been in two other life-threatening situations in his entire career. Those two involved gun fights. Having survived both of those and now his current situation, he knew how to count his blessings.

Beyond the most important one, being alive, he could count three more. The big man had cuffed his hands in front of him, that was one. Two, he was still wearing his duty belt and his cuff key was attached. After he removed the cuffs, he drew up his pant leg, and unholstered a compact Glock. Some of his buddies, who were state troopers, used to tease him for having an extra sidearm, but his old man's voice had always stuck with him, *Always come prepared, son.*

He checked the magazine and to his disappointment he found only three rounds. He always kept his duty weapon fully loaded, but must have forgotten to reload this one after his visit to the range. He gently eased the slide seating a round into the breach of the Glock, then scanned the area. He thought that he heard the big man mention another officer, and he hoped that Deputy Douglas Phillips was still alive. He checked his duty belt and realized he was missing his radio and cellphone. The big man must have disposed of them, he thought.

With his head still spinning, he took slow and deliberate steps toward the structure. He saw an open entrance at the base, with a door lying on the ground. Deputy Dodson wondered if someone kicked the door off its hinges in order to escape, or maybe the big man did it in a fit of rage. He still felt too dizzy to climb the steep slope, so instead he approached the open doorway, stopping every few steps to listen. Shuffling sounds came from within the structure. He took a careful glance inside from the edge of the doorway. From within the shadows he made out the silhouette of the big man, who appeared on a floor above. The big man was dragging a body. Deputy Dodson's jaws tightened as he thought about Deputy Phillips. Before he could formulate a plan, the big man dumped the body over the edge of the floor above. It crashed on the debris-covered dirt floor and lie motionless, not more than thirty feet from where the deputy stood watching.

The big man turned and disappeared back into the shadows. When Deputy Dodson heard the man's footfalls fade, he figured that it was safe to enter. Deputy Dodson moved as silently as he could to check on the victim. The lifeless body was of an older male. Deputy Dodson turned the body and found the man's wallet. It was Bob Warren, the owner of the white pickup truck that Deputy Phillips was investigating. He noticed that the body had a gun shot wound to the chest. The body also had no pulse. Deputy Dodson knew that he needed to get upstairs before his attacker had a chance to make a run. He found some crates, which he used to climb to the upper floor.

The room was dark, and Deputy Dodson expected the big man to lunge out at him at any moment. There was just enough light from the next room to define the doorway at the far end. He saw a dark stain on the floor in front of the doorway and assumed that it was Bob Warren's blood. He kept his steps light for fear of announcing his presence, as well as to avoid anything hidden in the shadows that he might trip over. He directed the compact Glock forward; he knew that he had to make each of the three 9mm rounds count.

As Deputy Dodson approached the doorway, he heard the man grumbling in the other room. It sounded like he was talking to himself. He wondered if he still had the girl with him, and where was Deputy Phillips? When he made it to the doorway, he took a quick peek to assess the situation. In the far corner of the room he saw Deputy Phillips's boots, then his legs. Deputy Dodson's heart sank when he saw Doug Phillips's body face-down and motionless.

Deputy Dodson could hear the big man, who was somewhere within the room. He watched a knapsack fly into view and land at the base of a makeshift ladder. He then was unable to believe his eyes. Deputy Phillips rolled onto his side. He still had his weapon and was directing it within the room, to where the big man must be. There was a lot of blood on his fellow officer's shirt. He could tell that Deputy Phillips was hurt bad. Deputy Dodson's muscles tightened as he stepped into the room.

Samuel Piejak looked around before approaching the pickup truck. He only heard the sounds of a circling horsefly and the crackling of the gravel beneath his feet. It occurred to him that maybe the police were chasing this guy through the woods. Maybe they were nowhere near this place, he imagined. When he glanced in the driver's side window of the truck, he was paralyzed by the sight of his daughter lying on the seat.

"Oh dear God," he gasped. He found that the door was unlocked, so he swung it open and slipped behind the wheel.

"Coleen—Baby—Wake up!" he cried. He gently shook her, aware that she might have broken bones. His stomach turned and he felt like he might be overcome with sickness as he looked at the bruises and markings on her arms and legs. He caressed her cheek and cradled her head.

"Baby, wake up," he whispered, as tears filled his eyes.

"No," she mumbled, "no, no, please."

"It's okay baby. Daddy is here. It's going to be okay," he whispered.

"Dad?" she asked, her voice as hopeful as a small child's. She turned her head, but winced at the pain.

"Oh God—Dad—we need to get out of here. He'll come back. He'll kill both of us," she struggled to persuade him to move, while she fought to move her own limbs, which were stiff and sore from skin to bone.

"The police are here, honey, we're safe," he told her, as he tried to convince himself as well.

"No dad, you don't understand, they're dead, they're all dead," she cried out.

Lance grabbed Coleen's knapsack off the dusty workbench and tossed it near the base of the ladder that led to the upper floor. He had forgotten to take it earlier, but now realized that he would like to have it. Lance remembered his aunt asking his cousin if he would like his father's watch after he had died. When Lance looked at Coleen's knapsack, he thought that this must be how his cousin felt. The look on his cousin's face, the wonderment in his eyes when he received his dead father's watch. Lance's own mother had never offered him any of his dead father's belongings. It was just as well; his father had nothing he wanted, at least that was what Lance tried to tell himself.

An almost inaudible groan drew Lance's attention. Deputy Phillips had rolled onto his side. One arm was tucked under his chest and now held his .357 revolver. His arm trembled to keep it leveled at Lance. His other hand covered the wound on his chest. Enough blood had already left the officer's body to paint his hand red. The blood reminded Lance of Roth's Meats on the other side of town. Old man Roth could be seen in the back room, covered in blood up to his elbows as he worked his knife or cleaver.

Deputy Phillips fought to stay awake. With his eyes half open, he lowered his weapon so that the base of the grip touched the ground, but angled the barrel up in an attempt to keep a bead on Lance. Even as he was dying, he was hell-bent on bringing in Lance alive.

"Take your best shot," Lance said in a gritty whisper as he took a step toward the deputy.

Deputy Phillips was too weak to squeeze the trigger. The heavy revolver tumbled to the side with a dry hollow thud.

"Get the fuck back!" a voice exploded to the right of Lance.

Lance heard the other officer before he saw him charge into the room. It was the other officer that he had tossed down the hill earlier. His clothes were dusty now, and he moved like a sack full of pain. Lance grinned at the man's resolve. The officer pointed a small black handgun at Lance. To Lance he looked comical, as if he were holding a child's toy pistol.

"I said backup."

Lance held his position.

"Turn around."

Lance paused, then turned to face the opposite direction.

"Hands on your head, and get on your knees."

Lance put his hands on his head, then knelt on the floor. Deputy Dodson removed his handcuffs from his duty belt.

"This time it's your turn to wear the cuffs."

Lance said nothing. His thigh muscles tightened as he heard the officer approach. Deputy Dodson rapped one end of the cuffs against Lance's wrist. Half of the cuff swung around and locked in place in one single smooth motion. Lance could feel how tight the officer held the chain link between both ends of the cuffs. Deputy Dodson shifted his weight, but then Lance was on his feet, drawing his cuffed hand downward and using his free hand to land a heavy blow against the officer's exposed face.

Deputy Dodson fired his weapon; the round put a hole in Lance's pants and grazed his thigh, but did more damage to the workbench leg that was in the middle of the room. Stunned, the officer lost his hold on the cuffs and stumbled backward, tripping over Deputy Phillips. Lance moved with the falling officer, taking away any space he might obtain to use his weapon. The two landed heavily across Deputy Phillips's body.

The deputy rolled on his side and pushed away from Lance. He had to keep from allowing the big man to get a hold of him. The weight of the big man crushed Deputy Dodson's forearm and his weapon tumbled across the floor and into the shadowy corner of the room. As Lance moved, the deputy was able to slip his arm free.

Deputy Dodson got to his feet and moved away from Lance. As he watched Lance stand, he was astonished; he had expected the big man to take one of the firearms and simply shoot him. Deputy Dodson came to the realization that this man liked to kill with his hands. Lance stepped toward Deputy Dodson. He was now between the officer and any weapons he might use. The fight was now down to sheer muscle and one's will to live. Lance loved it.

Deputy Dodson watched Lance move toward him. His body tensed at the thought that he might not walk out of this place alive. As the big man stepped forward, he paused and a confused look came across his face. Lance's head tilted and his gaze rose above the deputy to peer at a white cat's head that seemed to be floating on the wall.

An instant flash behind Lance lit up his silhouette and a deafening thunder filled the room. His expression went from anticipated glee to a look of indigestion. Lance then dropped to the floor like a marionette whose strings were cut. First his legs buckled then he came crashing forward on his face.

Deputy Dodson saw Deputy Phillips beyond Lance's fallen body. Doug Phillips fought to hold his .357 revolver upright. After he saw that Lance was on the ground he relaxed and allowed his weapon to fall to its side. Deputy Dodson turned to see what had entranced Lance, but only saw a softball-sized hole in the wall, with a small view to the outside world. He then hurried to Deputy Phillips.

"Come on Doug. Hang in there," Deputy Dodson shouted as he tried to assess Doug Phillips's injuries.

Deputy Phillips's body felt heavy, his muscles made no attempt to move or even tighten in responses to the pain of his injuries.

"Dammit—Doug—hold on. Do you hear me?" Deputy Robbie Dodson pleaded. He had no clue how he was going to carry Doug Phillips up the ladder and out of this hellhole. He hated to leave his fellow officer, but he forced himself to climb the ladder to look for help or the means to move Deputy Doug Phillips.

* * *

Samuel and Coleen Piejak stared at each other in silence when they heard muffled popping sounds coming from inside the old mill.

"Can you walk?" Samuel asked Coleen. She nodded and he opened the driver's side door. The door hinge creaked even though he tried his best to not make a sound. He helped her slide across the seat, and then they hunched down at the side of the truck. He removed his shirt and gave it to her.

"Here, cover yourself," he said.

Samuel stepped in front of Coleen when they heard movement coming from within the old mill. They both froze in place as they watched the sheriff's deputy stumble out of the gloomy doorway and into the sunlight. Samuel ran to help the deputy. He was a different officer from the one Samuel had spoken to earlier about his missing daughter and the suspicious man at the hardware store.

Deputy Dodson was relieved to see that Samuel had one of their police radios. He quickly radioed the station to get an ambulance rolling their way. He also requested Sheriff Birch's presence as well as the assistance of the state police.

"Can you help me move some cars so that emergency services can get up here?" Deputy Dodson asked Samuel.

"Here, kitty, kitty. Here, Snowball," Coleen called out.

Both men turned to see Coleen kneeling down and calling to a white cat that was crouching under some young pines. Only Samuel looked surprised that Coleen knew the cat's name.

Earlier in the day, anyone who happened to be at Gracie's Diner watched with curiosity as several state police cars raced by with their lights flashing blue and red. Those living in East Waterford were lucky to see a state police cruiser maybe once every two weeks. It was now early evening and the waitresses and cooks at the diner were eager to get home and turn on the local news. They were hoping to see what all the fuss was about.

Nancy Berry had just filled a young man's coffee cup when she saw the sheriff come through the door. She imagined that damn Robert Warren must have called the police to come and question her. She told Bob earlier that she didn't know where Lance was. She put the carafe on the counter and approached the sheriff. Might as well end the suspense right now and give Bob Warren an earful later, she thought. Charlotte, who was working the cash register, pointed out Nancy as she approached.

"Hello, Nancy Berry. I'm Sheriff Glen Birch. Is there a place where we can talk in private?"

"There's no place in here. Did Robert Warren send you?"

Sheriff Birch glanced around the diner.

"No ma'am, this is regarding your son Lance. Let's step outside for a moment," he said. His voice was soft and careful. The kind of voice that suggested pain and loss. Nancy marched out ahead of Sheriff Birch.

"I'm sorry to inform you Ms. Berry, your son Lance is dead. He died during a struggle with the police. He was to be arrested for kidnapping and possible murder," the sheriff explained.

Nancy made no eye contact. She stared silently out at the road.

"Since Robert Warren was your neighbor, I also wanted you to know that he died as well. He died at the same location. I unfortunately can't tell you more due to the current investigation," the sheriff added.

Nancy gave no reaction—no changes in facial expression or in her posture.

"Can I get someone to take you home?" he asked.

Nancy drew in a heavy breath and released it, "No—no—that won't be necessary. I don't want to leave my car here," she said.

"I'm sorry for your loss. If you need any further information, please feel free to call or come down to the station," he said.

Nancy watched the sheriff drive off before going back inside. Her mind shifted into neutral and she let her work habits take over. She emptied the carafe of coffee that she had left on the counter and set the Bunn up to brew a fresh batch. She then took the carafe of decaf to see if anyone wanted a refill. She walked halfway down the line of booths then stopped.

"That boy was a force of nature. I always thought it would take fire or flood to do him in," Nancy Berry said aloud, but addressed no one in particular. Only a couple of patrons looked up from their meals or table conversations to see who she was talking to. She knew that hell would one day find her son and it did. As for Bob Warren, she was too bitter to weep for him. Apparently seven years was too short of a time to heal from his rejection to marry her.

Nightfall settled over the ridge, darkening the old timber cabin that sat on top of the hill. Dim lights shone through the few windows and a mixture of sounds came from one that was open. The white cat took a quick drink from its water dish, then weaved its way through the array of table and chair legs. It folded its body tight around the corner and disappeared into the living room. There the stealthy creature compressed its body and slipped under the side table, then crept under the footrest of the open recliner, and leapt onto the lap of an elderly woman. The woman's gaze did not leave the television. She raised her arm, sensing the approach of her furry friend. After the cat had settled onto her lap, she lowered her arm, like the automated safety bar on a roller coaster. A soft smile appeared on her face as she ran her hand down the cat's back.

Lights from the television pulsed on the faces of the couple. After both news anchors made their introductions, the camera focused on one of the lead anchors.

"Tonight we begin with some breaking news. Earlier today police found a missing girl, Coleen Piejak, along with a grisly discovery. We are going live to Becky Jensen in East Waterford."

Becky Jensen nodded, acknowledging the handoff from the anchor newsroom to her location. "Thank you Stacy and David. We are live on Route 101, not far from the border of East Waterford and Briarwood townships, at the abandoned McKinney Saw Mill. The East Waterford Sheriff's Department found Coleen Piejak, a girl from East Waterford, who has been missing since early August. Her kidnapper and captor, Lance Berry, also of East Waterford, was shot by the police. He died at the scene. One of the sheriff's deputies, Deputy Douglas Phillips, died from injuries sustained during the attempt to arrest Lance Berry. Police have also found the body of an unidentified female, as well as the remains of two other unidentified bodies. State police, along with the East Waterford Sheriff's Department, have secured the scene and will be setting up a staging area to continue their investigation at first light tomorrow morning. We will be here at the scene to report any new information as it becomes available. Becky Jensen reporting live. Stacy, David, back to you."

Gwendolyn Schiffer turned the volume down on the television and turned to her husband.

"When those reporters find out who helped the police stop that evil man, they're gonna want to take pictures of Snowball," Gwendolyn said. She held a smug smile on her face and knew that he was well aware of her joy.

Jasper Schiffer was lying back in his recliner. His gaze remained fixed on the television, with a blank look on his face and the corners of his mouth turned down.

"I'm surprised the sheriff didn't keep her as evidence, with all that blood on her fur. Could've put her in a large *Ziploc* for all I care. As for those TV people, it'll be a cold day in hell before I let'em 'round this house," he mumbled.

"Temperature outside dropped prednure twenty degrees this evening, is that cold enough?" she said with a snicker.

He let out a heavy and almost hissing sigh, like a radiator with a broken valve, then rolled his eyes toward her and let out a conceded chuckle. He never stood in the way of his wife's joy, even at the expense of his own discomfort.

"Could be, Gwen, it certainly seems like hell if you don't get to cutting that pie soon."

THE TALE

"Matt, it's me," crackled a familiar voice out of Matt Scott's phone.

Matt stood in the dark next to his Mustang, which was parked under a broken lamppost. He peered across the dimly lit parking lot of the Pine Grove strip mall. He was confused by the voice. The Regal, the town's second-run movie theater, sat at the far end of the parking lot, and it was the only lit facet to the row of buildings. The theater often showcased art films and classics, some a bit too old and crusty for Matt's taste. He thought about his friends that must be waiting for him inside. They were gathering to see Hitchcocks's *Frenzy*, a classic Matt had seen before; yes it was crusty, but it had left an impression on him.

"Matt, are you there?" the voice called again. It sounded detached from any source.

"Darren?" Matt asked. He sounded doubtful of the caller's identity.

"Listen, this pay phone is going to cut off. Meet me at Gracie's," the voice said.

"Wait, Darren, where the hell have you been?"

Matt stood at the front of his car. He knew he had to go. It had been three days since anyone had seen Darren. The police had questioned Matt, and he assumed they had interrogated his friends as well, but no one had a clue of Darren's whereabouts. Matt thought of Darren as a troubled soul. They had grown apart over the years, but Darren seemed to always find his way back into Matt's life. Matt swung open the door to his Mustang. The hinges groaned with a warped metallic sound. It would take him almost thirty minutes to drive to Gracie's Diner, and it had started to rain.

The Mustang's wipers swiped in a slow delay across the windshield. Through the rain, Matt saw the scrolling red and blue neon letters of the diner's sign. As the rain washed over the windshield, the letters bled into streaks of colored light. When the windshield wipers swept away the twisted aberration, Matt pulled his thoughts back from wherever his mind had wandered. As he got closer to the diner, two other cars passed in the opposite direction. Aside from the Mobil station, Gracie's Diner was the only other friendly stop for weary travelers exiting the turnpike.

There were no defined entrances or exits to the diner; there was just one large swath of blacktop leading into the parking lot. Matt parked at the end of the row. An old white Dodge pickup sat at the opposite end.

Matt scanned the lot looking for Darren. A phone booth sat in the shadows at the edge of the lot. *Must be where Darren called me from,* Matt though. The sodium light mounted on top of the pole above the phone booth was either burned out or shut off. The only customer in the diner was a big man sitting in one of the booths. *He must be the owner of the white pickup.*

"Darren?" Matt called out toward the dark side of the building.

He scanned the lot once more and even peered up and down the street in case Darren had walked away.

"Great. I ain't waiting out here for you bro," he grumbled.

Gracie's diner prided itself on maintaining the style of a 1950's diner, even though it officially opened in 1985. The floor had a black-and-white checkered pattern, the booths and counter were composed of dark stained wood with chrome accents, and the waitresses wore pale yellow dresses with white trim and embroidered name tags. Only one waitress was working tonight; the cursive stitched letters on her name tag spelled *Nancy*.

"Would you care for a warm-up, Dear?" the waitress asked her lone customer.

"No, mother I'm fine," the big man grumbled.

"Better eat your pie Lance, before it gets cold," she told him, and then she filled his coffee cup anyway.

He continued staring blankly at the table top and only turned his head when he heard the door open.

Matt nodded to the cook, who recognized him as one of the high school boys who frequently ate at Gracie's. He also knew Matt as the star running back for Lincoln High School. When Matt glanced down the row of booths, he noticed a young man sitting in the farthest one. As he walked toward the young man he noticed the waitress; she wore an artificial smile as she spoke to the big man in the booth, whose shoulders and head rose above the back of the seat like an NFL linebacker. When Matt reached the last booth, he slipped into the seat opposite Darren.

Darren stared at his hands, which were resting on the table. He made no attempt to acknowledge his friend's presence. His hands were dirty, as if he had been working in a garden. His black cargo jacket was also dirty and disheveled. Matt wondered if Darren had been sleeping outside.

"Hey? Buddy? Where the hell have you been?" Matt whispered.

"Do you remember the cop that came to assembly after that girl, Gina Pierce, from Westlake went missing? I think I know where she went, and I think you do too," Darren said. His voice was weathered and hollow.

"What? Were you with that girl? Were you kidnapped? Everyone has been looking for you," Matt said.

"Not you."

"Of course I have. I couldn't find you."

"You didn't look hard enough."

The waitress appeared at their table.

"Hi, I'm Nancy. What can I getcha?"

Matt looked at Darren and supposed that she had already asked him, or maybe he had no money.

"Two Cokes," Matt said.

"We have free refills on the drinks," Nancy said, her smile now more genuine.

"Actually make one a water," Matt said, thinking that water would be better for Darren than a soda.

"Did you want anything to eat? The grill is closing down in fifteen minutes. After that we only have apple pie, coffee cake, or—" she paused and looked over her shoulder.

She yelled back to the kitchen, "Any soup left Petey?"

"Just the drinks for now, thanks," Matt said.

"Sure Hon, but it looks like we have soup, chicken noodle if you change your mind," she added before she headed back behind the counter.

The boys looked at each other. Darren then lowered his head and curled his fingers into fists.

"You're not going to believe me," Darren said. He stopped speaking when Nancy returned with the drinks.

Matt pushed both drinks to the center of the table, offering either one to Darren. Darren stared into Matt's eyes, and Matt turned away. Matt gazed out at the dark corner of the parking lot. He glanced over at his car, which sat in half shadow. The neon lights of the diner's sign glimmered off the wet pavement in electrifying currents of red and blue. He recalled some of Darren's past tales, which he thought were a bit too unbelievable. If Darren confessed now to running off with a group of stoners to get high and hang out for a week, then he could buy that. Besides Darren's disheveled appearance, there was an angry raised scratch that ran from his chin to the end of his jawline. Matt awoke from his thoughts when he heard Darren's voice. He listened as Darren spoke.

"Remember last month when we played Westlake?" Darren asked.

Matt cupped his hands in front of him on the table and nodded.

"Well, after the game, one of the Westlake cheerleaders smiled at me. It was Gina Pierce, the girl who later went missing. We crossed paths in the parking lot behind the bleachers."

"How'd you know her name? Did you two hook up?" Matt asked, now meeting Darren's intense gaze.

"No, we'd never met before. I'd seen her at some of the games. The first time I heard her name was at Starbucks last weekend. She was with some of her friends. They were laughing and looking at me. The only one not laughing was Gina; she was smiling and trying not to look at me," Darren said. He looked down at his hands, and his body shook as if he had a chill.

"One of her friends told me that they were heading to a bonfire after the game, and she said that I should come. They were meeting in a field off Route 101, you know, near the old abandoned mill?" Darren lifted his gaze, following the thin space between the two glasses on the table, until he met Matt's eyes.

Matt gestured for Darren to take one of the drinks, but Darren shook his head.

"Some say that the mill is haunted. I don't know about that, but while we were hanging out around the fire, I thought I saw some lights up there. As far as I know, no one from the party had gone up there," Darren said.

Matt took a sip of the Coke and raised his eyebrows trying to look intrigued, but he wondered where this was going.

Darren looked at Matt with contempt.

"Anyway, as it got closer to midnight, everyone started clearing out."

Matt returned his gaze to the window. The rain had abated, and the shadows drew his mind outward into the lot. The puddles looked like reflective pools randomly scattered about the earth, like fallen pieces of a broken mirror. He let his eyes wander from the wet street down the road into darkness. Matt continued to stare out the window in a trance as Darren's words flowed through Matt's mind like passing clouds.

* * *

I recognized the tall skinny kid from Westlake High; his name was Mike something. Even without his varsity jacket, I remembered that he ran track. He was emptying the remains of the keg into a two-liter bottle for anyone who was planning to stay.

"That's the last of it," he said to no one in particular. He then sat the half-filled bottle against one of the lawn chairs and loaded the empty keg into the trunk of his race-tuned Honda Civic. His girlfriend was sitting in the passenger seat, leaning out the window.

"C'mon, Michael. I told you that I needed to be home an hour ago. My dad is gonna kill me," she yelled at him.

"Keep your panties on! I'll get you home in a jif," he yelled back as he closed the trunk. He tucked some pastel pink panties into his back pocket, while she continued to fumble around in the car looking for them.

I watched the Honda as it rode over the once tall, but now matted down grass. As the guy drove away from the light of the bonfire, the car's taillights tipped and tilted with the uneven contours of the field. After a while all I could see were two glowing red dots, like eyes peering back at me, and then they disappeared. The car's performance mufflers roared from the distant darkness. I figured the kid punched it when he finally reached the paved road.

Laura, the girl that invited me to the party, and her friend Gina, the cheerleader in the varsity jacket, were sitting in some lawn chairs alongside the fire. They were whispering and looking at me like two conspirators. With the fire light dancing across their faces, they looked like witches planning to add me to their stew. I found myself focusing on their lips as they spoke, and I was surprised to find that I was raising a tent in my pants. I think just about everyone at school knows that I'm not with anyone, but I still felt some strange guilt. Maybe it was confusion. I've never had girls look at me in such a way, or perhaps I never noticed. Maybe it was just the alcohol clouding my thoughts.

"Hey Darren, come sit with us," Gina called to me. I noticed a bit of a tease in her voice.

As I approached, Laura held up the soda bottle with the remaining beer.

"Looks like your cup is empty, gimme," she demanded with an alluring smile.

I handed Laura my cup, and I sat in one of the chairs next to Gina, who had been glancing at me all night. I wondered if she had kept her distance earlier to dilute any gossip. Gina was warming up to me, now that almost everyone else had left. She had been holding the same half-full cup of beer most of the night, while everyone else was on a mission to empty the keg.

"Don't you live over in Parkside?" Gina asked.

"Yeah, but my mom is looking for another place. Parkside is a dump. I think those apartments were built in the Seventies, and they haven't been maintained since," I explained.

"Maybe you should get a mood lamp, Mr. Dark and Moody, to match the décor," she told me with a smile. She kept her eyes on me as she took a sip from her cup.

"Since you live at Parkside, why don't you go to school with us at Westlake? You know that Parkside sits right on the district border? There are some students at our school that live there," Laura said.

She filled my cup and handed it to me. I took a sip of the warm beer.

"Lincoln is a better school, plus we have a better football team," I said with a challenging smirk.

"You don't seem like the type who's into sports. Every game we play against your school you're always watching the cheerleaders, or you're not even there," Laura said.

"Yeah, what's that about?" Gina said, nudging me with her elbow. She knew that I watched her at every football game when our schools competed.

"I don't know Genie, maybe he's in the closet," Laura teased, trying to hold back her laughter and retain a look of concern.

"You've been watching me?" I asked. I raised one eyebrow and gave both girls a suspicious smile.

"Oh honey, we know all about you," Laura said.

I enjoyed flirting with both girls, but something told me not to trust them. Just as that thought struck me, both girls laughed, which made me feel even more uneasy.

"We're just messing with you," Gina said. She touched my shoulder and gave me a pouty look like a child seeking forgiveness. I smiled and started to chuckle, trying not to look too uptight.

"Have you been up there?" I asked and gestured toward the direction of the old mill. It was too dark to see anything. The moon was down, which would have backlit the treetops and at least given an indication of the mill's roofline.

"Do you mean the old spooky mill?" Laura asked.

"Yeah," I replied.

Laura gave Gina an inquisitive look and tight lipped smirk, as if she were trying to hold back a burst of laughter.

"No, as a matter of fact we haven't. Maybe you want to take us up there and do naughty unspeakable things," Gina said, teasing me.

"We shall see; I can't make any promises," I replied, trying to sound confident and clever. They both laughed. Gina gave Laura a quick glance, got out of her seat, then leaned over my chair. Our noses almost touched, and I became lost within her fiery gaze. I could smell the slight scent of alcohol on her breath and the faded remnants of her perfume. The chain of her necklace glinted in the firelight like a golden thread that directed my eyes to her breasts.

"If you're brave enough to go up there, you might get to see me naked," she teased. Her expression changed to one of deep concern, and then in a more serious tone she added, "Or you may disappear up there and never be seen again."

We lost track of time as we joked and talked about the other kids we both knew. The temperature had dropped some, so I gave Gina my cargo coat, and she gave Laura her varsity cheerleader's jacket. Gina rolled up the sleeves of my coat to better fit her; her smile gave me a sense that she belonged to me. She seemed to be inviting me to ask her out. We listened while Laura told a ghost story.

Gina stood abruptly. "I have to pee," she declared. After Gina strolled off into the shadows, Laura gave me a look of disappointment that her storytelling was interrupted. We both just stared off into the fire.

"Do you like Gina?" Laura asked.

"Yeah she's cool," I said, trying to sound noncommittal. The truth was, I found both girls fun to hang out with. Gina was more obvious, but I felt like Laura had a thing for me too.

"Boring," Matt said. He rolled his eyes to one side, put his hands behind his head and stretched back against the booth's back cushion.

"Asshole," Darren growled. He sent the word toward Matt like a punch. He looked up to see if anyone else in the diner was looking back.

"Get to the sex parts. If there are any," Matt said.

Darren's face tightened and his expression became more pronounced.

"Please tell me that you hooked up with both of them or at least one of them," Matt added. He tried to sound encouraging.

"Really, is that all you care about? What if I told you that both girls died up there," Darren said.

Matt lowered his hands to the table and sat forward.

"What?"

Gina seemed to be gone for some time. As we sat by the fire, Laura kept talking about some of the jocks at her school. I guess she was waiting for Gina to return before continuing her ghost tale. Her voice trailed off after a while. I hadn't said anything. I think she probably felt like she was talking to herself, like when you're talking to someone and you finally realize that they're not there.

"Gina babe, please tell me you're not taking a crap in the woods," Laura called out over her shoulder. We waited but there was no answer.

"Gina! Don't make me come and get you," Laura shouted.

"Maybe you should go check on her," I said.

"Great, I get to play mom. Always the responsible one, never the one that gets the guy," Laura muttered. Even if I hadn't heard her, the tone of her voice gave away her frustration.

When she stood, I stood as well. I then took her hand and kissed her. I don't know what I was thinking; I just acted.

She looked stunned, but I caught a subtle smile before she turned away.

"Let me get the flashlight out of my car," she said.

I waited by the fire with my hands in my pockets. I shrugged my shoulders against the cool night air. A moment later, the white light of her flashlight bounced as she approached. I squinted when she pointed the light at my eyes.

"Come on," she said. I followed her into the underbrush.

We had wandered quite far from the fire. I couldn't imagine Gina coming out this far just to pee.

"Hold up. She couldn't have come out this far. Do you think she's trying to play a joke on us?" I asked Laura.

"Oh, I think I know where she's at. Look over towards the old mill," she said. She lowered the beam of the flashlight, and we both could see a faint light bobbing up and down in the darkness.

"What the fuck did she go up there for?" I asked.

"Maybe she wants to show you something," Laura said. She started walking toward the mill. I followed close behind, not wanting to get lost in the dark.

We climbed an embankment and worked our way through the tree line until we stumbled onto a dirt road. It was so washed out from the rain that I almost tripped over some of the larger exposed rocks.

"Wooooooooooooah… Wooooooooooooah…" murmured a ghost-like voice from up the hill.

Laura placed the flashlight under her chin and turned toward me so that only her face was illuminated. Long ominous shadows stretched upward, giving her a sinister and ghastly appearance.

"Do you dare go any further?" she asked in an ominous tone. She was attempting to challenge my courage, but I rolled my eyes when I detected her restrained chuckle.

"Oh, why not? Lead on Samwise," I told her. She withdrew the light from her face, so I wasn't sure if she was smiling or frowning.

"Samwise? Really? Maybe that's why you don't have a girlfriend," she said. She then started walking toward the mill. I considered telling her that she sounded just like my mom, who had come to the same conclusion as to why no one wanted to date me.

"Come on. Let's go find our ghost," she said in a flat voice. I followed and wished that I hadn't kissed her.

When we got to the entrance of the old saw mill, Laura directed her light around the structure. The wood siding showed years of enduring icy winters and blazing summers. Its appearance reminded me of an old woman who had outlived her children. Laura stepped into the doorway. I reached out to stop her, but I missed catching her arm.

"Hey! You're not going in there?" I hissed. I don't know why I muffled my voice. I guess I had imagined that the old building had swallowed Gina. It looked alive to me.

"Seriously," Laura said. She then walked inside. I wasn't sure if she knew something I didn't. I watched the white dot of her flashlight, but then she disappeared. I went in after her, and I stumbled a couple of times as I tried to feel my way. I was totally paranoid that I was going to be impaled on a pitchfork like in those slasher films.

"Laura," I called out into the dark. I jumped when I felt a hand touch my shoulder.

"You've got to learn to relax," she said. She turned on the flashlight, which lit the ground near my feet, and then she directed it up between us so that we could see each other. Now I could see her look of contemplation, as if she were searching my face for any hints of attraction.

"Wooooooooooooah… Wooooooooooooah…" cried the voice again, but now from deeper within the mill. Laura crept forward toward the sound, and this time I followed close behind her. It was too dark to see the interior features of the building, but it felt like we were in the middle of a larger space. The floorboards creaked under our feet and the moaning got softer as if in response to our presence. Ahead was a square patch of dim light. When Laura directed the flashlight forward, I realized that the patch of light was a hole in the floor. Rough slats of wood formed a makeshift ladder that descended to a lower level.

"After you," Laura said.

I peered down the hole. The dim light in the room below flickered against the walls like a moth trying to find a way out. I could tell that the room was lit by candles, maybe only one. The nails that pinned the slats of wood to the wall complained when I put my weight on them, but they held. I lowered myself one rung at a time, and I didn't bother to look back at Laura, or ask her to shine the flashlight so that I could see. When I made it to the bottom, I realized that it was a dirt floor, which creeped me out. I don't intend to climb down into anyone's grave, certainly not my own. When I turned and saw where the light was coming from, I almost shot back up the ladder. There was a single jack o'lantern in the middle of the room on an old worn-out workbench. Its carved out face was staring at me with a *Look who's come for dinner* grin.

"What the hell is this?" I muttered.

"Don't come down," I called up the ladder. Laura didn't reply. I thought that maybe she had left. I could feel a presence hiding within the shadows, and I wanted to get the hell out of there. When I was half way up the ladder, something slid over the hole blocking my way out. I got to the top and pushed first with my hand then with my shoulder.

"Laura!" I shouted.

Whatever was covering the hole was heavy. I beat on it several times. Below me, I felt like a tiger was circling in the dark. I pounded my shoulder upward against the panel. Each time it shifted some. After what felt like an eternity, the panel moved enough for my hand to slip through, and then I was able to shove it out of the way. After leaping from the hole, I didn't look down the ladder to see if anything was following me; instead I ran and fell three times as I struggled to find my way out.

The cool air rushed into my lungs as I stood at the mill's entrance and tried to catch my breath. Between my gasps, I heard muffled laughter at the side of the building. Laura and Gina emerged from the shadows. Gina held her hand over her mouth and her shoulders shook. She was laughing so hard that she was unable to speak.

"Great! Nice, real nice," I said.

Laura turned on the flashlight and pointed it at my face. I noticed that both girls carried battery-powered camping lanterns, which were off.

"Oh come on Darren, you know you loved it. We had to get your blood pumping to other areas of your body so you wouldn't pass out," Laura said. I was embarrassed when I realized that she was alluding to the bulge in my pants earlier in the evening, which apparently hadn't gone unnoticed.

"Did you two put that jack o'lantern in there?" I asked.

"No. Another girl on my squad was up here the other night with her boyfriend. She left these lanterns and some beer, too," Gina said.

"You're not mad at us, are you?" Laura asked.

Before I could reply, Gina looped her arm around mine and said, "Come on." They turned on their lanterns and Gina led us back inside.

Four empty bottles of Molson's sat next to the jack o'lantern. Its face was now dark; the candle had burned out almost an hour ago. Gina and Laura had positioned the two camping lanterns on both sides of the room. There was also an extra one, which they had sitting on the table.

"I hope that you like our private little party," Gina said. She took a sip from her almost empty bottle. I was surprised at how much she was drinking, since she only had one beer at the bonfire earlier. She glanced over at Laura and then back at me.

"Come on let's take a look around," Gina said. I hadn't considered wandering around the damp and creepy old building. The last thing I needed was to fall down some dark hole, never to be seen again, as Gina put it.

"If you two wander off, I'm leaving," Laura declared. Gina just ignored her and gave me a wicked smile. Laura sat in silence with a stern look on her face as she watched Gina stand and pick up one of the lanterns. Gina then took my hand. As Gina led me from the room, I noticed that Laura looked hurt.

We stumbled around in one of the dark rooms. I walked close behind her, and several times she stopped suddenly so that I would run into her. The last time she stopped abruptly, she turned and we were face-to-face, and she kissed me. Her velvety lips melted against mine. When we parted, she was staring into my eyes. I looked away.

"Don't be shy," she said. Her tone was one of confidence and experience. She took my hand and led me to the corner of the room. In the dull light of the lantern, I saw a sleeping bag and a wool military blanket on the floor. Both appeared to be slept in. She hooked the lantern on a nail that protruded from the wall.

"Let me guess, your friend left this here? Looks like someone got busy."

"Sit down," Gina said.

I looked at the rough wooden walls; it wasn't the most inviting place to make out. With only a little apprehension, I sat down.

"Remember what I promised?"

I leaned back on my elbows and looked up at her with a smile. As she slipped out of my jacket, her eyes never left mine. The corners of her mouth curled into a devilish smile. She started to unbutton her cardigan sweater. It was a V-neck, with a neckline that was modest enough not to display any cleavage, especially since she had it buttoned to the top. After she undid the second button, I could see the flesh between her breasts. There were a few flecks of glitter on her skin. Her lacy bra pushed her breasts together. Through the thin fabric, I could see the outline of her hard nipples.

"You like?"

I started to clear my throat, but I was worried that my voice was going to crack into a high-pitch response, so instead I whispered, "Yes."

She pinched together the clasp in the front, releasing the tension so her breasts parted, widening the valley between them.

"Take off your shirt," she said.

"I never said that you were going to see me naked," I replied playfully.

She tilted her head, but before she could protest, I tugged my shirt over my head. She knelt down and put one hand on my thigh. When I leaned forward she backed away, so I relaxed back on my elbows. She was giving me the "Look but don't touch," tease.

As she leaned forward to kiss me, we heard rustling from the other room and footsteps.

"I guess we're alone now," Gina whispered.

"Did you really think she was going to stick around?"

"I drove, so she can't get too far."

"You're terrible," I said. She then leaned into me. I felt her breath on my face, just before our lips touched.

Tiny pulses of light twinkled from beyond the diner's window. Raindrops created the effect as they fell from the overhanging roof. It was like someone on a deserted island trying to signal a passing ship. Matt turned to look at Darren, but he was no longer sitting across from him. Matt blinked a few times and shook his head, as if trying to wake from a dream. He thought of asking the waitress where his friend went, but then he heard the bathroom door's hinges. *What a fucking loser; I shouldn't have come here,* he thought. He felt like an idiot caught up and drawn into another one of Darren's fantasies. At least in this one, maybe Darren would get lucky. Matt rubbed his eyes and chuckled to himself. He felt a headache coming on. Tension from the base of his skull was creeping over the back of his head. After rubbing his eyes, he rested his chin in his hands and placed his elbows on the table. When he glanced up, he met his reflection in the window.

The sound of the bathroom door closing caught his attention. He turned, expecting to see Darren, but the huge man he saw earlier was standing there. The man observed Matt briefly then took a cursory glance out the window and walked away. Matt listened as the man exited the diner. He then peered out the window and watched the man in the white pickup pull out of his parking spot and drive the length of the diner. As he approached Matt's window, the big man stared at him from the vehicle. Matt thought for sure that the big man had winked at him, but he decided that was absurd.

"I know that you want to leave," Darren said.

Matt turned to find that Darren had returned.

"Huh?" Matt muttered.

"Go if you have to go."

Matt considered leaving. Hell, Darren was alive with only a minor scrape. He wasn't in any danger, at least not now, Matt thought. But what about the two girls? Matt found himself attracted to the girl named Gina, who Darren made out to be quite sexually vivacious. He tried to remember which football games he'd seen her cheering at. Matt grumbled internally; *Darren was an idiot.* Did he really want to know if Darren slept with Gina?

"No, I'm good," Matt said. His voice was somber with a subtle hint of anticipation. After Matt made no motion to leave, Darren continued.

We were both tucked into the sleeping bag. Gina touched her cool hands to my chest and stomach. She twisted around for a moment, and then she popped her hand out the top of the sleeping bag to show me that she had taken her panties off. Even in the dim light, I could see her eyes sparkling. I could tell that she was into me, but I still felt bad about kissing Laura. I knew that it was a sympathy kiss, but I'm sure that she thought more of it.

Gina kissed me as her hands explored my body. I touched her breasts, which felt lighter than they appeared. Her skin was soft yet warm, also unlike what I imagined.

"Do you have a condom?" she whispered in between kisses. Her question seemed to wake me from a trance, and then sudden despair hit me.

"Um… No… I don't… have one," I whispered. I hoped that my face didn't appear too desperate. She looked into my eyes as if weighing her options, or maybe she was trying to decide if she trusted me. She licked her lips to moisten them.

"Okay," she whispered. As I leaned in to kiss her, she stopped me.

"You better pull out before," she said. There was a fire behind her eyes that told me she was serious.

"Okay… I will," I promised.

We kissed more and our bodies moved so that I was on top of her. I fumbled around, and she took notice.

"Is this your first time?" she asked. Her eyes widened a bit. When I looked away from her, she knew without me saying a word.

"It is your first time!" She tilted her head back as if to get a better view of my face and to gauge my expression. A sudden smile appeared on her face.

"Great," I muttered.

"Aww, that's so sweet," she said. I think she relished the thought that she was going to be my first.

"Don't worry. I won't hurt you. At least not that much," she teased. Her tone had shifted from concern to sated confidence. She guided me on my back and straddled me.

"You better tell me when you're close," she said. She guided me inside her. I felt like my blood was cycling through me at a million miles an hour. I had my hands on her thighs, which she moved and placed on her breasts. After a moment, she then moved my hands to her throat.

"I want you to choke me," she whispered.

"What?" I grunted, confused. I could barely think, much less speak.

"It heightens the experience."

"I don't want to hurt you."

"If I look like I'm going to pass out, then just let go."

I wasn't sure if she was getting ready to climax. She moved her hips faster and each time she crashed down on me harder. She covered my hands with hers and squeezed, signaling me to tighten my hold on her neck. Each time our bodies collided I felt like an electrical charge was racing through me and building at the point where we connected.

I strengthened my hold around her neck. Her mouth opened wider, but she was still able to release soft moans. I tightened my grasp on her. She pressed her hands into my chest and began clawing at me, digging her fingernails into my flesh. She drove her hips down, pounding against me as if to match the level of pressure around her neck. I was wildly aroused by the pulsing in her neck and the feeling of her nails breaking the skin on my chest. I grasped her neck as hard as I could, and I felt her flesh and muscle bottoming out against bone. Her movements slowed. I forced my hips upward, slamming my pelvis into hers. Her elbows unlocked and I felt the full weight of her body on me. I was unable to control myself, and I continued to ram into her. My labored breathing turned into grunts. I thought I had heard sounds that weren't my own; other grunts layered beneath mine, as if the mill too shared in my pleasure. Without warning I released before I could pull out. I lowered her onto me. She didn't protest, so I thought that she was in a state of ecstasy. I gasped and released heavy breaths. I tried to move a bit, because the weight of her body made breathing difficult.

"Are you… Are you… okay?" I pushed out the words between breaths. She seemed to have passed out on me. I didn't intend to hurt her.

Matt relaxed back into his seat. He looked deflated.

"Are you insane? Why didn't you have a condom? To top things off you came in this girl," Matt growled, as he tried to keep his voice down.

"Well, what the fuck happened? Is Gina okay?" Matt asked. Darren was surprised that Matt called her by name. He always flouted his female conquests but never seemed to remember their names. As Matt's eyes burned into him, Darren muttered, "I don't think so."

"Oh my God! What the hell did you do?" Matt asked, as if demanding a confession from Darren. Matt then turned to look around the diner. They were the only two patrons.

"Need something hon?" their waitress Nancy asked. She was standing only two booths away, which startled Matt.

"No… No… we're good," Matt assured her. He turned to face Darren and hoped that Nancy would just walk away. A few seconds later, he heard her back behind the counter chatting with the cook.

"So she's dead. How do you know?" Matt asked.

Gina remained still; I waited for her to take a breath. Her body felt limp, but not the "I'm asleep" limp. Remember when we found that bluejay that hit the back window behind your house? Remember when you held the bird in your hands and you said that it felt strange, lighter than what you thought it would be, lighter like it was missing something?

I don't know why I didn't panic. I don't know CPR, so there was nothing I could really do, right? Also, there was something about Gina; she looked strangely beautiful in her stillness. I laid her on her back and gazed at her as if in a trance. But then I was startled by the sound of wooden floorboards creaking under shifting weight. Someone was there in the shadows. I sat up. For a brief moment I thought I saw a large figure standing in and filling the far doorway. My attention was drawn away as I heard footsteps behind me. When I looked again there was nothing there.

"Laura?" I called in a hollow voice. After a brief silence, I heard erratic footsteps again that sounded like someone stumbling and tripping in the dark.

"Laura?" I shouted, louder this time. I heard a dull thud, which sounded as if it came from below the floor.

"Aaaaah," a sharp cry followed. I pulled on my pants and grabbed the lantern. I shuffled toward the sound, but stopped abruptly as the floor suddenly ended. I held the lantern over the edge, but all I could see was a dark shape moving below.

"Laura?"

"I think I broke my arm, and I can barely move my leg," Laura moaned. She could barely speak without whimpering in pain. I felt death calling me from the shadows where Gina's body lay. Had I killed Gina? It felt more like an accident. It was as if we were playing near a cliff and one of us fell. Although she hadn't moved since I left her, I thought I could feel her presence. I felt her touch, her hands on my shoulders, and heard her whisper, "Have her."

"Try not to move. I'll get my shoes and then look for a way down." Laura didn't answer; all I could hear was her crying.

I slipped on my sneakers, but I didn't bother fishing my socks from the bottom of the sleeping bag. I stood at Gina's feet. Her gaze was forever trapped skyward, but there was no view of the heavens from within the walls of the mill. I looked away from her peaceful body when I heard subtle coughing sounds from behind me. I looked once more down at Gina. There was no indication that she spoke; she hadn't even moved since I had touched her last. Was that my mind telling me to *have her*? Have who? Have Laura?

Laura's groaning caught my attention. I decided to return to the ledge where Laura fell rather than stumble around the building looking for stairs or another means to reach the floor below. When I brought the light over the edge, I could barely make out her form, but somehow I knew that she was staring up at me. I could sense fear in her unseen gaze, like a rabbit hiding from a wolf.

I walked the length of the ledge until I reached the wall. In the faint light, I could barely make out the top of a carelessly assembled woodpile. I feared landing on it; I didn't want my legs to fall through and be cut up on sharp pieces of wood or stuck on rusted nails. I dangled my legs over the edge and hoped that the distance down was shorter than it appeared. Surprisingly the woodpile withstood my weight and awkward landing, but I sprung off it quickly as it was unsteady.

"Don't hurt me," Laura pleaded. Her voice was just above a dull and painful whisper. I held the lantern out in front of me so I could see where she had landed; apparently she was unable to see my expression of concern.

"Relax, it's going to be okay," I told her. Even as I spoke, my words struck me in an odd way. It seemed disingenuous to use such words even when things were clearly not okay. Not that I would tell someone that they were dying if that was the case. Wouldn't they already know?

As I approached Laura, she attempted to crawl away using only her good arm. Her ankle was twisted and her foot was pointed at an odd angle. She had moved less than a foot from where I'd initially found her. Her clothes were dust-covered from her fall. There was a split in the back side of the gray tights she wore, and I could see her white panties. When she twisted on the floor, the seam that spread across her ass opened and closed, like an eye winking at me. She was still wearing Gina's varsity jacket, which had flipped up along with her shirt, exposing the flesh of her lower back. When I moved closer to Laura I noticed the dirt floor was different. I was standing on a dried up creek-bed.

"I don't think that you should be moving around," I told her. She looked at me with eyes filled with fear and uncertainty.

"What did you do to Gina?"

"You shouldn't be sneaking around in the dark. Did you enjoy watching us?" I asked, avoiding her question. As I knelt near her, she struggled to pull away from me.

"Don't touch me," she hissed.

"We need to get you help."

"Why don't you call the police? I'm sure they would like to talk to you about Gina."

"Yeah why don't you call the police? I'm sure they would like to talk to you about Gina. You're so full of shit," Matt said. The more he listened to Darren, the more he felt like a fool for being drawn to the diner and listening to Darren's cockamamie story.

"You've always been a loner. Your disappearance was all an act, right?" Matt pressed him. Darren stared at Matt but appeared detached. Matt lowered his voice and leaned into the table.

"Are you some kind of psycho? If Gina is really dead, you don't seem too choked up about it. I know I always say, *love 'em and leave 'em*, but I never said, *leave 'em dead*," Matt accused in a low growl. Darren was unfazed by Matt's sarcastic comment.

Darren maintained his emotionless mask and leaned toward Matt, matching Matt's aggressive posture.

"If I am some kind of psycho, then maybe I killed Laura too," Darren whispered.

"Stop fucking with me," Matt grumbled and then sat back in his seat. He had become uncomfortable with the conversation and needed space from Darren. Darren focused on his hands and said nothing. He rubbed his fingers as if lost in thought and contemplation.

"I tried my best to help Laura," Darren muttered. He tightened his jaw and bottom lip. As he shifted his eyes, he transformed his calm concerned appearance to one that was energized, like storm clouds preparing to unleash thunder and lightning.

I moved to Laura and crouched over her. She remained frozen, with her head sharply turned and her gaze fixed on me. I was surprised to find myself aroused by her; perhaps it was her vulnerability. The next things happened so fast. When I touched her hip, she tried to tear away from me, but I caught the waistband of her tights and suddenly her buttocks were exposed. I remember straddling the backs of her thighs and pressing on her back to keep her pinned to the dirt floor. Her skin was warm and inviting. I became electrified when I felt her muscles tighten as she tried to oppose me.

"Get off me," she yelled. It was all she could say or do.

I don't know why I had to have her. I heard those words in my head again, "Have her," and it was definitely Gina's voice I heard. I shifted my weight off of Laura so I could yank my pants down far enough. That's when she tried to raise up on her knees.

I only fumbled momentarily before I was inside her. I tried to be gentle with her, and soon her struggling subsided as she gave into me. It was too easy. I guess I wanted her to protest more; I wanted her to dig her nails into my flesh like Gina had done. I wanted her pleasure converted to my pain. Instead she remained still and detached. She groaned a few times, but I suspected it was from her injured arm and ankle. My rhythm became more aggressive. I wanted a reaction out of her. As hard as I fucked her, she only grunted a few times. I slapped her on the ass like in the porn videos. Her cheeks became rosy and I could almost see my handprints despite the lantern's soft light. I was excited to see my marks on her, but it only helped a little. Finally I flipped her on her back. She fought to keep me from getting back in between her legs.

Her struggle was brief since she only had one good arm and leg to fend me off. She relaxed. Her expression showed discomfort more than fear or anger. I thought for a moment that she had come around and wanted me like I wanted her. When I was once again inside her, I bent close to kiss her, but she clawed at my face. She only managed to catch me under the chin and near my jawline. I reveled briefly in the pain, but then I got angry. I grabbed her around the neck with one hand, and I watched as her face reddened.

I felt like I had stepped off a cliff and was falling. The only direction was down, and I was speeding towards a harsh conclusion. It was scary and exhilarating at the same time. Laura clawed at my arm, digging her nails in and trying to make me bleed. Hell, I wanted her to make me bleed, but I was too excited watching her expression as I fucked and choked her. I wanted to give her the same experience that Gina had desired. Her fingers slid down my forearm and her body became limp, but I continued to pound inside her faster and harder to take her to a place beyond bliss.

"You fucking maniac," Matt shouted. He rose up from his seat to reach across the table and strangle Darren. His rage gave way to confusion, because the seat across from him was empty. All he could see was his reflection in the diner's tall window. Beyond his reflection, Matt noticed the waitress, Nancy, standing behind the counter as if she were taking refuge from behind a barricade. She had a look of anticipation. Embarrassed, Matt sat quickly and turned his attention away. He glanced down at his lap nervously, and he noticed that his shirt was dirty and sweaty. As he rubbed his fingers down the front, minuscule grains of dust and dirt fell free from the wrinkled folds. He was perplexed. Why was his shirt dirty, when his jacket was as clean as always?

He peered outside. The rain had been coming in intermittent waves, but now it was coming down at a steady pace. Through the murk and shadows outside the diner's window, Matt saw himself rising from Laura's lifeless body. He then heard his voice rather than Darren's.

I made one girl's dream come true, and I fulfilled another's desire to know and experience the things that only a popular girl could. Opportunity for all, I'd say. I remember now: climbing up the woodpile, jumping as high as I could, then pulling myself up. After I retrieved my varsity jacket from where

I'd imagined Gina had hung Darren's cargo coat, I showed myself out. I was alarmed to find a white pickup truck parked outside. It was parked off to the side under some trees. Maybe it was there the whole time and I just missed seeing it in the dark. I can't remember.

Matt turned his head to peer out the diner's window. He thought about the man in the white pickup. *Did he really wink at me? Did he see me with those girls?*

Behind his reflection in the window he saw two sheriff's deputies enter the diner. One was not much older looking than Matt, while the other was probably in his late thirties. Matt recognized the younger deputy. He was Deputy Doug Phillips, who came to his school about a missing girl. Nancy, the waitress, was nowhere in sight. The sheriff's deputies approached Matt with caution.

"Matthew Scott?" Deputy Phillips inquired.

Matt drew in a heavy breath and glanced once more at his reflection. He thought that he caught a glimpse of Darren, but after a longer look he only saw his own image.

The deputies arrested Matt for the two missing girls. The state forensics lab would later find traces of both girls' DNA on Matt's body and clothing, but their bodies were never found. Matt confessed to "loving them and leaving them," but he never said that he *murdered* them. Even so, he was consigned to a state mental facility, where Matt pondered the disappearance of both Gina and Laura. Had they just gotten up and walked away? It was more of a mystery to Matt than anyone, since he'd made no attempt to hide or dispose of their bodies.

UNDER THE INFLUENCE

Cynthia had almost fallen asleep during her evening soak, but the water had grown cold. Without opening her eyes and with dexterous toes she turned the knob for the hot water. The bathroom door was open and provided a view down the hallway. Even with the blinds closed, a sliver of sun still on the horizon burned through the bone-colored vertical nylon strips. It painted the living room with a dull peach tone. The lights from the TV pulsed on the walls, more noticeable now that the sun had completely set. She had left the TV on as usual to listen to the evening news and her favorite game shows.

With a raised eyebrow, she took stock of the week's tribulations and was relieved that Friday had finally arrived. Last week, her company had hired a new manager, and he was a true know-it-all. His name was Nathaniel H. Nichols. Every time she thought of him, she envisioned his initials, "NHN… No Hell No!" He was a tall ectomorph; even his head was tall and slender, as if he had been stretched by some medieval means.

Soaking in the hot water for some time had melted her cares into mere soft grumbles. The fresh hot water had raised the tub's water temperature to a desirable level. She reached behind her head and poured in more bubble bath. The scent of white gardenias rose with the hot steam.

She peered down the hallway through half-closed eyes. The television illuminated the living room with bursts of hypnotic light. She saw a strange shadow that seemed to spread along the back wall and up onto the ceiling. It remained, even as the light from the TV held steady. She imagined that the show's cameras were trained on one of the contestants, which caused the aberration.

"What is the Bay of Biscay?" she whispered aloud.

Seconds later the host replied, "No, sorry the answer is, *What is the Bay of Biscay?*"

She blinked several times as if waking from a trance, and she noticed that the strange shadow had vanished.

Although she had lived in her apartment for almost two months, it still didn't feel like home for her. She had always lived with roommates until now, which had provided some level of comfort and security, but the frustrations of sharing a space outweighed the companionship. She thought that getting a place of your own was just one of life's eventualities. The silent and lonely existence was a price to pay, but she hoped it was something she would get accustomed to over time.

She heard the game show's closing music, which was followed by commercials and then the opening of the evening news.

"A decomposed body was found in a wooded area behind the Meadowbrook Apartments in Smithfield today. Several students of Smithfield Middle School discovered the body during their walk home this afternoon. Police have yet to make an identification or determine how long the body has been there," the news anchor said.

What the hell, she thought, *that's right behind the complex where I live. So much for all the online research for a safe and friendly neighborhood.* As the news shifted to the weather, she stared out at the room and watched as the lights still played along the walls. She felt nervous about the body, and she had an odd feeling that it was of a child, perhaps a young boy's body. She could only recall seeing a couple of residents with children, but she was fairly certain that it was a boy, and that he was not from this area.

She was annoyed that she forgot to turn on the lights in the living room before her bath, so now the hallway was dark and the living room only intermittently lit by the television. The shadow appeared again, but this time it was on the adjacent wall. Now more vertical, it resembled a standing figure with arms down to its sides. She watched closely for any movement. The shadow remained motionless and appeared like a silhouette of someone standing in front of a projector. When the room went dark between the broadcast and commercial break, she felt like her heart stopped beating. She tried to recall if any of her belongings might be causing the shadow. The room was again lit and the shadow was still there. "So much for a relaxing bath," she whispered. She stood and grabbed a towel to cover her wet body. Careful of her footing, she stepped out of the tub and paused to peer down the hallway. The shadow was gone. *Ok, I need to calm down, I haven't been afraid of the dark since I was nine.* She fastened the towel around her body and stepped into the hallway, leaving a trail of glossy footprints. Midway down the hall, cool air tightened her flesh and the presence of something brushed passed her. It was followed by a musty scent. She pressed against the wall, then she slid silently toward the living room, pausing every couple of feet. Every time she stopped, her body trembled uncontrollably. When she reached the living room, there was a lingering presence and the smell of musty clothes again.

The light from the television pulsed, which added to her confusion and gave cover to the invisible predator, real or imagined. She could feel something moving unseen through space towards her, like a panther that was advancing in the underbrush.

She ran her hand along the wall, searching for the light switch. A warm sensation climbed her back and as it reached her shoulders, she knew that whatever was in her apartment would soon be upon her. The room blazed as she found the switch; her corneas contracted in response to the intensity of the light. With the room and hall brightly lit, peace returned in an instant, except for the volume of the TV. With the volume already louder than necessary, the always-excited sports anchor seemed to be even more energized. She turned the television off and sat on the sofa. Still wrapped in her bath towel, she drew her knees up and held herself until she stopped shaking.

All she could think of was that she had to get out of there and get a drink. She recalled her coworkers discussing a new dance club called JAX. She wasn't sure if she was up for the stupid pick up lines this evening. She supposed that it was better than just sitting alone at some late night diner or coffee shop, which as of late had a strange appeal for her. In those quiet places, she thought she could almost hear people's thoughts, or even hear their blood running through their veins. She took a deep breath and decided to give the new place a try. "Live a little Cyn," she joked to herself.

She got ready and decided to leave the lights on in her apartment, convincing herself it was for safety reasons. Before closing her front door, she noticed that it was unlocked. She was unsure whether she had locked it earlier when she got home.

A third of the parking lot was sectioned off by police tape, including the exit to the side street, which forced anyone parked in the lot to use the exit on the far end of the complex.

"Wonderful, how can I get out of here," she grumbled under her breath.

A lone police car sat on Pine Street, which ran along side the apartment complex. The car's dome light highlighted the officer inside filling out his report. She imagined that the police were almost done with their initial inspection of the site where the decomposed body was found. She hoped that this last officer would soon get the all-clear call, remove the tape, and be done protecting the crime scene.

She debated turning off her car and just staying in for the night. A dark older model sedan passed by her parked car, turned hard at the end of the row, then drove up the service drive behind her building before it disappeared. Maybe he knows a way out, she thought. She put the car in drive and followed.

The club's music pulsated and invaded her senses as if it had a life of its own. She made her way to an array of tables and took a seat at the only one available. *Where the hell are they,* she wondered. *It was a few minutes after 9PM, perhaps they hit another spot, or maybe they couldn't get enough people interested in going out.* The crowd was mostly in their late twenties; although she was thirty-one she thought she fit right in. Her coworkers, who were a bit older than her, would have balanced things out. She resolved to wait another fifteen minutes, and then maybe she would head over to Reggie's, a local pub and familiar spot. She was reluctant to return home so soon as the police tape might still be up.

She thought about the body that the students found. The strange intuition of knowing that it belonged to a child, a boy no less, disturbed her. It was a terrible and sad tragedy that left her feeling both sorrow for the boy and anger toward his parents. *So many people these days seemed to be only charmed by the idea of being parents. These parents' lack of commitment and responsibility create an unfortunate situation for some kids. Those set-it-and-forget-it parents seemed content with letting their kids wander wherever, and if they happened to get hit in the street, well it was an act of God or Darwinism, take your pick.*

"Hello Cynthia," a voice came from behind her.

It was Stanford, a friend of Gina's. He was tall and wiry and was wearing a conservative but stylish dark gray suit. His angular features sometimes seemed attractive to her, but other times he appeared dark and ghoulish. Apparently he had met Gina at an office party. Cynthia had difficulty recalling if he was a lawyer or just another typical corporate exec. Regardless what he did for a living, she hated that he ingratiated himself to her longtime friend.

"Oh… hi Stanford," Cynthia said.

"You can call me Stan you know," he said, as if trying to up their relationship to an actual friendship. He then flagged the waitress to order drinks.

"A Cosmo, thanks," she said.

Stan placed his drink on the table, which seemed to appear out of nowhere, as if he had it hidden in one of his pockets. When the waitress returned with Cynthia's drink, Stan remained alongside the table. Since he seemed to be sticking around, and he made her nervous standing at the table, she invited him to sit with her while she waited. She thought that Gina or one of her other friends better show up soon. Although his appearance seemed familiar, it was odd that she could only vaguely remember what he looked like. The visions in her mind were like melted wax; the original or previous shapes of his face had softened and became distorted. When she tried to recall where they met, that too was an out of focus vignette. The best she could conjure was a mental picture of Stanford and Gina, but only Gina's face was in focus. The blurred portions of her mental images felt deliberate and hidden.

"How's life been treating you? Are you still working nights for some distribution company? Working the late shift can be grueling. I've done it most of my life. Getting home before morning and catching up on sleep during the day makes you feel like you're living underground," Stan said. His voice sent a charge through her. Although he was stating the obvious, she felt like he was attempting to convince her of something. It upset her that he seemed to know more about her than she did about him.

"Yeah, I still work for Landis. I'm one of their logistics managers," she said. Her words sounded distant and unsure.

"That's right, I remember you mentioned Landis. Does your job make it difficult for you to go out in the evening?" he asked.

"Working nights isn't so bad. I've always been sort of a night owl. I like sleeping late. Mornings suck with all the rushing around, everyone fighting to get to a job they probably hate," she said with a bored look, gazing out into the crowd of people dancing.

She checked her cellphone, but there were no calls. *Ten more minutes then I'm out of here,* she thought.

While Stan continued to engage her in more small talk, she wondered why she despised him so much; on the surface he seemed like a nice guy, dull yes, but nice. When she found out he was a Taurus, she thought that explained everything, especially why she felt unexplainable disdain towards him.

Cynthia finished her third drink, with Stan buying; she found it difficult to refuse his generosity. Before he could order another for her, she finally put an end to it, and put up a sign of surrender, waving at the waitress to cease and desist.

"Well, this night was a bust. I'm sure I thoroughly bored you to death," she said, hoping that it was true. She wished that he would walk away, especially since none of her coworkers had shown up.

He rotated his glass with delicate agile fingers and offered her a gentle smile.

"You're being too kind. And, I think it was you, who was on the receiving end. Are we becoming friends, or is that the alcohol?"

"Nope, we're good. I've got to pee," she said, and touched his arm for reassurance.

The alcohol that filled her body with warmth and softened her thoughts had settled between her thighs. She stood and held the edge of the table for a moment to regain her balance. After scanning the room, she spotted an opening to a hallway and assumed that was where she would find the ladies room. She aimed herself in the desired direction, while Stan watched her stumble off. She realized that she had been warming up to him, albeit artificially.

He had seen her intoxicated quite a few times, unbeknownst to her, and usually with substances much stronger than alcohol.

His long-time confidant and mentor always teased and balked at his weakness for troubled girls. It was something about their careless vulnerability that he was drawn to.

Cynthia's fingers glided across the glossy lavender-painted cinder block walls. They were smooth from all of the previous layers of forgotten colors. A dark lavender panel opened; it was the door to the ladies room, so she slipped past the girl exiting and went inside.

She sat in one of the stalls and thought about how she could get out of there without Stan seeing her. Then she heard a sniff, followed by a moan from next stall.

"Are you okay?" she asked.

She heard muffled giggling from behind the abused metal door. It was unlocked. Trying to be considerate, she pushed the door in slowly. There was a young woman in her twenties wearing a black blouse and a plaid miniskirt. She sat, knees together, balancing a piece of cardboard on her lap with two lines of coke. Her head bobbled when she looked up at Cynthia.

"Want some?"

Cynthia closed the door behind her and knelt in front of the girl. The girl handed her a rolled dollar bill. Cynthia stared at the neat rows of powder. She held the girl's knee as she drew in one of the lines. The girl licked her lips and smiled, engrossed in watching Cynthia. Cynthia slumped back against the stall door.

"Good, huh?"

Within seconds the drug started to burn inside her nostrils like an untamable wildfire. She had done coke before, but it had been a while. Something was different. The back of her head slammed against the metal door, and she clawed her fingers under her hair, pressing against her scalp in an effort to keep her skull from exploding. She murmured and began to cry out. She felt like her brains were being scooped out by a melon baller.

The sharp, near-blinding pain exited through the top of her head, leaving behind a calm euphoria. Her knees buckled, almost bringing her to the floor, but instead she sat down on her heels. The girl had finished the other line unaware or disinterested in Cynthia's reaction, then tilted her head back and laughed in a muffled tone.

Cynthia knelt forward and placed her hands on the girl's knees for balance. Even with the green tint of the exposed florescent lights, the girl's skin was rosy and electric. Her top was cut low, offering a view of her cleavage. When Cynthia's gaze moved upward, the girl bent forward and kissed Cynthia. Their open lips drew in each other's breath. Delicate fingers felt their way under leather and silk to find flesh.

Cynthia stumbled out of the bathroom door. The large panel closed slowly behind her. She saw Stan at the bar talking to a younger man who wore an overcoat with a suit and tie. The only non-conservative thing about him was his hairstyle, which was longer and fuller than the typical business types she was used to seeing. With his coat on, she was unable to tell if the younger man had just arrived or was about to leave. Stan was leaning in close, and it appeared as if he were whispering into the man's ear. Since his attention was completely on the conversation, Cynthia crept along the opposite wall to the exit. The small clusters of remaining patrons offered cover for her.

She was relieved that she would soon be rid of him. She looked at the time on her phone; the evening had gotten away from her. A sign at the front indicated that the valet was closed for the evening, so she stopped at the coat check to inquire about her car keys. After waiting there for a moment, she announced herself. A woman in her early forties with a short blonde crewcut and overly applied mascara came from around a corner among the rows of hangers and shelves. To Cynthia it looked like the woman had emerged from a peculiar walk-in closet.

"Back from Narnia?" she asked with a smile.

"Excuse me?" the woman asked with a look of confusion.

"Nothing. Can I get my keys here?" Cynthia asked.

The woman nodded, and then rummaged through the small lower shelves at her feet. The coat-check girl had a look of fatigue beyond a hard night, or even a tough week, but rather years of working nightclubs, Cynthia thought.

"You look like you could use a little something," the woman said as she handed Cynthia her keys. Cynthia found the comment funny coming from this woman.

"You and me both sister, what do you got?" Cynthia said.

"Got some H, ten a bag," the woman answered. She glanced past Cynthia, then returned her gaze and presented the smile of a professional hostess.

Cynthia put a ten dollar bill and three ones in the tip jar. The woman handed Cynthia her keys with a bag the size of a quarter under them.

A police cruiser was parked on the shoulder of Pine. It sat under the only streetlight within six blocks. Officer Dale Morris had been on-scene near the Meadowbrook Apartments since four o'clock in the afternoon. He was one of the first officers to secure the scene. Earlier in the day, some kids had found a body on their way home from school. It had been hours, and now even the forensics team and detectives had come and gone. He hoped they got what they needed. While he waited to find out, he tried catching up on his daily paperwork. As he filled out the papers, he saw his cellphone on the armrest light up; it was Detective Mike Bennett.

"Hey Mike," Dale said, hoping this was the call he had been waiting for.

"Yeah, I'm still out at the Meadowbrook Apartments. The chief wanted me to sit tight until you and Kim gave me the all clear." Dale's tone was subtle but transparent. He wanted to ask how the investigation was going, but after hours of sitting idle, he was eager to get back on patrol. Prior to Detective Bennett's call, he had four calls that were close, but every time he was told to stay put.

"Thanks Dale. We're good to go. No worries about the tape, we can take care of that tomorrow," Detective Bennett said. Relieved, Officer Morris sat for another fifteen minutes to finish the paperwork, and then he keyed on the Crown Vic and headed toward town.

The two parking lot lights only illuminated the alleyway entrance. Her car sat further back, engulfed in the blackness of the night. As Cynthia approached the lot she thought, "Great, this is how young women get raped, killed, or both." She hurried and fished her keys out from her purse while she was still under the street light. Aside from the passing cab, she seemed to be the only one in the street, yet the safety of her car was well beyond her reach. As she entered the alleyway, her footsteps echoed among the three buildings surrounding the lot. Only one of the buildings facing the lot had any windows, but they were all dark. The tall ominous brick walls loomed before her. It reminded her of the courtroom when she was first arrested for drug possession six years ago. She imagined the judge appearing in one of the small windows looking down at her.

"Hey, where are you going?" A crackling voice with a tone of laughter came from behind her and echoed between the buildings. Her muscles tensed and her heart hammered in her chest. She held her car keys and walked as fast as she could without twisting an ankle. Her five-inch Louboutin's created a sharp staccato against the concrete.

"Are you sure you're sober enough to drive?" The laughter had been replaced with a serious tone. She turned at the sound of a familiar male voice. The man's silhouette under the streetlights looked equally familiar. Her first instinct was to dash to the car for safety, but she almost never followed that inner voice; instead she stopped to see who the stranger was.

As the figure approached and finally slipped from the shadows, she realized it was Stan. He was taller than she first remembered. *Perhaps he does have a redeeming quality.* She still knew very little of him. His conversations kept her at arms length, offering no real depth to who he really was. Regardless of his protective nature, she was fairly sure he was single. At least he wasn't a jerk; his enthusiasm and compliments were growing on her, and it had been five weeks since she last had sex (with a man). Still she had mixed feelings, and although guilty of worse things, she decided to test how far and fast he would chase her.

"I'm fine. You don't need to worry about me," she replied over her shoulder, with her hand in the air trying to wave him off. She had known men who were sweet at first and later became violent, so she kept her distance.

"Let me drive you home," Stan said.

Cynthia raised a hand in protest. "Really I'm fine."

"You don't look fine to me, you're stumbling all over the place. Come on, it's late. Let me take you home. I won't try to hit on you; you made it clear earlier that you're not interested," he said.

She thought about the bag of heroin in her purse; it was calling to her. She wished he would just go away, but having dealt with him earlier, she knew it was going to take some finesse to get rid of him.

"I can't leave my car here overnight," she said.

"I'll drive you home in your car, and I can take a cab back to get mine," he said.

"Look Stan, you seem like a really nice guy, but I've only known you for less than two weeks, and within that time we've only seen each other on a few occasions."

"I am a nice guy, and we do usually finish last as the saying goes. Since we're both friends of Gina's, what would she think if I didn't get you home safe?"

"I'm a big girl," she said through pouty lips.

The few drinks she had earlier on top of the line she did in the bathroom assured her that she was a very sexy and clever girl.

After all, two younger guys had hit on her before Bozo-boy Stan had shown up. She now regretted rejecting their advances, as she could have easily gone home with one or both of them instead of talking to Stan in this empty lot.

The more she thought of it, she realized that maybe it was his overly helpful and caring attitude that she found so irritating.

"I don't need someone to take care of me," she said. "No, nope, no, not going to happen. I'm going home, and I don't need you to drive me," she added.

Stan said nothing more; he just watched as she walked to her car, got in and drove off.

The Toyota's gas light warned that E now truly meant empty. She knew that the car was running on fumes.

"Fuck it figures," she said, cursing under her breath as she pounded her palm against the steering wheel.

"I think I can make it, but what about tomorrow?" she thought. She knew that skipping the station now would mean a possible trip to the gas station on foot later.

While waiting at an intersection for the light to turn, she noticed a brightly lit Mobile station a block away down the cross street. It was out of her way, but the streets were otherwise lifeless with nothing available in the direction she was heading, so she turned the corner.

After giving the young man her last eight dollars through the metal slot in the booth, she noticed the headlights of a car parked down the street. With the town's plan to save money by limiting which street lights would be on, the car stood out more than usual. *Just another night owl like me,* she hoped and went about fueling her Toyota. The gas seemed to flow slower than usual. She could hear a police siren off in the distance. *Never there when you need them,* she thought. It felt like it took forever to fill the eight dollars worth of gas. The pump clicked off when it reached exactly eight dollars. With a nervous speed, she jumped into the driver's seat and locked the doors. When she drove off, her rearview mirror was dark except for the lights of the Mobile station, which vanished after she turned the corner.

The streets felt darker than usual; even the moon had taken the night off. She brushed her arm to her shoulder as if she had a chill. She turned the radio down to an almost inaudible level and kept glancing up at her rearview mirror. She wished she could drive with the headlights off to avoid being seen by whatever might be watching from the shadows. Being the only car on the road, she felt like a goldfish dropped into a tank of piranhas, like the one she saw at Penny's Paradise Tropical Fish store. The pack of menacing fish had waited, huddled in the far dark bottom corner, while the bright orange fantail fluttered its fins in lazy strokes under the tank's hood lamp.

Detective Daryl Kim was hunched over a keyboard cycling through case records. He was scanning for a single common element in ongoing, closed, and cold cases, trying to find anything that matched the Sheri Cole murder. "Dammit, I know I've seen this before," he grumbled under his breath. A paper coffee cup appeared on his desk.

"You know Quasi Kim, didn't your mother ever tell you, if you sit like that you'll be stuck that way the rest of your life?"

"Thanks Mike," Daryl said, his tone exhausted and unamused.

"Anyway, doesn't that only apply to facial expressions?" Daryl asked.

"Probably, but your mother should have at least told you to sit up straight."

At six foot two inches, Detective Mike Bennett loomed over Daryl's shoulder. Both detectives focused sharply on the screen, scanning the records that Daryl was calling up and flipping through. Although Mike was tall, he was slender and lanky. His warm friendly face looked more suited for a sales job at a computer store, but it made it easy for him to conduct interviews.

Daryl, on the other hand, was only 5'5". He was the only Asian within the Smithfield Police Department. Among the rest of the department, they were referred to as the Geek Squad, because both were well versed in utilizing the various criminal databases as well as all local departmental computer systems. Daryl thought it was due to his race and Mike's gangly body that they were given the term of endearment.

"Still looking for other cases that involved biting?" Mike asked in a speculative tone.

Daryl kept his eyes fixed on the screen, and then lifted the coffee cup and peeled off the plastic lid.

"Well, yeah… until forensics can tell us otherwise. I'm not seeing any type of object that could have been used to tear the flesh off that woman. Besides, they looked like bite marks to me, do you agree?"

Mike, who was sipping his coffee, raised his eyebrows in temporary agreement.

"It looks like they were trying to torture her, but that doesn't match up with the location. Typically and individual that tortures others tends to favor someplace private, where they can take their time. Sheri Cole had chunks of flesh removed from three locations: thigh, breast and neck. The whole thing certainly looks like a crime of opportunity: the time, the place, the victim. How could they know someone wasn't going to just walk in to use the bathroom?"

"What about the lack of any signs of a struggle? Maybe she knew her attacker?" Mike asked.

"Or maybe she was just too wasted to care, or she could have been unconscious. We did bag some drug paraphernalia. Once the tox screen is back we'll have a better idea," Daryl added.

Daryl Kim swiveled his chair toward Mike. He pinched the bridge of his nose between his eyes and took a long slow sip of the scorched coffee. Mike crossed his arms and stared at their whiteboard where they had a collection of photos and a barrage of handwritten notes in various dry erase colors. The notes were names, addresses and lists of objects, some of which had lines connecting to the photos. The board was also divided into two sections separating two cases: the left side was devoted to the body that was recovered near the Meadowbrook Apartments, the right side for the murder of Sheri Cole at the JAX nightclub.

"You know the body that was found by the Meadowbrook Apartments, it had strange bite marks, like an animal. Do you think this could be the same person, or maybe animals got to it?" Mike was thinking aloud.

"Got it covered. I'm already having the ME look for any saliva or traces of DNA that might connect the two," Daryl said.

Behind him, Mike heard the clicking of the keyboard as Daryl resumed his search through the records.

* * *

Most of the apartment parking lot was well lit, but the only available spaces were near the tree line, furthest from the buildings and the comfort of any adequate illumination. Cynthia's Toyota sat in the shadows near two large pines. The pavement was littered with dirt, small fallen branches, and other debris that the wind or tiny dust devils had deposited there. The landscapers and maintenance folks never seemed to keep this area clean; it was the forgotten zone of the Meadowbrook Apartment complex.

When she cut the engine, the lot fell silent. She would have to pass several rows of cars before reaching the walkway and path to her building's entrance. As she sat in her car, cool fingertips of fear slid up her back and rested on her shoulders. She had come home late many nights before, but tonight something felt off.

She got out quickly when the dome light came on and swung the door in a fluid controlled motion, then used her hip to close it tight. Her heels made dull taps as she walked toward the buildings. When she passed the third row of cars, she turned and noticed the orange parking lights of a car that was idling across the lot. She walked steadily and increased her pace. When she glanced back again, she saw a silhouette of someone sitting on the driver's side. *You just stay put,* she thought.

She quickened her pace to an almost jog and tried not to trip on the curb when she reached the sidewalk. Beyond that was the path between the buildings, and then she would soon be inside. As she made her way up the path, she paused to take another quick glance back toward the lot. All of the vehicles were dark and motionless. She wondered if the lone driver had driven off. She located the spot where she had seen the car; it was still there, lights off and unoccupied.

She panicked at the sound of a distant whip-like snapping; she instinctively pulled her arms up close to her body and raised her hands to protect her chest and face. She turned and looked down the sloping pathway to one of the other parking lots. Wind rushed between the buildings, and out of the shadows a yellow ribbon snapped in her direction. It was some leftover police tape that must have come loose and blown this way. Her chest dropped with a release of breath, but her neck and shoulders remained tense. When the wind picked up once more, the tape reached out to her like a hand pleading for someone's life, her life. Standing only twenty feet from the entrance, she thought she saw movement in the shadows. First under the tree at the side of the building, then closer against the unlit wall. She felt it coming, unlike the goldfish, which was stunned when it was finally aware its lower half was missing. At that moment her legs moved, her body took over, she hurried up the short path and prepared her keys for the lock. The darkness moved in on her and a man's shadow cast long, extending in front of her; someone was coming.

In a single motion, she keyed the lock to her building, turned the knob, and slipped inside. As the mechanism seated, she heard steel thudding against steel. The lock's plunger was all that opposed the outside force. She wanted to race up the stairs to the safety of her apartment, but instead she crawled to the narrow glass pane at the side of the door and peered out. Her chest heaved as she attempted to catch her breath. A quick glance revealed nothing. The wind brought the trees alive and they seemed aggressive in their movements; their shadows were morphing into frightening shapes. The door thundered again on its hinges, but the lock held. She saw no one. Feeling amply warned, she quickly slid out of her heels and ran for the stairs.

Cynthia stood at the kitchen work island and poured a second glass of Castello del Poggio. She cradled her arm to steady the glass as she brought it to her lips; her body continued to tremble. She switched on the living room lights hoping to dispel any unseen evil. Curling up on the sofa, she pulled her knees to her chest and tried to enjoy her glass of wine.

"Jeez, what a fucked up night," she muttered, rubbing her temple with the tips of her fingers.

The wine began to warm her, but she felt like it was battling the cocaine. One had her mind racing between excitement and fear, while the other felt like a heavy blanket dulling her ability to rationalize. She thought about the heroin in her purse, which was hanging from one of the barstools in the kitchen. It would certainly chase away her fears and would cover her in a tranquil yet paralyzing embrace. When she was first experimenting with various substances, she could recall those delightful feelings with ease, but now it took more effort for her to find those happy places. She would need a little help.

"Evening gentlemen. You know if you had given me another hour, I would have called and saved you the trip," said Marsha Rollins.

She was the appointed medical examiner for Smithfield. She sat behind stacks of papers; if not for the phone, name plate and lamp, it would be anyone's guess whether or not there was a desk hidden there.

"Great to see you too, Marsha," Detective Mike Bennett said.

His jacket had creases like he had slept in it or on it. The day had left his face looking ragged, but he offered her a sincere smile.

Detective Daryl Kim nodded and said, "Hi Marsha, what do you got for us?"

"Well, of the three files you sent over, we can rule out two of the missing boys, and I was able to match up the dentals with the last one."

She tossed the two still-cold-case files on top of her other papers closest to the detectives, then handed them the one matching.

"Jonah Sawyer," Daryl read from the top of the folder.

"Cause of death?" he asked.

"It looks like he bled to death from several bite wounds in three areas on his body. There also was some blunt force trauma to the left side of the head. It was minimal. I would guess that the boy was struck in the head to incapacitate him but not as a blow to kill," Marsha said.

"Three bite marks? We only found two," Mike said.

"Aside from the two major ones on the left side of his neck and shoulder, which were readily visible, there were two small punctures on the right wrist, hidden under the victim's coat sleeve. The wounds on the neck and shoulder, on the other hand, look chewed either by the original attack or by some animals that came across the body. Based on the tests I ran I've determined that the marks were made by a human, female."

"Is that right? A woman did this?" Daryl asked, stunned.

"What about any DNA—" Mike started, but Marsha held up a hand to stop him.

"Hold on. Yes, the DNA from the saliva sample confirmed that the bite belonged to a female in her late twenties to mid-thirties. Sorry I can't give you race, height, weight, or the person's address," she said.

Her tone was serious and both exhausted detectives almost missed the trail of sarcasm. After a moment, Mike raised his chin and smiled, message received.

"If only you could," he told her.

"Tell us more about the two punctures on the wrist," Daryl asked.

"I was just getting to that, Detective Kim. They are probably the most compelling aspect of the examination. They were within the bite marks, and actually part of the bite pattern," she said.

"So you're saying that this woman has fangs?"

"It would appear so. Do you gentlemen believe in vampires?" she asked with a sarcastic smirk.

Both men looked at her as if she had two heads.

"What about the Cole girl, did you get a chance to examine the body?" Mike asked.

"Just a preliminary work-up. The toxicology results have yet to come back from the lab. You guys are going to love this—the three sites where she was attacked display bite marks similar to Jonah Sawyer's body. Close inspection of one of the sites revealed two puncture wounds among the masticated tissue. Last item, both bodies only seem to have around two pints of blood remaining," Marsha said.

Daryl glanced at Mike, who was lost in thought.

"You know Mike, there wasn't that much blood where we found Sheri Cole. So where the hell did it go?" Daryl asked.

Mike glanced over at Marsha. "Let us know as soon as you have the tox results, I'm betting both victims were killed by the same nasty little biter." He turned and walked out of her office. Detective Daryl Kim thanked her and hurried to catch up to his partner.

Another night and Cynthia found herself soaking, but not remembering how she got there. Steam from the bathwater formed cold droplets of water on her face and arms, while the rest of her body was submerged in warmth. The thick fragrance of creamy white gardenias that gathered around her breasts and under her chin, welcomed her. Her eyes surrendered heavy and dreamy. The volume of the living room television was all that kept her from sailing off into her dreams.

"Police have yet to find a suspect in last night's brutal murder. The body of Sheri Cole was found in one of the bathroom stalls at the dance club JAX in Smithfield," the news anchor stated.

"That's it for that place. Won't see me there again. They're not off to a very good start," she thought.

Her limbs felt airy and with subtle movements under the soapy water, her fingers glided between her thighs. Not sure if she were dreaming, she saw lights pulsing; they were the lights hanging over the dance floor at JAX. Mental images washed in and out of focus. She was getting high in the bathroom stall with some girl, then they were kissing. She could hear herself moaning, not from within the stall, but from some speaker over head. Her voice sounded foreign and pre-recorded. The girl started laughing, and Cynthia felt herself laughing. The girl smiled at her and Cynthia smiled back. She felt her face contorting, like a sheet being drawn tight over an object, so only the object's major contours remained. Her mouth lay agape with lips pulled back, air ceasing to enter or exit. The girl was laughing again, but her eyes were like that of a dead fish, washed out, and behind her beautiful full lips were large sharp teeth.

Her head jostled, jumping from the dim waters of her dreams like a fish leaping from one world to another. The television called to her again from down the hall as if announcing its presence. "The body that was found yesterday in Smithfield has been identified as eleven-year-old Jonah Sawyer of neighboring Trenton. Police are still investigating how the boy's body ended up in Smithfield. Mindy Upton is live at the Smithfield Sheriff's Office with the latest, Mindy. Thanks Sheila, we're here at the Smithfield Police Station where Sheriff Downing just released a statement. He said that the police have interviewed Mary Anne Sawyer, the boy's grandmother. She resides on the north side of town opposite of where Jonah Sawyer's body was found. She told the police that she had not seen Jonah since he went missing on the twenty-second of August. Aside from the boy's grandmother, police are telling us that he has no other family or fiends living in Smithfield. The sheriff's department would not comment on any possible family issues and said that they do not have any suspects at this time. They did say that they spoke to the boy's mother in Trenton as well. She was distraught when she got the news that her son's body had been found. He had been missing for little over a week, nine days to be exact. Both the Trenton community and Jonah's mother were hopeful that he would be found alive. Truly a sad, sad turn of events. We will continue to stay with this story and bring you any new information as soon as we have it. Sheila, back to you."

Cynthia stirred under the foamy bathwater. Visions of a boy surfaced in her mind, as if called up from some unknown depth. From down the hall, the news broadcast droned on, but the sound seemed faded and distant. The more she thought of the boy, the sharper the details became. As she drew in a long slow breath, her back and shoulders stiffened. She realized that she knew this boy, and that he was Jonah Sawyer, the dead boy on the news. She could see him standing in front of her. "He's... he is... afraid," she muttered.

Two male figures sat in a late model Buick Century at the far end of the Meadowbrook Apartment parking lot. The vehicle would most likely be reported missing in a few days, if the homeowners returned anytime soon. In its place they would find a year-old silver E-Class Mercedes parked in their garage.

"Even if she does come to terms with what has happened to her, she has other urges that will ultimately destroy her and maybe expose you as well," the younger man sitting in the passenger seat said.

"I thought I could save her," Stanford said. He gripped the steering wheel, as if to brace for a collision.

"What, by prolonging her tortured existence? You always had a thing for the damaged ones. Giving her eternal life isn't saving her soul. She overdosed; she wanted to die. Why did you interfere with that?"

"I wanted to give her a second chance. Maybe she wouldn't have had my nightmares, the endless procession of haunting faces," Stanford said.

"What makes you think she wants to continue? You know she can't serve two masters," he said, staring at Stanford. Stanford stared straight ahead and refused to engage him.

Detectives Daryl Kim and Mike Bennett sat in an unmarked Crown Vic parked alongside the sidewalk to the Meadowbrook apartments. They were waiting for Wayne Distelrath, the building manager, to meet them with the keys to the complex. Wind buffeted the car, as if God were trying to blow them away.

An economy-sized Ford sedan caught their attention. It pulled into the maintenance spot near the side of one of the buildings.

"Must be him," Mike said.

Both detectives hopped out of the vehicle, braced themselves against the wind and headed toward the parked Ford. A stocky man, who was shorter than Mike, but taller than Daryl, got out of the Ford and lumbered toward them. He had a well-developed waistline cultivated by years of leisure. Daryl was wondering if the man was going to make it across the lawn before he would need to stop and rest.

"Mr. Wayne Distelrath?" Mike asked.

"Yea—Yeah, that's me," Wayne replied, huffing the words out.

Before Mike or Daryl could thank Wayne for coming out late in the evening, Wayne found enough air to push out his complaint.

"Couldnah—cod—couldn't this have waited 'til tomorrow?"

The wind picked up and Mike stepped closer.

"Afraid not," Mike said.

"You suspect one of the tenants had something to do with the boy's body that was found nearby?" Wayne asked.

"Not exactly Mr. Distelrath, we just have some follow up questions for some of the tenants."

"Oh, come on now. You know something like that could have waited until tomorrow."

"Thanks, Mr. Distelrath, for meeting us this late. We apologize for interrupting your evening. Now if you can please open the door to the building we can take it from there," Daryl said.

All three men made it up the walkway as the wind tried to shove them every which way except the direction they wanted to go. Mike noticed the police tape had been blown across the lot and was tangled on the railing to some stairs. He wished he had told Officer Morris to remove it before leaving the scene.

When they got inside the main floor entry way, Daryl asked Wayne to stick around. He wanted to follow the detectives, but Daryl told him to wait downstairs or in his car. The detectives climbed the stairs while Wayne stood there with a disgusted look on his face.

"What do you want, it's late." a woman called from the other side of the white steel door.

"Police. We need to ask you some questions," Daryl said, trying to be loud enough to penetrate the door and at the same time low enough as not to disturb any of the other tenants.

A dull metallic tumble came from the seam where the door met the frame. It was followed by the delicate noise of polished metal surfaces passing one another. A woman in her early thirties with wet dark hair against creamy milky-white skin stood in the half opened doorway. She was wearing a burgundy bathrobe, which she clenched closed near the collar.

"Ms. Cynthia Albright?" Detective Mike Bennett asked.

"Yes," she replied.

Both men withdrew their credentials from their jackets and offered them for her inspection.

"What's this about?" she asked.

"We would like to ask you some questions about the boy's body that was recently found nearby. Maybe you've heard about it on the news," Mike said.

"Oh. Yes. Please come in," she said.

"If you don't mind waiting here in the kitchen while I put some clothes on, I'll be with you in just a minute."

They nodded and stood around the kitchen work island while Cynthia shuffled down the hall to the bedroom. The Meadowbrook Apartments had been built less than three years earlier. The contemporary cabinets and granite countertops were in keeping with the road sign's tagline, "Embrace Modern Luxury Living in Smithfield." Mike raised his eyebrows as he glanced at Daryl; they agreed without speaking that it was a nice place. Cynthia's kitchen was immaculate, with the exception of the empty wine bottle and cork extractor near the sink. The space smelled and felt sterile. No faint or distant aroma was present to indicate that anyone had ever cooked a meal there.

On the work island was a small wicker basket with a few letters and coupon fliers. One of the three tall barstools had a purse draped over the back. Daryl noticed a single earring that was almost hidden under the contoured side of the basket.

He was mindful not to disturb anything as he searched around the basket, but its mate seemed to be missing. He knew that he was looking at something important, but he failed to make any connection.

"Mike," Daryl whispered, pointing. Maybe his partner could see what he was missing.

Mike furrowed his brows and shook his head, not picking up on what Daryl was suggesting. They could hear the sounds of Cynthia getting dressed down the hall. Mike glanced around the corner and turned quickly away after seeing Cynthia naked through the half open bathroom door. She was wearing only a bra and brushing her hair. He wondered why she had left the door open, but doubted that she had seen him looking.

A door closed and echoed down the hall. Daryl shuffled through his jacket, retrieved his phone from the breast pocket, took a couple of quick shots of the earring, and then slipped his phone in his pants pocket.

"Sorry to keep you waiting," Cynthia said. She wore pink satin pajamas. She noticed the Asian detective leaning against one of the empty barstools next to her purse. She tried to recall if she had removed the bag of heroin. *No such thing as drug sniffing cops, are there?* she hoped. An abrupt chuckle almost passed her lips.

"Can I offer either of you a drink?" Cynthia asked.

"No thanks, we're good," Daryl said.

She needed a drink as much as a distraction. She moved to the refrigerator and placed an unopened bottle of wine on the counter.

"Ms. Albright, your apartment faces the location where the boy's body was found," Detective Mike Bennett said.

"His name was Jonah, at least, that's what they said on the news," she muttered, almost as if she were in a trance.

"Yes, that's correct. Can you tell us if you saw anything out of the ordinary, in particular out toward the field near the parking lot?" Mike asked. His partner Daryl said nothing; he just stood there observing Cynthia's reactions.

"I don't remember seeing anything strange. Whoever dropped the body there, I would imagine, did it at night, otherwise you would already have witnesses. I work nights, and I don't remember seeing anything strange coming or going," she explained.

She opened the bottle and poured herself a glass of wine, and she kept her eye on the Asian detective, who stood silent. Her purse hung on the back of the stool, dangling her guilt in front of Detective Daryl Kim. Thank God it wasn't weed, she thought, or anything that might give off a recognizable odor. He stared at her, making her feel like he was waiting for her confession, all while he held the damaging evidence right in front of her. She directed her attention to Detective Bennett.

"Was there anything else?"

"Were you working last night?"

"That boy, Jonah, was found only yesterday, don't you mean Friday night?"

"Yes, that's what he meant. Or rather do you work on the weekends?" Daryl jumped in before Mike could press the question.

Cynthia shook her head, "Nope, no weekends for me."

Mike held back waiting to see where Daryl was going.

"Okay, Ms. Albright. I think we're done. Come on Mike, we have some more doors to bang on," Daryl said with an assured smile. He slid his card across the granite work island toward Cynthia.

"If you do happen to see anything or hear anything, please give us a call. You would be surprised how many times these psychos return to the scene of the crime. Thanks for your time," Daryl said.

The footsteps and voices of the detectives had diminished moments ago, but Cynthia was having difficulty prying herself from the door. She peered through the door's security peephole a second and last time. With the outside hall empty, she returned to the kitchen and poured another glass of wine.

Looking over at the barstool and her purse, she shook her head. "Stupid, stupid, stupid," she thought. She sipped the wine, feeling the thin stiff glass between her lips and the cool fragrant liquid that filled her mouth. Her cheeks tightened and her lips curled into a devilish smile, as she struggled to keep from bursting into laughter.

Prancing on her tiptoes, wine in one hand and her purse in the other, she danced to the couch, and then dumped the contents of her purse onto the glass coffee table. She focused on the tiny plastic bag that slid out with everything else. It sat partially under her Tiffany compact with the mirrored finish.

The decorative edge of the compact case had several thin steps, each one casting a reflection. Parts of the usual bright and shiny case looked dull. She tilted it around, wondering how it got damaged. Every surface that turned away from her became bright and reflected the room and its furnishings. Every surface that faced her became dull, gray and darkened the more she inspected it. She felt as if she were looking inward, into a space with almost no illumination. She thought she saw figures moving within, calling her, drawing her inward. She pushed the compact away, and it slid to the middle of the table.

The uncovered plastic square, not much larger than her thumb, seemed to stare up at her, enticing her. She stretched across the length of the couch to fetch a small wooden cigar box. It sat on the lower shelf of the end table. *Time for a rendezvous with Mr. H,* she thought as she eagerly assessed the tiny square *Ziploc.* The plastic surface reflected the room's lights, obscuring the powdery contents. She retrieved her lighter from the scattered contents of her purse, and then removed a spoon and syringe from the cigar box.

The wheels of the Crown Vic almost separated from the pavement as the police cruiser crested the hill and floated over the railroad tracks on Darby Street. Detective Daryl Kim struggled to keep control of the vehicle as he made a hard right onto Featherstone Avenue at the bottom of the hill. Mike mashed his palm into the ceiling and held onto the dash as the car rounded the corner.

"I love an old-fashioned police chase just as much as the next guy, but Daryl, there's no one in front of us," Mike said.

"Sorry Mike, I need to check the evidence taken from the Cole murder."

"So you think Cynthia Albright is connected?"

"Yeah, didn't you see me pointing at the earring?"

"I thought you were referring to the mail in the basket on the counter."

"Don't worry about it. I got a few shots with my phone. We can compare it to the one we bagged. I tried calling Teri, to see if she could shoot me over a photo, but she's not picking up," Daryl said, his face tightened in a concentrated scowl.

Mike could hear Daryl's frustration. He knew that Daryl had excellent observation skills, but early on when he was trying to impress their chief, Daryl had arrested an individual based on what he thought was a clothing match. Lucky for him, the person let it drop and Daryl got to keep his job, but lost a year getting his detective's shield.

"Got it," Mike said.

He rang the main desk number for the evidence department on his cellphone, but after thirty seconds, he just shook his head.

"She's not answering," Mike said.

After turning on Church, Daryl gripped the steering wheel and mashed the pedal. The Crown Vic leapt forward. Even as the engine roared and the car's speed increased, Mike relaxed back in his seat. It was now just a straight shot to the station.

Insistent echoes of a phone ringing came from an office down a long tiled corridor. The ceiling of the hallway was lined with florescent lights that led to the twin steel doors of the Smithfield Police Department's evidence storeroom. The phone's ring was dull through the metal doors, but the tiled walls of the hallway gave it extra life and carried it.

Officer Teri Warren sat at the security desk, which was not much larger than a student's desk. The surface was only able to accommodate a lamp, a few files and not much more. Her head was resting over folded arms and her less-than-shoulder-length chestnut hair covered her face. If not for the glossy crimson outline around her forearms and the stillness of her body, she could have been accused of sleeping on the job.

One of the steel doors opened, and its weight screeched on oil-deficient hinges.

"Fuck sake Teri, we've been calling you. Don't tell me you've been sleeping off a hangover?" Daryl snarled.

Mike took two steps forward and saw the spread of blood fenced in and hidden by her arms and head. Her lower right cheek, jaw and lips were pressed into the pool. Daryl snatched up the phone and pressed the button for the front desk upstairs. The line was dead, and he had no cellphone service in the basement, so he ran through the steel doors and bolted down the hallway to get help.

Mike moved around the desk to check to see if Teri was still alive. Her body showed no signs of life. He scanned the room, which was only twelve shelves deep. It would be difficult to hide among all the open steel shelving, even with the scattering of banker's boxes and archival sealed envelopes. He returned to Teri's body, which was now a crime scene, and started his routine investigation pattern, taking photos with his phone and jotting down quick notes in his log book.

By the time Daryl returned with two other officers, Mike had already laid out Teri's body on the floor and was performing CPR. No matter how many times he compressed her chest, her face remained void of color. Each downward motion felt hollow; it was a futile attempt to push nonexistent life-sustaining fluids and air where they were needed.

"Paramedics are on their way," Daryl said, pushing the words out between breaths.

Officer Lindsey O'Rourke got on her knees and assisted with the attempt to revive Teri. Daryl inspected the phone and noticed the line was pulled from the wall.

"We have to check all of the items in evidence. Let's start with drugs and weapons first," Daryl told the other uniformed officer. He handed the officer a heavy binder.

"Check everything, and make note of any items that were released and follow up with whoever had last chain of custody," Daryl said.

Daryl watched Mike briefly then headed down the rows of shelves. Nothing looked disturbed and the floors were clear of any boxes or items. Two rows from the back he stepped into the aisle where the boxed evidence of the Sheri Cole case was kept. He found the box; it appeared undisturbed with the lid secure and in place, but his heart sank when he grasped the sides. It felt like an empty shell. He knotted his jaws and slammed his fist against the shelf after removing the lid.

"Son of a bitch," he growled.

As Cynthia lay in bed, she noticed that her body felt airy and lighter. *Must be the high,* she thought. The ceiling appeared to be getting closer. A delicate pull of gravity tried to reclaim her. She looked with fascination at the caustic light patterns across the ceiling. She remembered that the television was off, besides it would have produced different kinds of flashes and bursts of light, unlike what she was witnessing. The lamp on her nightstand was on, and the bulb burned bright.

"What is this?" She pushed out the words on soft air between subtly open lips. It was as if something dark was swimming above her, forcing shadows among the light. She smiled at the thought of an all-new adventure with Mr. H.

"Where are you taking me Love?"

Her skin drew tight and appeared emaciated, which accentuated the rope-like muscles in her limbs and face. Her lips opened to a gasp of frozen breath. The marbling of shadow and light swirled above her, and waves of dark began swallowing the light. She held her hands out before her as her body ascended toward the darkness, like an astronaut adrift with a broken tether.

The ceiling was pitch as the night sky; there were no stars, just a yawning gape of blackened void. The walls to the room were being consumed as well. She wondered if she were dying. She had a fleeting memory of someone telling her that she had overdosed, but that couldn't be, she was alive after all. That memory, among others, lurked in the dark crevices of her mind.

A cool chill crawled up her back, like delicate fingers tracing her spine, visiting each fleshy protrusion. Fingers gave way to palms, caressing around her, following her ribs from back to front, outlining her breasts before traveling over the contours of her abdomen to her hips and thighs.

Cynthia's body twisted, electricity surged through her limbs and her skin became tight with a chill. Lips touched her shoulder and neck, and a nose brushed her ear.

"I'm sorry," a whisper drifted from behind her.

"Whaa—t," she tried to reply, but the volume of her own voice trailed off into silence.

Like the needle she had used earlier to inject the heroin, burning sharp points penetrated her flesh. She arched her back in a violent motion, and she thrust her chest forward. She felt remnants of herself being pulled, like air through a vent. Her penetrated flesh felt like an open doorway to a new beginning. She felt transformed, a new kind of alive.

"They took everything. Her clothes, jewelry, shoes, handbag, everything," Daryl said, his face a mask of frustration.

Mike watched the paramedics wheel Officer Teri Warren down the hall. He and Officer O'Rourke had done all they could, but they knew that she was gone. Both left their thoughts unspoken to avoid crushing each other's spirit. Even with no signs of life, the EMTs kept working on her. The emergency room physician would make the final call to pronounce her deceased.

"Let's check the security video, I want to know who the son-of-a-bitch was that did this," Mike demanded.

Mike and Daryl finished securing the evidence room. Police tape was tied around the handles of the two steel doors, and a crime scene seal was taped across the seam between both doors. Checking the entire inventory against the manifest would have to wait until they could figure out who had entered the station, made it to the secure evidence room, removed various items, killed Officer Warren, and walked out without being stopped or questioned. Those thoughts raced through both detectives' minds. Mike tried to formulate various scenarios but came up short on anything that seemed plausible.

"I've got to stop by my desk first. I'm going to prove to you what I already know," Daryl said.

Obscured in a cloudy shadow, Stanford rose beneath Cynthia's floating body. Both ascended toward the ceiling of the bedroom like two submerged figures gliding to the water's surface. He embraced her with limbs that reached out from the deepest blackness where light had never existed. Her body made subtle movements, as if she was turning in her sleep.

Like sharp thorns hidden among soft petals, Stanford's viciously sharp teeth were surrounded by gentle, soft lips. He kissed her cheek, then her neck. The usual thump of a heartbeat and pulse of fluid being pushed through arteries was no longer there. Their flesh was the same: soft, cool and damp. His lips pressed against her. He retched and almost withdrew as the icy and lifeless fluid filled his mouth.

In his early years of walking in the shadows, he pondered his new existence as a kind of thief. He would steal life from the living to pay an ever-perpetuating debt of the dead. Every attempt at suicide only led to his dark nature taking over, often brutally pushing his once human moral instincts to almost unreachable corners within himself.

Drawing in her blood would be a payment of the dead, an insult to his new gods. His sponsor held little remorse for his situation, and none for the girl he had brought into their circle. Tonight he hoped that he and Cynthia would escape together.

Daryl leaned over his desk, arm locked and fist planted on the surface.

"Here it is Mike. I knew we should have arrested that girl," Daryl said tapping one of the pictures in the case file.

He handed the open folder across his desk to Mike. Mike examined each photo as he flipped through them. The second photo was a close up of the side of Sheri Cole's face. Since one earring was missing, forensics had photographed the one that remained. It was a match for the one Daryl had seen at Cynthia Albright's apartment.

"Son-of-a-bitch," Mike said under his breath.

"Yeah, son-of-a-bitch," Daryl remarked. His deflated voice trailed off.

Randy Evers was already trolling through the station's security video footage when Daryl and Mike came knocking. Randy opened the security door to the double-sized closet space. With only one chair, the two detectives chose to stand; they loomed over Randy's shoulders like two vultures waiting for their meal to die. Randy had that day's video paused on one of the five monitors. The others gave a clear view of the current activity within the station.

"I've cued up the evidence room footage from the camera with the clearest view of Officer Warren," Randy said.

He engaged his keyboard and put the video in motion.

"It should also be approximately thirty minutes before she was assaulted."

He moved the video forward at time and a half.

They watched Officer Warren at the desk handling her daily paperwork and taking a couple of calls. The image seemed to dim as if the contrast was turned up, but instead of the bright areas washing out, they remained at their current levels. Only the shadowy areas on the ceiling became darker, as if smoke were crawling across its surface. If they had watched the video at normal speed, the change in light would be unnoticeable.

The dark mass slid to the side of one wall, and then rode the seam above the rows of shelves.

"Can you increase the speed? Whoever came in should be showing up soon," Mike said.

Randy pressed a series of command keys to increase the playback speed.

A dark mass appeared behind Officer Warren. She made no motion to suggest that she was aware of its presence. Its shape morphed and whipped in violent patterns, seizing Officer Warren from behind with almost invisible speed, like a spider drawing in its prey, caging it within spiny legs and immobilizing it.

"Whoa—whoa—whoa!" Daryl shouted.

Randy paused the playback.

"What the hell is that?" Mike demanded.

Randy scanned the video back to where the shape first entered the frame, paused it and started playback at half speed.

All three men watched as the form dripped downward from the seam where the wall met the ceiling, then amassed behind their colleague. Alternate frames revealed a figure within the black mass, appearing then vanishing as Randy moved the recording forward frame by frame.

"Stop there. Is that a man in there?" Mike said.

"Looks like it, but what's all that smoke?" Daryl asked.

All three men stared at the monitor trying to comprehend the shadowy mass with the man emerging from it like some dark jinn, magic lamp and wishes not included.

"I don't get it. Look at the rest of the picture, Officer Warren and the rest of the room are as clear as day. I don't think there is anything wrong with the video or the camera," Randy said, as he turned to face both detectives.

A contemplative silence filled the room, then Daryl and Mike broke their gaze and looked at Randy; their expressions were an unspoken approval of his reasoning.

"With the evidence missing, I'm telling you, Mike, that Cynthia girl is involved and connected to this," Daryl said.

Cynthia was still floating facing the ceiling of her bedroom. The black open space remained a vista before her. Her serenity was replaced by a feeling of dying. As her essence flowed from her, she struggled to break free. She shook with fear, not from fear of dying, but from a sense of uncontrollable evil filling her. She clenched the arm that held her and managed to break free, then spun around to face her captor. Her vision was a blur, but she recognized Stanford's stunned expression. She could only watch and witness as her body responded beyond her control. Her arms and legs wrapped around him, held him fast, and her sharp teeth snapped at his face and neck. He fought to push her away, and then opened his arms to accept her assault. Maybe this would be the end, he thought, as his blood flowed from his body. An overwhelming thirst came over him. He opened his mouth and emitted a subtle guttural sound. A distant knocking came from outside the room and down the hallway. Each note was dull and reverberated in his head as if he were descending underwater. He felt himself slipping into a different sort of darkness. He had a feeling of landing softly, almost weightlessly, like autumn leaves floating and settling on the forest floor. The numb, almost calm, feeling was brief. His last vision came in the form of dark, abstract, silhouetted shapes that broke apart. The shapes became larger and more recognizable. They morphed into a pack of wolves that circled his body, growling, and then rushed to devour him. They tore at his body as if it were a paper doll, until nothing remained.

Pounding came from the other side of the steel door, and after several heavy blows it swung open to Cynthia's apartment. A man appeared in his mid-thirties, clean cut and dressed in a suit and overcoat. He paused just inside the door to listen for any movement. After a brief scan of the kitchen and living room, he stepped down the hall. Halfway to the bedroom, he spoke in a delighted tone, "My dear boy, now that wasn't so bad, now was—," his voice trailed off when he reached the doorway to the bedroom.

A contorted body was seated on the floor at the foot of the bed. The clothing confirmed that it was Stanford. His flesh was blackened and drawn tight to his bones, giving him the appearance like that of an ancient mummy found frozen in the Himalayas.

"Well, that's unfortunate," the man whispered.

He stared at the body, but then a coldness settled over his shoulder. His brow furrowed in an expression of concern, then his nostrils flared and his eyes shot to the corners of their lids as he felt a presence in the room.

Detective Kim rousted Wayne out of bed, to again gain access to the apartment building. This time Wayne held back on his complaints, as he was sure that this time they were there to make an arrest. He had watched enough cop shows and was eager to be part of the action. Of course they made him wait downstairs, when he wanted to see the looks on people's faces. The expressions of guilt and surprise when they found out they were being hauled in for whatever wrongdoings they had committed. Instead, he watched both detectives climb the stairs and disappear as they rounded the first landing.

Mike stopped a few feet away from Cynthia Albright's door, blocking Daryl. Without a word he pointed, directing his partner's eyesight to the door, which sat ajar. The door knob was bent and the steel encasement surrounding it was caved in as if it had been hit with a sledgehammer. It looked like a SWAT team had made entry. They glanced at each other with puzzled looks, and then drew their sidearms.

Both detectives scanned the kitchen and living room. A small wooden box lay on the couch, along with an empty purse and all of Cynthia's belongings spread out across the coffee table. Among her things they noticed the all-too-familiar items that came with drug abuse and assumed that she was probably the one who dumped her purse—not an intruder.

With caution they stepped down the hallway toward the bedroom. Glass shards crackled under their shoes as they reached the doorway. As they had many times before, they entered the room with smooth tactical precision. Daryl entered first, followed by Mike; both directed their firearms forward, ready for any confrontation.

They were greeted by a rush of wind that entered through the broken window on the far side of the room. Surprised at the body of what appeared to be a male wearing a gray suit, seated on the floor at the foot of the bed, both detectives moved to opposite sides of the doorway. They had only come across one other similar scene during their combined twenty-seven years, when they found the charred remains of a murder victim.

Mike hurried to the broken window, expecting to see another body laid out on the winding stone walkway below. All he saw was the dancing shadows of the windswept trees. The shadows moved across the pathway, convincing him that there was something more there. He felt like someone was looking back at him from the dark, and could almost hear his name being whispered.

"No ID," Daryl announced, his eyes still fixed on the body, which looked like a contorted soul.

"What on Earth happened to you?" Daryl muttered.

After further inspection of the victim's sport coat pockets, he found an old expired driver's license. The photograph was of a blonde woman.

"Leslie Rogers? You look awfully familiar Ms. Rogers," Daryl said.

Although it was a blonde female pictured on the ID, she resembled a younger and less tattered Cynthia Albright. He finally looked up to see if his partner was paying attention.

"Mike?"

Daryl scanned the back wall of the room and stopped when his eyes arrived at the open window. The black square seemed to float on the wall. Rather than being a portal to look outward at the surrounding world, it felt like an opening to a smaller space.

"Mike—" Daryl cried out and ran to the window, catching himself on the frame. The walkway below was too dim to see anything.

"Mike!" he yelled out the window.

His voice was swallowed by the darkness and swirling wind. He spun around to an empty room, and then ran to the hallway, even though he knew very well that he would have seen his partner pass him if Mike had left the room through the doorway. The living room was also empty, so he returned to the bedroom; he was nervous that somehow the body they found would vanish as well.

Daryl jammed his hands into his overcoat pockets. He found his cellphone and called Mike's cell, hoping to locate him. At first he heard nothing, then there was the faint familiar ringtone of his partner's phone. He moved to the window. The wind had abated some, so he could hear his partner's phone ringing from the dark walkway below.

"Mike?" he yelled from the window. The familiar ringtone of Mike's phone was all that he could hear. He ended the call and cried out once more before he ran from the apartment to find his partner.

Cool air descended from the open window to the bathtub below and was met with the rising sound of gentle musical humming. The scent of white gardenias swirled within the steam as it rose from the bathwater.

Cynthia's knees protruded from the water like the soft tall hills of Guilin China, while her shoulders and breasts were hidden within the sudsy clouds of the bubble bath. Her face was half covered by newly dyed locks of deep auburn. She held an eerie gaze down the submerged length of her body. Her expression was void of any thoughts or daydreams; she was like a spider in repose, neither preparing to strike, nor busying itself with its web, just existing in utter stillness.

Voices came from the adjoining room. A flatscreen that faced two queen-sized beds presented the local news. The anchor, in her dark suit and helmet-shaped blond hair, looked into the camera as if she were looking into a mirror.

"Last night two detectives of the Smithfield Police Department made a gruesome discovery of an unidentified man's body at the Meadowbrook Apartment complex in Smithfield township. The body was found in the apartment of Cynthia Albright, whom the police were there to question. Police have still not located her. One of the detectives, Detective Daryl Kim, has been put on administrative leave, pending the investigation into the death of his partner, Detective Mike Bennett. Detective Bennett was found impaled on a metal fence with a broken neck. Police believe that Detective Bennett was either pushed or fell from the window of the apartment belonging to Cynthia Albright. We will bring you more details on this story as it unfolds."

NORTHERN LIGHTS

David was in a deep sleep after the exertion of yesterday's hike, but the pain at the side of his head and sudden shock to his ribs was alarming. In his groggy state, the signal felt like a long distance connection, with his body at one end and his brain at the other. When he managed to crack his eyes open, a blur of color and intense pain flooded in.

The inside of his tent, the temporary ceiling of red nylon, was torn away to reveal the open sky. A heavy fur-covered figure stood over him, acknowledged his awakening, and drew back to deliver another strike. Alarmed, David instinctively drew his elbows up and cupped his hands to the sides of his head in a defensive posture. The crushing impact against his hand, radiated inward, like a multi-car accident, ending in head trauma. His knuckles crunched within his glove, passing the pain from his hand to his head.

His vision blurred and nausea washed over him as he was violently flipped over onto his stomach. The matted down sleeping bag padding did little to protect his stomach and scrotum from the rocky campsite. He was pinned to the hard surface by what felt like the attacker's knees. His arms were drawn back and bound first, then his ankles.

He turned his head to his side as he struggled through the pain, and he saw that his wife's sleeping bag was empty.

"Jessica!" he cried out.

He turned his head again, trying to see what his attacker was doing and where his wife Jessica might be. Before he could gather much information, a sack was slipped over his head. Blind, he continued to cry out his wife's name, only to be struck in the head again. The blow caught his nose with a muffled crack, and his lips became wet, warm, and salty. He licked the blood from his upper lip. He stopped moving and quieted himself, knowing that if he was beaten unconscious his chances of survival would drop considerably. Not knowing where Jessica was made him feel that much more vulnerable.

"Hey, I can get you money, you can have my watch, just tell me what you want," he pleaded as calmly as he could.

No reply came. Unable to see and hogtied, he rolled onto his side and was able to shuffle onto his knees. The snow crunched around him, and he heard the familiar sound of a fiberglass sled sliding over the snow behind him. He was shoved backwards onto a stiff synthetic surface. He wondered if he was on the pack sled he had used to tow the camping gear.

It was a two-day trip by cross-country skis to reach the cabin he and his wife rented for their five-year anniversary. They were both competent outdoor enthusiasts, with a particularly great love for hiking and camping. With lots of past experience, they felt confident in this adventure. Neither had ever been to the Alaskan wilderness, but they were excited at the prospect of just the two of them in a cozy cabin and later venturing to witness the aurora borealis.

The weight of his body caused the sled to drag; based on its speed and jerkiness, David guessed that only a single person was pulling it.

"Where's my wife, Jessica?" he demanded.

Only the crunching sound of the snowy surface breaking beneath careful footing was returned.

The farther they got from the campsite the more concerned he became. It was like descending into a dark well, with the light from the surface slipping away. He turned his head side to side trying to slip from the nylon sack. The blood from his nose was almost dry and had stuck his mouth to the inside of the nylon bag. He shook his head more aggressively and felt tearing pain as the nylon peeled from his lips. It might as well have been duct tape.

The sack now rotated freely and the drawstring had loosened as well. After a bit more wrangling and twisting, David was able to free his head. The air felt good on his face, but the sky was a blinding white. Closing his eyes only half helped, but his eyes would adjust eventually. Squinting, he noticed that indeed he was on the camping gear sled, which had come to a stop. He sat up and tried to turn to see his captor.

He looked up and saw that the stocky fur-clad figure was right beside him. The only feature he could discern were dark eyes that glinted with a honey-yellow amber glow. He blinked his eyes in an attempt to confirm what he was seeing, but then he lost consciousness and everything went dark.

He opened and closed his eyes several times, not sure if he was dreaming. A small fire near his feet cast soft, but limited light on the stone walls surrounding him. His ribs ached, both from being attacked and now from lying on his side. The rocky surface was unyielding and unsympathetic. He sat up, and first noticed immediately that his hands were no longer bound, nor were his feet. A small pile of sticks lay against the wall. He took two pieces and placed them over the fire. There were a few charred fish fins and scales among the ashes. Someone had eaten here before and must have been maintaining the fire while he was unconscious. The thoughts put him on edge.

Taking stock of his condition and resources, he noted that he still had his wristwatch, and it was now five p.m. He estimated anywhere from twenty minutes to half an hour that he'd been awake, which left much time unaccounted for. He knew that he had been unconscious while either further traveling on the sled or lying in this cave. There was nothing to indicate one over the other. Rifling through his pockets he found that he still had his keys with a small pen light and a pocket knife.

Now that the fire was a bit higher he could see that the cave led in two directions. Nervous about calling out, he remained silent and thought about how a wounded animal's cry usually attracts predators. Steeling himself against that thought, he twisted on his pen light and started down the right tunnel. After almost twenty yards, it sloped downward at a sharp angle. He was careful of his footing as there was a hole, which was definitely large enough to swallow him. The blackened shaft gave no indication of a bottom. Door number one was not a winner; let's try door number two, he thought and backed out of the tunnel.

* * *

Slowly working his way back, he quickly turned off his pen light. He caught a glimpse of shadows moving near the fire; someone was there. He stood frozen in place while his mind raced. The only option that entered his mind was to fight. He had no desire to jump down the black hole behind him, which would most likely leave him bloody and broken. Even if he survived the fall, a slow death from starvation down a dark hole held no appeal.

As he stepped forward slowly and deliberately, doing his utmost not to make noise, he advanced on the glowing junction of the cavern where he awoke. He felt his jaws tighten, and he clenched his fists even tighter.

A figure was kneeling down by the fire, adding more sticks to keep it alive. The figure was not dressed in fur pelts, but wore cold weather clothing similar to his. Observing the figure's movement and build led him to believe it was a woman.

"Jessica?" he whispered under his breath.

He drew back his arm with a tightly clenched fist; he was ready to strike if needed. He moved silently half crouching and kept close to the wall in the relative safety of the shadows. As the figure rose he sprang forward, tackling the person in a bear hug. He turned over the stranger to find an olive-skinned woman. Her lips were held tightly open, her teeth clenched.

"Please don't hurt me," she pleaded, as tears filled her eyes.

He backed off, kneeling and held his hands up with his palms open.

"I won't hurt you," he told her repeating it a second, then a third time, each time slower and softer, "I won't hurt you."

"My name is David," he said, trying to draw his mouth into a comforting smile.

"Who are you, and where are we?"

"I'm Ava. I'm, well, I'm not sure where we are," she said, her body trembled.

David thought he detected a British accent.

"How long have you been here?" he asked.

"I think maybe twelve days. There is a shaft above us where a bit of light comes in. I've been counting each time I see it. Since you already know that way is a dead end, the other way just leads to a set of metal doors. We are indeed captives, but to what end I do not know." Before he could continue his questions, she stopped him and pointed at his face. "You're bleeding."

He covered his mouth in embarrassment, thinking he must look like some cannibal with the lower half of his face covered in blood.

"I was hit quite a few times before being carried off. I think they wanted to make sure I was unconscious and wouldn't make any trouble."

Ava retrieved a clay jug and bandanna, "Care for a drink? You might want to tend to the blood on your face."

He thanked her, took a sip from the jug, then wet the cloth and put it to his face. The water was cool, giving him a subtle slap of clarity.

"Have you seen anyone else, a woman perhaps, with blonde hair? She's my wife, Jessica."

She stared into his eyes for a brief moment.

"No, I'm afraid not." The corners of her mouth turned down as she answered.

He sat back against the wall and peered into the fire. His wet eyes were empty of hope.

"I haven't seen any of my friends either. There were five of us. Noah was our guide. We hired him from Glennallen for our hiking trip. Joan, Katie and Michael are my friends from San Francisco. I'm from Essex, in the United Kingdom, that is."

He looked up at her.

"My wife, Jessica, and I were hiking to a cabin. We were going to see the aurora borealis. I was taken hostage this morning, but when I was dragged away I noticed that she wasn't there. It seemed like only one attacker. Oh, and he was wearing furs like Grizzly Fucking Adams."

She raised her eyebrows at the last bit of information.

"I only saw one person as well, and they were dressed as you described," she said.

"What the hell does he want? I offered him money, my things," he said, staring at her. He was sure that she had no clue either; it only made him feel better vocalizing it.

"Well, we're wanted for some reason. Water, food, and wood for the fire are always left inside the doorway when I wake in the morning. If he wanted me dead, then I wouldn't expect to be cared for," she replied, trying to apply some logic to their situation.

He gave her an agreeable look and half joked, "If he's not going to kill us, I'm sure as hell not going to become a slave to some Eskimo tribe."

They both chuckled.

David felt a bit more galvanized and got to his feet.

"I'm going to the door to see if anyone's out there. Maybe I can talk some sense to him," he said.

She looked at him for a moment, and then nodded. "All right, maybe he'll respond to you. No one has answered my cries."

* * *

The tunnel curved and tapered down, ending where the metal doors stood. The light from the fire had limited reach, so he twisted on his pen light. The doors were heavy and ornate. David wondered who might have put them there and how long ago. He looked back toward the fire, but only one of the walls was illuminated as the tunnel curved toward him.

Figures in relief, like Rodin's *The Gates of Hell*, lined the edge of the portal as well as the doors themselves. They seem to be emerging from or descending into the doors. Toward the top, there were four small square openings, out of reach and maybe even too small for a child to fit through, he thought.

After touching and further examining the protruding figures, he put his foot on one and pushed up. Confident that it was taking his weight, he held onto one of the higher figures and stepped up on another one until he was within reach of the openings. He felt like he was on one of those rock climbing walls with the plastic rock protrusions, only he was climbing on dark bronze figures of the damned.

He paused and listened, but heard only the wind's haunting whisper through the openings. He breathed out heavily and sprung upward, his hand finding one of the holes. Using his grip on the opening to pull himself up, he stopped when a sudden sharp pain blazed across his palm and he withdrew his hand. He flexed his gloved hand, which was cleanly split open, down and into his flesh. He groaned with pain and held his fist to his chest. The inside of his glove started to fill with blood.

Pressing his chest into the door for balance, he used his good hand to point the flashlight. From his elevated vantage point he could see that the openings were all designed with sharp edges; anyone hanging from them would be sure to lose their fingers and perhaps their hands. Although the patina on the doors was dark he saw what appeared to be bloodstains. How many people were held here?

He jumped down, knelt on one knee, and cradled his cut hand. He pounded the bottom of his clenched fist against the door, making a dull thumping noise.

"Let me out of here, you bastard!" he yelled then stood and half stumbled back towards the fire and Ava.

"Any luck?" she asked.

He shook his head, his mouth turned down, and his eyes blazed with anger.

"I almost lost my hand on those fucking doors," he shouted, holding his wounded hand up for her to see.

He sat by the fire and removed his glove, then took the still wet cloth she had given him earlier and wrapped it over the cut. The coolness felt good, but he winced at the sharp pain.

"You said that they leave you food. Well, I plan on being ready when those damn doors opens," he declared, staring at her with vengeful eyes.

"I've tried catching them, with no success. Perhaps they knew when I was sleeping. Maybe they are even watching us."

He acknowledged her encouragement and tried to calm down so that he could get a better perspective of the situation. He pulled his jacket hood over his head, crossed his arms, and stared into the embers of the fire until pain and exhaustion gave way to sleep.

* * *

David was a practical man; his dreams even seemed to fall within strict guidelines. Tonight he saw himself lying in wait for his captor. He pressed his body against the curved wall, just outside the sight of the doors, or better yet crouched down on either side of the doorway. That would allow him more time to make his move and less space to traverse before striking. His dream allowed him to explore options before making the decision where he would make his assault.

Even in his dreams he stared upon the doors, watching, and putting himself into a comfortable crouching position. The wait would be anyone's guess, but he would be ready. His eyes grew heavy and part of him was cursing himself to remain awake, but even in his dreams he was surrendering to sleep within sleep.

In the darkness of his dreams he heard the doors opening.

"No dammit," he cried out.

It was like watching an accident unfold and being in no position to change the outcome.

"It's ok. It's going to be ok," a soft voice filled his ears. The gentle words were followed by a kiss, dry yet delicate lips pressed against his.

He felt comfort and his body gave in, falling to deeper depths, beyond the realm of dreams. In his dreams he stood naked before the heavy metal doors. The bronze figures were animated, and they were reaching out to him from their place of unimaginable damnation.

The doors opened and light poured in, first as a thin strip then widening to completely cast light over David's body. The light was warm like sunlight and as his eyes adjusted he saw

Jessica. She too was naked and stood with her arms open to him, but her eyes were closed. He stepped through the open door and reached out to her. A smile formed on her lips and her eyes opened to reveal amber glowing globes. David's mouth fell open and he stumbled backwards, back inside the tunnel. The doors closed, shutting out the light and Jessica. Her laughter echoed from the other side.

David's body jerked, his eyes opened to slits and a sideways world came into focus. The fire between him and Ava was almost out. He propped himself up on his elbow and cast back his hood. She lay facing away from him, her bare back exposed, snow pants still covered her legs. Her body shivered. He stared confused by her naked back and was still shaken by his dream.

He knelt over her, removed his jacket and wrapped her in it, then tossed the last few sticks onto the fire. When the flame began to rise, he shook off his fears and turned her toward the warm flames.

"He came in the night. I thought he would rape me, but instead he took my clothes. I think he wanted to punish me," she said, as tears filled her eyes.

"H—how? Why? I was right here," David muttered in disbelief. He looked hard down the passage toward the doors. He felt her trembling. "Let's get you warmed up," he said, wrapping his arm around her.

"I don't think I can last much longer here," she said. She then turned over on her back and looked into his eyes.

He touched her hair and wiped the tears from her cheek. "It will be ok."

His comforting and compassionate face turned to stone when he heard the cold shriek of metallic parts grinding together from down the tunnel. The metal doors were opening. He rose quickly and ran on the balls of his feet, trying to be as quiet as he could.

He slowed his pace as the wall rounded and the doors came into view. It was only open by a third; a familiar arm reached through, placing things on the floor. It was covered in the same fur coat that his kidnapper wore. David rushed forward and hooked his hands around the open door's edge. He brought up his foot to brace himself but missed and his knee crashed into one of the bronze figures sending pain shooting up his leg. He pulled with all his might, but only managed to hold the door open long enough to see the amber glowing eyes of his fur-clad captor. David's hands burned from the deep cuts he sustained earlier. He tried to hang on, but the door began to close smoothly, almost with a dreamlike slowness, taunting him. He let go for fear of having his fingers crushed.

He pounded on the door and yelled upward to the four openings, but only the whisper of the wind answered him. Even the faintest signs of movement were nonexistent: no shuffling of feet, no rustling of clothing, nothing. He crouched down and listened with greater intensity, but heard nothing. After a moment, he heard Ava stirring and looked back down the tunnel. In the dim light by the base of the doors, he found a jug of water, a wrapped fish, and a bundle of sticks, just as she told him.

He returned to the fire and Ava with his arms full, but remained silent and sullen.

"Is that all the wood?" she asked.

"Yeah, why?"

"Well, that's not going to last us the night, and I have your coat," she replied.

Before she could go on, he said, "I want you to keep it, I have three layers. Maybe I can even spare my sweater."

She shook her head, not wanting to further compromise him.

"Put the fish down the tunnel, it will stay cool until we're ready to cook it," she told him.

They decided it would be best to ration the wood for the late night chill yet to come. He asked her how she kept her sanity, being alone for so many days. She mentioned that she grew up as an only child with few friends. It taught her to cope with being alone, and most of all, to learn how to entertain herself.

After moments of sharing personal life experiences, they asked each other trivia questions. She knew more about American culture, entertainment, and food, than he did about the United Kingdom. Regardless of each other's level of knowledge, it was a much-needed distraction.

The day vanished quickly, like a timid rabbit. David wondered if it was overcast outside. Most of their light had come from the shaft above, but now it was the fire they relied on. Sharing the small fish gave them little nourishment, but it was better than nothing at all. David had cooked fish over a fire on several trips with his wife Jessica. He missed his utensils and spices. Now, even the simplest of things that had kept him civilized carried a greater appreciation.

Their conversation grew softer, as they both stared into the fire and beyond. The temperature dropped, forcing them to toss more sticks into the flames. They looked at each other skeptically. She saw the shiver on his lips and moved closer to him.

"We'll stay warmer if we sleep closer," she said.

He said nothing, even when she opened her coat and revealed her breasts, then leaned forward and embraced him. Face to face, he felt her breath on his lips. They kissed and he drew her tighter into his arms. Both needed reassurance that someone was there, and that they were more than just two people sharing the same plight.

He dreamt about making love to Ava, her beautiful olive toned body, sensuous lips, and long wavy dark hair. He saw them both still within the cave, their bodies unclothed and intertwined. Warm sunlight penetrated from above and illuminated the space with intense brilliance, enclosing them in a large band of light.

David awoke, spooned behind Ava. His clothing was still on, his dream just a dream. His joints felt stiff, almost petrified. Rolling on his back, he moved sloth-like, as if he feared his body would crumble like burnt bits of wood. Holy shit, he thought. He had not felt this weak since his first mountain climbing experience. All of his muscles were tight, and his body felt dehydrated. He was sure that sleeping in the cold cave was taking its toll.

Getting to his knees was a huge task. He leaned forward, bracing himself with his elbows locked and palms firmly planted. He rose like a ballet dancer, pushing up slowly, and trying not to topple. He stood up straight and rolled his head back, then looked upward at the light filtering in from above. The shaft rose at least fifty feet, following the soft contours of the walls that tapering upward. Even with proper climbing gear, they had no chance at scaling the walls and escaping from above. He thought again about the hole down the opposite tunnel; was there a way out by descending? He had read about climbers going deeper into a crevasse and later finding an exit, a way out.

He stepped slowly in the direction of the doors, hoping to find more rations. The fire had burned out hours before the morning came, so wood would be welcome. Halfway down the tunnel, he fell against the wall, his knees almost giving out. Cursing his weak limbs, he braced himself until he reached the doors. A jug of water and a few pieces of wrapped bread lie on the floor, but no wood. With his back to the wall, he slid down next to the rations on the floor. He felt like he had not slept at all. The stress of captivity was bearing down on him. Where was his wife Jessica?

Returning, he found Ava was sitting up, a hopeful smile on her face.

"Good morning," she said, her tone comforting and positive. Her warm greeting helped to remove his cobwebs of sarcasm and doubt. He smiled in return.

"I'm beat. I guess I didn't sleep well," he told her.

He sat, then placed the jug and wrapped bread between them.

"That's all our host left us this time. Bread and water, the meal of champion dungeon dwellers," he said.

She smiled at his sarcasm.

"I need to rest, but I want to examine that hole again before we lose too much light. The daylight helps some, and the battery in my flashlight should be good for a while. You game?" he asked.

"All right, let's have a look. Before you arrived, I dropped some of the lit wood pieces down the hole. The drop appeared to be about ten meters, or a little over thirty feet I think, then angled off to the left. If you were lucky not to break your bones from the fall, hitting the incline might send you off to some unknown drop. We'll need to be careful."

He nodded in agreement and his face reflected her concern. Lying on his back, he stared upward at the soft light above, until his eyes became heavy.

David dreamt of wandering in the woods. It was night, a full moon helped him discern the trees and contour of the land. Some dry fallen leaves crackled beneath his feet. It was early autumn and he was naked in the forest, but the seasonal chill had not yet arrived, instead a comfortable warmth flowed over his skin. As he walked, he felt the soft earth welcoming each of his steps. Before long he came to an opening. From the tree line, he looked out to a large field of knee-high grass and wild flowers.

A figure stood at the center; it was a silhouette of a woman. He went to her, and as he neared, he could see that it was Jessica. She opened her arms to embrace him, her nude body radiant in the evening light. He held her tight, she brushed her fingers within his hair and down his back, and they kissed deeply as if trying to fuse one another together in an unbreakable bond.

They lowered themselves onto the soft grassy plane, the flowers surrounding them, witnessing. He made love to her with the passion of when their relationship was young, when their bodies were new and undiscovered. Guilt from kissing Ava lingered in his mind; he even saw visions of her as he lay with Jessica. Even in his sleep he wondered if it was something that all men felt, some great need to save the damsel in distress. He wondered if perhaps the act of protecting Ava would somehow bring safety to his wife.

As they lay in the soft grass, before he drifted off to sleep he heard her whisper, "I could be her for you."

A warm hand on his cheek and a soft voice seemed to come from the star-filled sky, "Are you ok? David, wake up."

He opened his eyes and saw a concerned looking Ava.

"I think you were having a nightmare. You were moaning in your sleep."

David rubbed his forehead and ran his fingers through his hair, trying to dispel the fogginess.

"That nap didn't help at all. I feel even more worn out," he said.

He still felt like he had to investigate the hole. Exhaustion aside, he was determined to find a way out of their current situation.

He sat up and unlaced his boots, then tied the laces end-to-end and attached his pen light to one of the ends.

"Well, that will give us a little more reach, so maybe we can see where the drop slopes."

She unlaced her boots as well and gave the laces to him to add to the cause. She dug through her pockets, and then offered a small Swiss Army knife and disposable lighter.

"I stopped smoking years ago, but some of my friends still do. I guess I keep it for them. Thank God I had it to light the fire," she said.

He held the tied laces at the ends and gave them a tug to further tighten them to ensure that his flashlight was secure.

"I think we're ready," he said.

They walked carefully into the shadowy tunnel. The hole was ominous not by size, but by the depth of darkness it contained. David felt it, almost alive, seducing him, trying to draw him in. He knelt before the opening, and for a moment felt the urge to just tumble forward and fall, wanting to give in to the strange invitation.

Ava touched his shoulder, waking him from his hypnosis.

"Careful. Maybe you should lie down and then lower the light. You won't fall as easy and you'll at least add the length of your arm."

He agreed and got on his stomach. She did the same. Lowering the light was like dipping it into a barrel of oil. As he got halfway through the laces he could finally see that the side walls were beginning to slope. When he arrived at the end of the laces, his light illuminated just enough for him to confirm that the angle of the slope was indeed sharp. He did have some level of hope, as the walls appeared smooth and less treacherous. He wondered if there might be another cavern floor not too far below.

Ava held her arm out straight and flicked the lighter. It offered little help, but one thing David noticed, the flame danced.

"Hey, look at that—must be a breeze down there—that could mean a way out!" he said with excitement.

He pulled up the laces and retrieved his light, and they both sat back against the wall. The once again black hole now provided a glimmer of hope.

"We have to think this over," she told him. He agreed and they both returned to the fire.

"If we can make it out of here tomorrow, then I don't care about freezing another night," he declared.

They turned in early, rationed the bread and water and discussed how they would get to the bottom of the shaft. David suggested they get as much rest as they could before taking on the task.

David dreamt of the forest again, but this time when he came upon the open field, he ran to the awaiting woman. As he drew near he saw it was Ava, and her arms were open awaiting his embrace. He slowed his pace, but as he peered into her eyes he felt his body levitate to her.

He kissed her soft lips. The look in her eyes, held an unspoken offering. They lay down on the grass as he had done before with his wife. As he made love to Ava, he saw Jessica's face. He was soon filled with oppressive guilt. Her embrace tightened as he attempted to pull away. Her thighs held firm around his hips, and her heels pushed into his buttocks.

He knew he must have awakened, as he was now back in the cave. It was still quite dark, with only the initial arrival of light from above. He was shocked that he was still in Ava's embrace, and more so that he was naked. Just as in the dream, he was on top of her, with her legs wrapped around his waist and her arms around his neck.

"Don't stop, don't stop," she chanted in his ear.

"No, let me go," he cried out.

He pulled free from her arms and looked upon her face. Her eyes reflected a honey-yellow amber glow. She started laughing, and glossy wet sharp teeth filled her mouth in contrast to her sensual lips, which she licked seductively. She lowered herself to kiss him, but with his strength only a fraction of the day before, it took everything he had to escape her grasp.

* * *

He stumbled naked and aimlessly down the tunnel trying to get away. Fear choked off any ability he had to think and reason before he reached the hole where the floor opened to swallow him. No time to even cry for God's intervention. The blackness came, instant and eternal. He seemed to fall forever, and then it felt as if a freight train hit him. The slope's curve was less than he anticipated, and not gentle enough to slow his descent. His limbs twisted and bones shattered. His left leg locked then snapped into an unnatural angle; his right wrist absorbed the weight of his body before the bones disintegrated. His limp body crumpled and rolled to a painful stop.

He lay face down and bleeding, but unsure exactly from which locations. A warm salty taste crossed his lips as blood pooled around his mouth.

A tiny spotlight played on the walls, growing larger until he heard her voice.

"Forget something?"

Ava lowered the shoelace-tethered flashlight and placed it in front of his face. All he could see was the white of the small pen light, but he could feel her moving around his broken body. His body trembled with pain as he reached up to take the light. He shone it around the space trying to locate Ava. Across the chamber his light indicated a pile of what appeared to be bodies. He involuntarily gasped, but his cracked ribs only allowed for shallow breaths. Ava stepped into his light, her amber eyes glimmering in the darkness.

"I could have been anyone for you," she told him.

Her body contorted and her head shook violently as she took on the appearance of his wife Jessica. David's breaths became rapid and tears filled his eyes.

"Your wife must have been out on an early morning stroll when I found you, otherwise I would have first taken on her shape and perhaps we could have avoided this misunderstanding. Of course you slept with Ava easy enough, didn't you darling? You could have even had Ava's friends if you liked," the thing that appeared as Jessica said. It morphed three more times, first appearing as Katie, then Joan, and finally back to Jessica.

After seeing Jessica with Ava's amber glowing eyes, he knew that she was dead, and he lost all desire to carry on. Like a fly without wings, he knew that there was no escape in his condition. Instead he dropped his hand that held the flashlight. It made a sharp tapping noise as it hit the rocky floor and echoed off the walls. He sensed that she was still standing before him in the darkness.

He cried out from the pain as he felt his broken body being dragged, then later dropped onto a pile of awkward protruding objects. He directed the beam of the small flashlight and confirmed his fears that there was a pile of bodies and he was its newest member. There were old corpses with flesh drawn tightly over their bones. They appeared to be past explorers who wore antique snow clothing made of wool and canvas. He then saw four bodies in modern cold weather clothing. They appeared the same: thin flesh pulled tight over their skeletons. He then noticed one that wore his wife's coat and snow pants. All of their mouths were open in silent screams and their eyes were missing.

"Jessica?" David called out in a muffled cry.

One of the other corpses had olive skin and he assumed that it was the real Ava. David thought that the male corpse next to her must belong to either Michael or their Alaskan guide Noah.

From the shadows appeared the naked form of his wife Jessica. She knelt down and began to remove the clothing from his dead wife's body.

"Don't you touch her!" David cried out.

She ignored him, but instead dressed herself in Jessica's clothing and walked off into the shadows. David was unable to move and could barely turn his wrist to direct the light to search for her. Instead he dropped the flashlight, refusing to look any further at the horrors that surrounded him, yet unable to cower away from their touch. He felt sleepy, and gave in to death's slumber.

Michael guessed that fifteen days had passed since he first found himself a prisoner within these strange cavern walls. The only mark of humankind was a set of two bronze ornate doors at the end of the tunnel. A bundle of food and supplies was dropped down from one of several shafts in the ceiling, which he had no means of reaching. Each day he yelled upwards into the shaft hoping whoever was dropping the bundles would rescue him. Days passed and all he was able to do was eat, sleep, and keep a fire going. Sleep was difficult as dreams gave way to nightmares. He woke sometimes to what he thought were screams of torture, but he only could hear the winds that howled through the cavern.

On what he guessed was the sixteenth day of his captivity, Michael awoke thinking he heard screaming from either the sharp openings in the metal doors or one of the vertical shafts descending into the cavern. It had been days since he last saw his friends: Ava from the United Kingdom, or Joan and Katie from San Francisco. Not to mention their perhaps too confident guide, Noah, who they had picked up in Glennallen. If the sounds were indeed screams, he prayed for the safety of his companions. Sitting up on his elbows, he was surprised to notice a figure in a fetal position. It was a woman with long blond hair tucked under her knit ski cap. The strange woman wore a heavy cold weather coat and snow pants.

"Hello," he said, trying not to alarm her.

Her eyes opened and she sat up, crawling backwards until she pushed against the wall.

"Don't hurt me, please, don't hurt me."

Michael stayed seated and held up his hands in an effort to look as unthreatening as possible.

"Calm down, I'm not going to hurt you," he said.

"How did you get here?" he asked.

"I don't know," she replied.

Not knowing exactly how he arrived either, he avoided pressing the question.

"I've been held captive here for weeks. Apparently you're now a prisoner as well. My name is Michael."

Her posture relaxed but she kept her distance.

"I'm Jessica."

THE FIELD

It was a cooler than normal October in 1960. Gloria Jean Swenson looked out the kitchen window of her Indiana farmhouse, across the almost endless rows of turned down corn stalks. Beyond her family's fields were the Carlisle's, and beyond that, the Webber's.

A tiny figure came into view. It was a speck of a man on the dirt road that separated the parcels. He seemed to just appear out of nowhere. Maybe he came across the Carlisle's land, hidden by a group of trees, and after traversing the deep ditch at the edge of the road made his surprise appearance seem so.

At first she thought he might be old Tim Carlisle, but after a second look she knew otherwise. Even at that great of a distance, she could see that he was a tall slender man. He reminded her of her late husband, Jack. In contrast, Tim Carlisle was shorter and had a stocky build.

The way this man swung his arms and shuffled up the edge of the dirt road sure did remind her of Jack. Even his dress, a dusty brown three-piece suit and fedora brought back memories. That suit Jack used to wear made his limbs seem even lankier, like clothes hanging on a scarecrow's stick body.

Gloria Jean brought her attention back to the dishes soaking in the kitchen sink. She was lifted by the fragrance of lemons as the soap bubbles swirled around her wrists and arms. She was a God-fearing woman, who maintained a clean house and did right by her fellow man. It gave her comfort that she was keeping in the Lord's good graces.

She took another look out the window to check on the man by the road and noticed that he had stopped and was wiping his brow, not far from where she last saw him. A load of school kids in a top down Chevy blew by him, kicking up a dust cloud that covered the man. Gloria Jean shook her head in sympathy. Poor soul … you're not getting anywhere fast, and you'll be needing a bath when you get there, she thought.

The man adjusted his hat and seemed to stare across the fields, past the picket fence, over the back yard and square into her window. She felt like he was looking right at her. He was still too far away for her to see his face or gather any clues to his identity.

He couldn't possibly see me, she thought, but he continued to look in her direction, making her feel uneasy.

She wished that she could shoo him away like a stray dog. Maybe he recognizes the house or something, she imagined. Before she could give it another thought, he was moving up the road again, with his pant legs flapping in a cross breeze.

The warm water and suds brought her back to task. She reached around until her fingertips caressed the edges of the dishes at the bottom of the sink. She peered through the patches of suds and saw her china plates, which were outlined with prints of swallows flying with ribbons in their beaks. For a moment she felt like God peering through the clouds at His creations below.

As the suds moved about and the plates turned within her grasp, the birds appeared to be flying under the cover of the soapy clouds. She thought of the days spent at the local pond. Jack would take their son Davy to splash at the water's edge. That was twenty-three years ago, when he was still in diapers.

The storm door swung open, and its springs squealed as they were stretched. Gloria Jean heard the familiar sound of the heavy wooden front door scraping against the thick nap of the rug at the entrance, creating a rough dragging noise. Weighty workman's boots scuffed the rug as the door closed and the latch sounded.

"David is that you?" Gloria Jean inquired with a raised voice, bracing herself in front of the sink.

"Temperature has dropped another five degrees. I brought your paper in," a familiar male voice said from the other room.

The wood floors in the hall creaked, then David appeared in the doorway, bringing with him a subtle chill of the October air.

"Hi mom," he said holding some roses wrapped in cream colored paper. Dark green W's were printed in a pattern on the outside, so she knew that he picked them up at Wringles, their local florist.

Gloria Jean sat up in her hospital bed and watched her son approach carrying a bouquet of flowers. It was an arrangement of lilies, chrysanthemums, and sunflowers, rather than the roses that she first imagined.

"Oh David, they're beautiful, what's the occasion?"

"I thought these might brighten up your day," he said with a comforting smile.

He placed the flowers in a plastic pitcher that one of the hospital techs had given him when he stopped by the nurse's station. He set the arrangement on her bedside table, which she often referred to as her kitchen table. She fiddled with a few of the stems until she was satisfied with how the flowers sat in the pitcher.

"How you feeling today?" he asked.

"A little under the weather, as to be expected for this time of the year, but I've managed to get my dishes washed," she replied.

He drew his mouth into a scowl of concern, but then his expression softened into quiet compassion.

"Oh, that's good. Keeping busy are you?" he said.

"Did you see that man outside?" she whispered with a curious look on her face.

David looked out her hospital room window, which was on the third floor, unsure where she meant or how she was seeing this man.

"No, where? Do you mean Doctor Clausen?"

"No, I saw a man out the window, off in the distance. He was a tall lanky fellow."

"What did he look like?"

"He was too far away to make out his face, but he was wearing a dark, three-piece suit." She had a sweet smile on her face, which gave her an innocent, childlike appearance.

"Your father always looked good in a suit," she said.

David said no more on the subject. Doctor Clausen told him that her condition was getting worse. Being the only child and with no other relatives to call on, matters of her health rested on his shoulders. He struggled with leaving matters in God's hands, but knew that there was nothing he could do.

* * *

The dust cloud from the passing Chevy finally settled and the stranger got a look at the kids in the car. The boys looked smug in their varsity jackets and the girls were youthful in their pastel dresses. He wondered how the young man driving was able to keep the car on the loose dirt road.

He looked up at the house, which was beyond several tracts of farmland. From that distance the house was the size of a postage stamp, but it was still recognizable. It seemed like a long time since he was last there. Although he knew the place, a strange apprehension came over him, making any forthcoming reunion feel small, foreign, and above all, unwelcome.

He removed his hat and wiped the sweat from his brow and the dust from his lips, and he thought of the woman he knew long ago. She lived in that house across those tracts of land.

That strange apprehension tugged at him again; he felt like an underperforming salesman sent to revisit a potential customer, with strict instructions not to take 'No' for an answer.

He stumbled down the incline of the ditch and into the Webber's corn field, covering his wingtips in dust. Out of fear that he might lose sight of the house, he wanted to take the most direct route. The uneven dirt tracks tilled by heavy farm equipment were not friendly to his attire. He could have stayed on the roadside and made his way there in a sensible manner, but he had to get there before dark.

He turned his ankle and cursed the terrain. Between his smooth leather bottom soles and the inordinate number of large stones in the field, the trek would be slow, rough and painful. He remembered the family in the nearest house; they were the Webber's, he recollected.

"They need to turn this damn field better than this, and get rid of all these stones," he thought.

Before he could reach an even patch, he went down on one knee, and pain shot up his leg and into his ribs.

A soft knock on the loose screen door caused it to rap against the inside trim, doubling the announcement. Looking across the flowers at her son, Gloria Jean raised her head and turned toward the hallway. She closed her eyes and heard the sounds of a struggle with the front door opening and closing as when David entered earlier. This time the footfalls were lighter and then Doctor Clausen filled the doorway. He was wearing a white hospital coat, penny loafers, and corduroys.

"Why it's Doctor Clausen," Gloria Jean said with a smile.

"You know you're going to catch a cold wearing just your shop coat in this weather," she warned him.

"Hello Ms. Swenson, how are you feeling today?" Doctor Clausen inquired as he moved toward David to shake his hand. David stood to take his hand and was pleased to see him.

"I was feeling a little sick after breakfast, but it passed," Gloria Jean said.

"Any pain or just the nausea?"

She shook her head and he nodded in acknowledgement.

"That's good. I'll be back around a bit later to check on you again," Doctor Clausen said. He then made his way to the door.

"It's getting cold outside. Be sure to wear your coat. Please close the front door tight, doc," she yelled after him, wearing a smile of satisfaction.

"You got it Gloria Jean," Doctor Clausen said, as he left the room and closed her hospital room door.

David caught up to him at the nurse's station down the hall. "How bad is she?" he asked.

"I'm sorry, but her condition is declining, and the rate appears to be increasing. I'm pleased that you're able to visit your mother as often as you do. With her condition and confusion, she needs a comforting familiar face, even if she has moments where she doesn't know who you are." He gripped David's shoulder and offered a reassuring smile.

As the stranger stumbled to reach the even patch of earth, the wind picked up and swirled dust into his face. He closed his eyes, grit his teeth and tightened his lips to seal out the wind. With one hand in front of his face, he clenched his hat and tottered forward.

Through slit eyes he located the house and directed his steps accordingly. There were few areas of easy travel, so he slowed his pace to avoid falling again.

His heel planted on a hard round surface, but he was able to keep his balance. He paused to recover and kicked at the protruding obstacle. A few gentle probing nudges with his shoe revealed holes, which he realized were sockets belonging to a human skull. He knelt down and ran his fingers over the top and down the side where the cheek would have been. It was too large to belong to a child, yet too small for an adult, unless it belonged to a small woman. Maybe it belonged to a teenager, he thought.

With a thumb in one of the sockets and his hand around its side, he gently unearthed the skull. Like the insistent winds that pelted his face, visions of the past filled his thoughts. He saw a beautiful teenage girl laughing and tugging at his arm to follow her.

It was 1936: he was at the county fair delivering an extra load of bundled straw. A familiar young woman was standing at the crowd's edge, on the other side of a white fence. It was Sarah Carlisle. He recalled that her father was a farmer and worked the land next to his.

He smiled at her when their eyes met. Two young boys started to unload the straw into stacks. He told them that he was going to take a look around and maybe get himself a cold soda. They both just nodded—they were more interested in finishing the task at hand—so he went about seeing what this year's fair had to offer. He noticed that Sarah was watching him and following him along the fence line. Her delicate hand glided over the top rails of the fence, briefly pausing at each post. She was one of those girls who wasn't interested in boys her age, instead she seemed obsessed with chasing young men. He was fully aware of girls like that when they were chasing other men, but now with Sarah's sights set on him, he was blinded by her amorous flirtations. Although he was twenty-seven, which seemed young, that was the age of a man well on his way for the time. She was just sixteen, but saw his age as a challenge. More than that, he was the most beautiful man she had ever seen.

She had been obsessing over him for weeks. She had first encountered him outside the general store, when he ran into her father, Tim Carlisle. The men spoke briefly as she stood by silently observing. She knew how to charm a man with just her eyes and shy smiles.

He walked past several stands. Mrs. Traver was selling her pies and other baked goods. He passed a couple of games of chance: a Hoop Toss, and Tin Can Alley with stacked milk bottles instead of cans, both only mildly catching his attention. When he reached a small corral of young farm animals, she was waiting on the other side of the fence. Her eyes drew him to her. They met at a break in the fence, and she looked about and then pulled him by the arm until they were both stumbling in the tall grass. They ran down the hill beyond the fairground to a brook that was lined by a shallow cluster of trees. She took off her shoes and knee-highs and waded in the water, then beckoned him to join her.

He returned to the present and cast his gaze on the house. Turning the skull within his hands filled him with an uncomfortable sadness. There was a crack leading to a rough oblong hole.

"Someone hurt ... murdered you," he whispered.

A wave of memories hit him. He saw a girl's face appear like a mask over the face of the skull. The image was blurry, but familiar.

"Sarah?" he whispered, a mere breath that passed his lips.

Ashamed that he had disturbed the skull, he returned it with care, placing it back into the dirt cavity that previously surrounded it. As he rose, the skull turned into a simple stone, like any other that he might have stumbled over. He looked toward the old farmhouse, and with cautious steps, continued onward.

Gloria Jean rose from her chair and went to the window. Her curiosity moved her to see if the man off in the distance was still there. Surprised to see that he was crossing the field toward the direction of her home, she steadied herself against the counter top near the sink. He was still quite far away and judging by his posture, he was having difficulty walking.

Observing the stumbling man brought back memories. She recalled when their station wagon was stuck in a snowy ditch and her husband Jack went for help. He staggered through the heavy knee-high drifts until he disappeared in a wash of white. To this day she still wondered how he managed to find his way back and return to her from the storm. He always had a knack for finding her. When they used to play *Ghost in the Graveyard*, she was never able to tag him before he yelled, "Ghost in the Graveyard!"

David sat on one of the breakfast bar stools in the kitchen of his girlfriend's apartment. Kate was making dinner. He appeared to be looking at the salad she was preparing, but his mind was elsewhere.

"I take it you stopped by to check on your mom. How's she doing?" Kate asked.

"She's hanging in there. Doctor Clausen said that her condition is declining. He didn't know or wouldn't say how much time she had left."

"I'm sorry to hear that. Did you at least have a good visit?"

"Yes, but she often brings up past events, like they are happening now. She even talks to me like I'm still a boy."

"You'll always be her little boy. That's a mother's bond with her child."

"Yeah I agree, but this is different."

"Maybe as her memories fade, the most significant ones remain until the end."

David nodded in silence, and just stared at his hands that were resting on the counter.

Gloria Jean sat alone and exhausted at the kitchen table, feeling like she had just served a holiday meal with all of her family present. Soft illumination came through the windows as the earth turned its back to the sun. The bright sodium light in the yard now shown through the kitchen window. She rose from her chair, drawn to the light like an insect. Before turning on the light above the sink, she glanced out the window to see if David had returned.

Just beyond the fence a dark figure stood. Its silhouette was in the shape of the man she saw earlier. He moved smoothly, shadow-like to where the fence opened near the barn. Her mind raced to discover some reasonable explanation as to what this man wanted and why he came at such a late hour.

David had yet to return from town.

"Maybe he ran into some friends," she thought.

With desperate anticipation she wished that she could just call out to him, and he would be in the next room. She wove her fingers together into a painful bond, and she fixed her eyes on the yard and the strange apparition.

"What do I do now David, since your father is gone?" she whispered.

The afternoon sun had warmed the air. David and his partner Frank Lionel had their latest roofing job more than halfway complete. They stopped to get a drink and wipe the sweat from their faces.

"How's your mom, Davy?" Frank asked.

Being seven years David's senior, he was given to calling anyone younger than him by his childhood name. David handed Frank a cold soda then sat on their plastic work cooler.

"I don't know really. Her spirits seem to be good, but at the same time she seems to be getting worse. It's like we're all waiting around for something to happen," David said.

Frank took a heavy sip and nodded.

"Is your mom still frightened by unfamiliar faces? Would be a shame if she couldn't meet your new girl."

David stared at the ground and paused to swallow.

"Kate understands. Unfortunately, her great aunt had dementia before she died last year. Her great aunt also had a hard time remembering faces, but at the same time she could go on about the past—people she used to know—events and stuff. I understand why it's important to Kate; she never knew her birthmother, so she really wants my mom's approval of our relationship. I just don't know if my mom is capable of giving it to her."

Without further discussion, both men crushed their soda cans and threw them in the bed of the pickup. Each shouldered a bundle of shingles and ascended their ladders.

Early afternoon pressed on. Kate's Ford Escort rolled up the uneven stone driveway. It rocked gently side to side over the loose gravel; stones crunched under the car's tires. David came down from the roof when he saw her hurrying toward the house.

"Haven't you checked your phone? The hospital has been trying to reach you," Kate said.

"Sorry, my battery is dead. Anyway we were going to finish up in a few hours, so I wasn't too worried about it."

"Well, thank God you put my number down as an alternate contact. Anyway the hospital called and said that they don't think your mother has much longer to live. Come on, I'll take you over there," Kate said.

Before David could say anything further, Frank called down from the roof, "You go on Davy; I'll finish up. Just leave me the truck and I'll bring it by later."

David closed the back gate to his pickup, tossed his work belt in the back and told Frank that the keys were in the ignition. He brushed his hands off on his pant legs and got in the passenger seat of Kate's Escort.

Dusk had arrived when the stranger finally made it to the house. He stood at the break in the fence near the yard's edge. At its center the sodium lamp on a high post shone like a beacon and drew him near like the many night creatures that stared out from the darkness. The light stretched and illuminated the back of the house and across the yard. It fell short of the barn doors, concealing him and everything outside its reach in shadow.

Looking upon the back porch steps his mind filled with visions of a young girl. It was years ago, when the screen door had a fresh coat of paint on it. He saw himself as a young man, talking to her through the screen. She was crying and asking for his help. The cloud of déjà vu cleared and memories almost knocked him to the ground. It was Sarah Carlisle and he could hear her.

"Jack, what are we gonna do? My dad will surely come after you when he's done with me. He might even send me away," she pleaded.

"You shouldn't call me Jack, at least not here," he said in an urgent muffled tone. He was surprised at how cold and distant his voice sounded back then.

"There's a doctor who sometimes passes through. People talk about him taking care of certain things."

"You mean you don't want me to have the baby?" she said.

"Sarah … I'm married. What did you expect—that you and I would just run away together?"

Sarah's expression told him that was exactly what she had expected. Perhaps she thought if he knew that she was carrying his child, he would decide to leave his wife to be with her. Sarah's eyes filled with tears at his rejection.

"I won't kill it," she declared with a shaken voice.

"Sarah it's not even born yet. It's so early, I bet it's like inside a chicken's egg, barely formed," he said.

His tone was gentle as he tried to convince her that there were no other options. She remembered when her mother gave birth to her younger brother and how big she got just before. She knew that she would not be able to hide her condition if she were to have the baby, even if her intention was to give it away.

He watched her as she mulled things over. Her expression morphed from troubled to terrified to confused and then back again. Before she could formulate another idea of how they would ride off into the sunset together, he told her that he would seek out that doctor first thing tomorrow when he went to town.

"Don't you worry. I'll take you to see him when he comes around. Now you go on home, nothing more we can do tonight," he said.

The vision of Sarah faded as she walked away; even under the bright sodium light she was gone. Even as she faded, his memories continued. He recalled that she decided to have the baby and in turn her father sent her away to live with her aunt. Her decision to keep the baby was an unsettling link that tied him to Sarah. A great secret, which was only concealed by distance and Sarah's love, both of which were unpredictable and most likely, unsustainable. He was amazed by her ability to keep the identity of the baby's father from her own father. He imagined the beatings she sustained. God help any of the boys that her father might have suspected, he thought.

The yard lay empty. Memories had played out and were now past. The light from the kitchen window carried him back to the present.

Gloria Jean watched the shadows in the back yard warp and mix together, the strange man's shadow combined with the others like a giant black organism, or a stream emptying into a larger body of water. There were no other sounds; all she could hear was her own breathing, weighted and deliberate. She gasped when she heard a rap at the outer screen door. She thought that he might have seen her in the kitchen window, but stood silent with desperate hope that she was mistaken.

"Gloria Jean," an old familiar voice called from beyond the door.

She remained still, like a rabbit that had evaded a predator, but now the predator was near, sensing her.

"Gloria Jean, open this door. I know that you're in there," he said.

"It's late; you shouldn't be here. I'll call the police if you don't leave," she announced. She was uncertain of the man's identity, but he did know her name, which troubled her. No reply came, and Gloria Jean's kitchen fell silent. She contemplated calling the police. "Oh David, where are you?" she whispered. She stepped slowly toward the door, trying to see if the man had left.

She saw subtle movements of the doorknob, then she heard a loud knock. Gloria Jean's body stiffened and she stood fixed before the door. The knocking became desperate, with each strike being heavier than the last. Soon he would force his way in, she feared.

David sat at his mom's bedside. She gazed at the ceiling of her hospital room as if watching a film projected above her. Her expression was one of worry then terror. It was how she looked when he saw her viewing traumatic events on the evening news, or during a suspenseful point in a movie.

"No—you—you can't come in," she mumbled. The hair surrounding her face was wet and matted to her skin. The pit of her neck glistened with droplets.

David spoke to his mother in a calm, yet elevated voice, attempting to awaken her. She instead remained captivated by the visions being projected on the walls within her mind.

A name popped into his head, as if he was searching for a tool in a garage and after almost forgetting what he had come there for, the item presented itself.

"Dammit Gloria Jean, it's—Jack. Open the door."

He tried the handle again, but this time it turned, and he eased the door open. With slow cautious steps, Gloria Jean backed away into the kitchen. She kept her eyes on the tall dark figure as he stood just inside the entrance. He advanced toward her with no human gait, but rather floated like a newspaper page caught by the wind.

"Gloria Jean … it's me—Jack. Don't you recognize me?" His voice was dry and hollow.

"You can't be Jack. My husband died a long time ago."

Although he felt truth in her statement he had to follow through with his obligation.

"Don't be afraid. I won't hurt you. I've only come to talk. We need to settle some things."

"You're not my husband," Gloria Jean said. With her arms crossed, she was visibly shaken but brazen enough to protest.

"Understand this, woman. I've come for your acknowledgement of the truth and for your confession. I'm beat and have no time for games."

"I've done nothing wrong," Gloria Jean declared in a raised voice. She crossed her arms in guarded disapproval, but started to accept that this man, or shadow of a man, was her late husband. The words Jack often used to start his objection during a heated argument were, "Understand this woman …" a telling sign that she was indeed speaking to the genuine artifact.

"I know what you did," he said in a soft voice that reached down into her soul and brought chills to her body.

David sat at his mother's bedside listening to her talk in her sleep. It was unclear whom she was addressing. Her words trembled, so David moved to the edge of his seat to hold her hand.

"What man, mom? Who are you speaking to?" David asked.

Gloria Jean's eyes were half closed and fixed on the ceiling of her hospital room, while her true gaze was still back at the old farmhouse. She turned as if emerging from a dream, recognizing David by her side.

"Oh David, my sweet boy, you're here," Gloria Jean muttered.

"Mom, I know that it's not a great time, but I have someone that I want you to meet," David said.

Through the tall and narrow glass pane of the door, he motioned for Kate. She opened the door slowly then moved toward Gloria Jean's bedside.

"Mom, this is Kate, my girl—," David said, but was cutoff by his mother's reaction.

Gloria Jean's eyes widened and her mouth opened, but she was only able to release a gasp. Even with her weakened body, her muscles stiffened and she moved away with all her might to the far edge of the bed.

"It can't be. Wha—What is she doing here?" Gloria Jean cried.

David touched her arm.

"Mom, it's ok. She's not going to hurt you," he said.

Gloria Jean kept her gaze on Kate when David spoke.

"Hello Ms. Swenson," Kate said in a gentle voice. She clasped her hands in front of her and held her distance.

"You died," Gloria Jean said.

"Mom, what are you talking about? You and Kate have never met," David said, with a hint of frustration.

He looked at Kate. Rather than being upset, Kate returned an expression of compassion and understanding.

"Of course I've met her. Why she—she's Sarah Carlisle." Gloria Jean turned and glared at Kate, then muttered, "but you're dead." Her chest heaved and she took in heavy gasps. Before anyone could press the emergency call button, the nurse came in. She was making her typical rounds. After seeing how distressed Gloria Jean was, she asked David and Kate to step out into the hall.

Outside Gloria Jean's room, David held Kate. Her eyes were glossy.

"I'm sorry. I hoped that she would be in better spirits," David said.

"I thought I could handle meeting your mom, especially after what my family went through with my great aunt Doreen. Your mom's reaction caught me by surprise. Do you know this Sarah Carlisle that she's talking about?" Kate asked.

"I never met her, but heard that she was the neighbor girl," David said.

The nurse came out into the hall.

"I started the drip again for her pain. It should calm her and help her sleep. I also called her doctor, who should be coming by a bit later. You can go back in," the nurse said as she pumped the wall-mounted container of hand sanitizer, and gave them a reassuring smile before she headed to the next room.

Gloria Jean felt lightheaded as her consciousness returned. The figure of Jack Swenson, her late husband, remained just inside the kitchen door that led to the backyard. A brief eight-foot space separated him from Gloria Jean. She regarded his statement of just wanting to talk with far more gravity, especially since she believed him to be a ghost or spirit. Her strong religious belief in God and angels kept her from total hysteria, but those beliefs also included a steadfast fear of God's judgment and God's wrath. There were things, moments in her past, that she had trouble reconciling. She always tried to avoid any conflicts, but sometimes that meant leaving important matters unresolved. Was this apparition here to judge her?

"Do you remember the summer of 1938? There was a young girl by the name of Sarah Carlisle. She was your neighbor, Tim and Jean's daughter," he said.

She remained still, listening quietly. She felt the familiar tightening in her chest as the hatred and frustration inside her came to a rolling boil.

"Do you mean the young trollop who was obsessed with my husband? I remember years ago, maybe around that same time, she got pregnant and her father sent her away. It was best for everyone. She couldn't seem to find a young available boy her age. Instead she was obsessed with chasing older men—married men. No one wanted her around, stirring up trouble," Gloria Jean shouted.

The shadowy figure's expression changed and became strained as if he were carrying a physical weight.

"You knew that Sarah was pregnant, but did you know who the father was?"

"You know damn well I knew it was you. I loved you, Jack, and you still took up with that girl."

Gloria Jean's emotions finally confirmed that she conceded to the stranger's identity. Her confrontation with this spirit felt like the day-to-day internal conflicts she struggled with frequently. Most times they were of no serious concern, only on occasion did they shake her enough that she had to call on God for introspection and spiritual guidance.

The fact that a dead man had shown up at her doorstep and she was now speaking to him, might have brought most to cower and think that the end of days had arrived. A single childhood experience strengthened her resolve. When she was ten, she witnessed her father arguing at great length with an invisible opponent. He later told her that his deceased brother's ghost had paid him a visit, and he was reminding him of her father's debts and promises. Gloria Jean's mother only laughed at her father, dismissing his behavior as being drunk and frustrated at their broken down tractor. Although he had been drinking that day, Gloria Jean knew better. When she was young she sometimes felt odd things. Her own visions came after her grandmother died when she was seventeen.

"Tell me what you did to Sarah," Jack's voice was cold and threatening.

"Don't you mean what *you* did to that girl? After her father sent her away, I only heard that she had the child but later died."

He stared at her with the dead eyes of a reptile. She could feel his contempt and knew the look on his face, although he was obscured by shadows.

"You know more than that. Will you not confess the truth, even to save your soul?" he urged.

"Jack, why are you trying to scare me? What is it you really want? I've done nothing wrong."

"Sarah came to the house after she had the baby. You spoke to her. I know that you remember," he demanded. Gloria Jean tried to hide her shock; how did Jack know that Sarah came to the house, and that Gloria Jean had spoken to her?

She sat at the kitchen table and looked up at him with heavy eyes.

"I must leave before dawn. Will you not confess the truth, not for my soul, but your own?" he said.

Exhaustion took hold of her. She no longer wanted to converse with him. He might be a spirit, but he was not God, and anything between her and her Lord would have to wait until they met face-to-face. She spread her arms on the table and rested her head on her forearms. The morning would come soon enough and she would be rid of him.

Gloria Jean lay deep in sleep, almost comatose. David noticed only subtle movements between hours of stillness. During the quiet periods, he had only the heart monitor to know if she was still within this world.

The door opened and Doctor Clausen came to the foot of Gloria Jean's bed. He only looked at her briefly then addressed David, who rose to shake Doctor Clausen's hand.

"I'm sorry, David. I've done all I can. All we can do now is make her comfortable," Doctor Clausen said.

As David thanked Doctor Clausen, his words came out dry and almost inaudible. He returned to his seat and held his mother's hand.

"I will tell the nurses to give you some privacy," said Doctor Clausen. He had closed the door so stealthily that David thought he was still there. Only when he looked up did he know that he was alone with his mother.

David watched her go in and out of consciousness all day. Sometimes when she spoke she appeared to be mentally visiting visions of her past, while other times she was incoherent. He picked up on some of the memories, especially the familiar ones from when he was a boy. Occasionally she cried out between quiet moments of introspection.

Gloria Jean looked out the kitchen window. She saw the young Carlisle girl in the backyard. It looked like she was snooping around, going to the side of the house where the car was usually parked. Jack's truck sat there with a bad starter. He had taken the old station wagon to town to get the parts he needed to fix the truck.

Gloria Jean heard a rap at the door. She moved to the side of the kitchen window to conceal herself.

"Jack, oh Jack, I've come back to you. We have a new baby girl. Her name is Kate," the young girl called from the other side of the door.

Gloria Jean stormed to the door and opened it in a rage.

"How dare you come here," she shouted.

Sarah stumbled off the porch steps, almost falling down, but made it to the middle of the backyard, keeping a safe distance.

"You get the hell out of here and never come back, do you hear me?" Gloria Jean screamed at the girl.

"Jack has a right to know," Sarah cried as she ran toward the fence.

Gloria Jean chased after her. Sarah reached the opening and quickly got on the other side, in order to protect herself.

"He has the right to know," Sarah said again.

"Jack is as wrong as you are and he has no rights. Now you get out of here or I'm going to kill you," Gloria Jean screamed.

As Gloria Jean ran toward the end of the fence line, Sarah took advantage of her lead and ran into the field. Gloria Jean was propelled by fury, and she gained on Sarah, rounding the fence and chasing her further into the field. As she got closer her lungs tightened and her thighs began to cramp. She stopped, but Sarah ran on. Before she could get too far, Gloria Jean grabbed a few rocks that were at her feet. The first one hit Sarah in the back, causing her to stumble. The second, larger one, hit her in the head and brought her to the ground. Gloria Jean dropped the third and stood frozen. Only after seconds, which felt like minutes, Sarah got back on her feet. She never looked back; she pitched forward and ran as fast as she could, stumbling, falling, then running again.

Gloria Jean watched as Sarah stumbled farther into the field, then she headed back to the house. Her breathing was still labored. She felt like she was going to pass out, so she knelt down in the dirt at the edge of the field. She felt the earth's coarseness against her knees and hands. The air became thinner and she was unable to draw a breath. Gloria Jean never looked back that day, but later learned that Sarah never made it out of the field. The newspaper reported that a young woman, Sarah Carlisle, died from a head concussion and was found in her family's field. No one suspected foul play; everyone simply thought that the girl had fallen and hit her head.

David held his mother's hand as he sat by her bedside. He could tell that she was agitated. She was whispering something about the neighbor girl, Sarah. She looked like she was arguing with someone. Her appearance gave David the impression that she was having it out with his dad. After her words trailed off, David felt the sudden heaviness in his mother's hand. He knew that she was gone.

Gloria Jean felt a hand holding hers from beyond her visions. She thought that Jack had come back for her, but remembered that he had said he would be gone at daybreak. A deep despair and sadness came over her, like she had missed the last train that would have connected her with family and friends. Darkness settled over fields and farmhouses as dusk arrived, its heavy blanket tucking the Earth into bed. She usually welcomed the closing of an honest hard-working day, but tonight she felt enveloped by unrest. Unknown and unseen entities brushed against her, then pulled at her hair and clothes, taunting and tormenting. A cacophony of whispered words swirled around her, taunting her with the things she imagined that the Carlisle girl would say to her husband Jack. Things only a dirty little trollop would say. Before Gloria Jean could protest, she was pulled and shoved in all directions. She ran as fast as she could, stumbling across the uneven ground. The voices behind her become louder as her tormentors threated to catch her. A sharp dizzying pain blazed at the back of her head. She fell to the ground and struggled to remain conscious.

Gloria Jean trembled with fear, as sweat chilled her body and soaked her dress. She got to her knees and turned, suddenly aware that she was in the field behind her house, where she had seen Sarah Carlisle fall all those years ago. A dark familiar figure stood less than twenty yards away. She was alarmed when she realized that the figure was her.

"You go to hell. You stay away from here. Stay away from my Jack," the dark reflection of herself shouted with rage as it began throwing rocks at her. She felt Sarah's fear and understood that her husband, Jack was more to blame. He should have fought off the girl's advances instead of giving into them, Gloria Jean thought. In that moment she found herself alone.

Drifts of ash blew across the field and clung to unseen bodies, forming dark and devilish forms. They were all around her, circling and drawing near. She saw that the closer entities had long sharp teeth. Gloria Jean screamed as they tore into her. Their numbers blotted out the light. The wounds they inflicted were not of flesh and bone, but of pride, contempt, and heartbreak. She knew that she would not find God in this place.

NO GOOD DEED

The night seemed darker than most, or perhaps Lester needed new glasses. He avoided wearing the ones he owned, not for vanity sake, but because he hated how they felt on his face. Of course driving was a different matter; getting in a wreck while not wearing his glasses could land him in a bit of trouble, especially considering the damage he might do behind the wheel of a 20-ton tractor-trailer. At seventy-two, he tended to lean more on the side of caution, but this evening there were few cars on the road, and it was one of his usual routes, so why the hell not live a little. For tonight's run, he was hauling ten skids of soda from Davison via the expressway. He thought he had seen everything along this stretch that there was to see.

The expressway was his, with the exception of a few cars that had passed him moments ago and were now absorbed into the darkness that lay ahead. Lester drove the 2001 CH601 Mack with pride, although it was the least likable truck in the Connors fleet. He was just happy and grateful to still be working and driving. He loved the open road and to Mike Connors, Lester was a solid, dependable asset, even at age seventy-two. The haul was an overnight run. Since the Mack lacked a sleeping compartment that left Lester either sleeping in the driver's seat or paying for a motel room. With work was few and far between, he slept in the truck to save money, and paid for it with a stiff neck. In some aspects the discomfort was a blessing, as it kept him awake once he was back on the road.

The exits and on-ramps seemed to appear out of nowhere as he rolled on by. Late nights on the road were often hypnotic and became more so as he got closer to his destination. He drove past one of the few rest stops, which was desolate with only a single car in the lot. He wondered if it belonged to a maintenance worker since the windows were clear. Usually he would see several cars with steamed windows, indicating sleeping occupants.

Beyond the rest area, he saw a car with its flashers on and someone standing behind it. As he drew closer, he could see that it was a woman and she was trying to flag him down. Sighing, hoping that no one was hurt, he slowed the truck to pull in behind her. The bright lights of his truck illuminated the woman and her dark gray Mercedes sport coupe. Being cautious, but also a bit nervous, Lester slowed and pulled the truck along the shoulder. He used the visual advantage of his imposing truck lights to assess the situation. Good luck or maybe street smarts had kept him safe all these years. If it were a man needing help, he probably would have kept on rolling.

"Thank you for stopping. My car seems to have stalled, and now it won't start," she called out towards his silhouette.

"No trouble miss. You're lucky I came by. It's not safe out here for you to be stranded. By the way, my name's Lester," he yelled back as he approached her.

She gave him a quick friendly smile, but withheld her name. He understood. Maybe she was just being careful.

"I tried my cellphone, but was unable to get a signal. Must be a dead spot," she explained.

She was dressed elegantly, as to be expected for someone driving such a nice set of wheels. Her hair was dark and long, face thin, skin fair like porcelain. She wore sunglasses, which seemed odd to Lester.

"How can you see with those on?"

"They're prescription sunglasses. I can't seem to find my other ones," she replied.

"Pop the hood and I'll take a look," he told her.

He peeked under the hood. The belts were all in place and everything looked clean and new.

"Try starting it," he said.

The engine turned over smooth but refused to start. Lester was good with older vehicles, but the newer Mercedes was beyond his level of automotive knowledge. He thought that maybe it was the car's computer or an electrical issue.

"How's your fuel level?" he called out from behind the hood. *At least he could discount the obvious*, he thought.

"It's above the half mark," she said.

"Well, I think the best I can do for you is radio for a tow truck," he said.

"I'd like that," she said.

He closed the hood and started back to the truck when he heard her car door open.

"It's all right, you can wait in your car," he said.

Before he could take another step he was thrown into the

ditch. He wondered if a car had clipped him, as he tried to get to his knees in the tall grass. She stood before him in an instant, no longer wearing her glasses. He could only make out blackened sockets where her eyes should be. Before he could stand she was on him in a rigid and unyielding embrace. Her nails clawed and dug into his cheek. He tried to push her away, but was unable to break free. She attacked like an animal, biting at his shoulder, then neck. As Lester struggled he knew that he was bleeding, his hands were wet as he tried to stop her. The more he struggled the faster he faded into unconsciousness.

Lester's lifeless body lay in the ditch, his eyes open with the side of his face pressed against the ground as if he were trying to listen to the Earth's heartbeat. No breath left his mouth or nostrils to disturb the micro-sized lunar landscape of dust and pebbles that filled his vision. Strange how the ground looked when closely inspected; his truck lights created long shadows from even the tiniest grains. A heavy sound of compressed air rushed by, telling him that he was lying next to the woman's car on the shoulder of Interstate 78. His mind was groggy and confused. His last act of going to use the truck radio was all that he could remember. Questioning thoughts eluded him ... *how long have I been here ... how many cars have passed by ... did anyone see me?*

He could see her feet from under the car. She was on the opposite side. Despite his haze, Lester noticed that her toenails were painted crimson red. He usually avoided looking at such things in detail. Simply knowing if a woman was attractive or not was his limit of observation. He used to tell his buddy, Herb Wallace, "If she's got a good smile that does it for me."

Her heels clicked against the asphalt as she walked around the car. He could feel her standing behind him, and then he heard the door open. Unable to move to see what she was doing, he felt himself being lifted, almost weightlessly floating into the passenger seat of the Mercedes.

"Can't leave you here like roadkill, besides a nice gentleman such as yourself at least deserves a fighting chance," she said in a sporting yet soft tone. He wondered if she was really talking to him or to herself.

Now in her car, it was anyone's guess where she was taking him, and to what end. *Perhaps they were headed to the hospital, maybe I had a heart attack*, he thought. A sudden chill of fear crept in as the memory of her attack came back in random flashes. A primal but distant sense of self-preservation stirred within him. He struggled to clear the fog in his mind. He thought that maybe if he felt anger, he might be able to pull himself out of this stupor and regain control of his body, but instead only a hollow paralysis remained.

She drove on in silence, appearing confident that she knew her destination. As the car sped forward, Lester watched the patch of road that the headlights illuminated from the darkness. After several miles they exited to a single lane road that opened to rolling hills and farmhouses.

It seemed like only minutes had passed when she pulled over in a wooded area, then headed down a small work road intended for farm equipment. After a hundred feet or so, she stopped the car and turned off the lights. He was only able to look at the dark silhouettes of the corn stalks, as she walked around the back of the car to open the passenger door.

She yanked him from the seat by the arm, and the rest of his body came along like a rag doll. As he lay on the mud-packed road, he noticed her black heels sitting by the rear wheel. The weight of her body let him know that she was straddling him. His neck felt tight and sticky. *Was I bleeding?* he wondered. Her hair moved across his chest, her lips placing soft kisses. *Was she some man-hater, like that one woman who killed all of those men in Florida?*

He thought of his wife Marion. It would be a day or two before she would start worrying, long enough for him to be well departed. Of course the big question also loomed in his mind: *Why me? All I tried to do was help someone.* The thought became bitter in his mind. Before he could get philosophical he could hear his dad telling him, "No good deed goes unpunished," a response to a grade school altercation where a young Lester tried to defend Annie Bartlett, an often teased girl who wore glasses.

The woman's fingernails scrapped the flesh on his shoulder; the dried blood peeled up in crimson flecks. Her soft cool lips kissed his neck; the pulse of his blood seemed to gravitate towards her. Pain radiated into his shoulder and down his arm, his fingers feeling the prickling of needles. His body became limp like a rapidly deflating tire.

Fighting to stay conscious, he could tell that she was dragging him down a path between the corn fields. Through his foggy haze, he noticed her bare feet sinking into the soft earth. Still unable to control his body or voice to protest, his mind wandered into a punch-drunk state. *Hey lady you're getting your fancy toes all icky in the mud, I guess that's why you took off your shoes darling,* he thought and laughed internally.

When she released her hold on his wrist, Lester fell lifeless into the mud. He was turned away from her, with only a view of corn stalks towering into the night sky. All Lester could hear were the primal sounds of laborious grunts and animalistic clawing, like a determined hunting dog trying to dislodge a rabbit from its hole.

He was once again hoisted up by his wrist, and then rolled into a shallow hole. *Will this be my grave and the end of it all?* he thought. She was covered in mud up to her elbows and knees, but was still strangely beautiful and dream-like.

She began pushing dirt over his body. He watched her like a child watches his mother tuck him into bed. His body unable to move, his lips unable to cry out, all he could do was feel the weight of the loose earth covering him. It soon filled his eyes and ears, and then all was dark, still and silent.

There was no way to tell how much time had passed; an endless void was Lester's only existence. Through the abyss he felt movement in his fingers, the muscles in his body twitched as if tiny electrical charges inched their way up and down. Although the weight of the earth that encased him was overbearing, his limbs were able to move through it; he reached and clawed upward until he penetrated the air. When he was above ground he rubbed his eyes to remove the caked dirt that impaired his vision. Although the night was moonless and pitch he could see clearly as if it were midday. He walked down the rough muddy path, through the walls of corn, and in the direction that he thought the road might be. With each step, an eerie feeling came over him. There seem to be no weight to his body; it moved fluid like silk within a breeze, yet he still minded his footing for fear of falling. Beyond that, there was something more troubling: He wasn't breathing. His chest did not fill with air. He could open his mouth and expand his lungs, but then he had to force the air out. He wanted to cry out, but instead he began to run, not stopping even as he exited the field.

The narrow paved road led to a small grouping of houses. As Lester crept between the single story structures, he noted that the siding and roof shingles were old but cared for as best as meager means could manage. Soft feminine moans came from a nearby window. He giggled to himself, like a schoolboy who was witnessing his older brother or sister having sex. The comedic tone soon became one of lust and longing, and a sinful hunger came over him.

All of his darkest thoughts, once held back and in check with his moral compass came rushing forth; they raced and rolled through his mind. The internal wall he had built over time as a child and young man attending church, now lay in ruins by the forces that drove him. He squatted down beneath the open window and listened as the couple carried on. After moments of silence he heard the man complain about having to be at work early. The woman's voice begged him to stay, but was later followed by the metal creaking of a storm door. The light in the window came on briefly as the couple said goodnight.

After waiting under the window, his face shrouded in the shadows, Lester spoke, "Do you still want me to stay? Can I come in?" Brief silence then in a delighted tone from the window, "I knew you couldn't stay away, of course, come in baby."

* * *

Lester awoke, half buried within some shallow space. A jumbled garden hose lay near his feet. To his right were a couple of old rakes, which should have been retired a few autumns back. On a hook was a kerosene lamp, which was a little rusty, but still serviceable. He had no need for it; even without light the space seemed well lit to him. In the diagonal corner from where he sat he could see a small square door, which opened into someone's back yard. This was the home of the young woman he met last night.

The steps near the side porch had police tape across them. His initial thoughts were about the girl's wellbeing, but those quickly morphed into bitter and strangely sweet desires for unwarranted vengeance. Trying to fill his head with reason and compassion only amplified his wicked spite. *The bitch must have gotten what she deserved.* He covered his mouth, ashamed of the words he just spoke. With a vacant stare, he broke into a maddening laughter. Part of him wanted to see if anyone else was home in the other small houses. Only the distant desire to return home to his Marion persuaded him to press on. *Did she miss me?* he wondered. He smiled at the thought of his wife's horrified expression when she finally saw him, looking like what the cat dragged in.

This night he felt stronger. Can a young woman make an older man feel young again, isn't that how it goes? He laughed at the thought. He took to the road, walking some, running some, even skipping some. Pace or time were of no consequence, his body was no longer held to this world, a world of common man. The only honest thing left for him was the desire to see Marion one last time. He held onto that thought, but moreover he tried to hold on to his last strand of sanity.

As the hours passed, the night took him across several roads, and through a small town until he came to some railroad tracks. He remembered the tracks running parallel with the expressway and decided to follow them.

There was an old underpass down an embankment from the rails. Flaming barrels lit a stone archway. The bridge's turn-of-the-century foundation was composed of stones and mortar that supported the passage of a single lane road. It once provided some shelter for the destitute, but now mainly attracted mischief seekers. For young teenagers in love, it was a hangout away from prying eyes and parental guidance. Two figures were visible standing near the fire, one was wearing a gray hoodie with a skull and crossbones pattern, jeans with holes at the knees and heavy military style boots, while the other wore a gas station jumpsuit. Beer bottles in hand, they were talking loudly and laughing even louder.

Lester moved down the hillside, almost floating. The hill was steep, one that a mortal man would avoid for fear of a twisted ankle, or worse a broken neck. The moon tonight was a mere sliver, leaving the hill dark and concealing. He watched the young men, one telling a story, his arms well animated. Their shadows danced tall under the arch.

At the other end of the underpass, two figures embraced in the darkness. Lester could see a couple kissing; the young man was standing with the girl's legs wrapped around his hips. The boy's hands cupped the girl's bottom, his fingers slipping under her panties. Lester licked his lips while he watched with anticipation. The other two boys carried on their loud conversation, giving the couple privacy.

Chris opened a cooler chest and pulled out two more beers, and popped the caps off with the opener on his keyring. His buddy, Brad, flung the two empties into the darkness; one landed in the tall grass at the base of the hill.

Before sitting down on the cooler, Chris farted loudly and handed one of the beers to his friend.

"Nice, just keep that zipped up," Brad demanded with laughter.

Chris was still wearing his mechanic's jumpsuit from work. Both had been drinking prior to their arrival and now were unable to stop laughing at each other.

One of the empty bottles came sailing back and landed just behind the boys. It shattered near the base of the arch. Their expressions changed and they stared in silence at each other. At first they seemed confused as to the origin of the projectile, even looking toward the direction of the couple.

"Hey did one of you mother fuckers throw that?" Brad called, as Chris took a sip of his beer.

"Fuck you. No," answered a voice from the darkened end of the tunnel.

They looked out into the darkness as a second bottle came sailing through the air and hit Chris in the left eye, causing him to stumble back and trip over the cooler.

"Fu—k … Brad my eye," cried Chris.

"Who's there? You're getting your ass kicked. Come on out," Brad yelled with a hint of panic in his voice.

Brad yanked the hood off of his head and stared menacingly into the shadows as he sidestepped back to check on his friend.

"Chris let me see it," said Brad, as he grimaced at his friends pulverized eye socket.

He dragged Chris into the tunnel and yelled toward Rick and Beth. Brad returned to the entrance with Rick, who was wearing a school varsity jacket and brandishing a baseball bat. Brad unsheathed a hunting knife and held it out to his side. They both called out ready for a fight, only to be answered with sharp sadistic laughter.

From the shadows Lester emerged, the darkness clinging to him like smoke to a smoldering building.

"You shouldn't litter," Lester said, smiling and taunting the two young men.

What they saw was a disheveled old homeless man, one that no one would likely miss.

Lester could have dodged the bat with ease, but allowed the blow to crash against the side of his head, only half knocking him back. The impact gave him new respect for the trauma a baseball must endure. Out of range of any follow up swings, he measured no pain, and wondered how shattered his face must appear.

The boys stood defensively, waiting for the disheveled man to attack or run. He moved closer and into the light, where they could see his face. Although he had a split on his forehead from their attack, a crooked smile formed on his lips. His eyes were dark pools of endless void. The two boys were captured within his gaze, first swimming in the black nothingness then forever falling.

Without a spoken word Brad saw Lester's violent thoughts, heard the whispering within his mind, telling him to do things. His lips trembled and his knuckles went white from clenching the knife. He swung his arm in an upward arc and slashed the blade deep across his friend's neck. A returned glance of horror and confusion fell on Rick's face. Rick's knees buckled, he released the bat and fell face forward, blood painting the ground under him.

Brad's eyes were wide and filled with tears, and his teeth were clenched in disbelief. An internal battle raged within his mind. He tried to fight Lester's dark commands. The bloody hunting knife flashed through the air once more and opened up Brad's own neck. A sheet of blood poured down his chest spewing forth like a magician's endless ribbon.

Lester was on him like a tiger, knocking him backwards to the ground. Brad's face was covered in deep red, then his body jerked twice before settling, alive no longer.

"Hey you guys, Chris is hurt real bad, his eye won't stop bleeding, we need to get him help! Guys?" A girl's voice echoed out from within the tunnel.

Lester left the two fallen boys and slipped into the darkness along the underpass.

Beth knelt next to Chris, who lay unconscious. She held a handkerchief against his wounded eye. She had long dirty blonde hair, a form-fitting top and plaid miniskirt. Lester licked his lips watching her from behind the barrel; the flames of fire in it still burned high. His dark senses were in a frenzy, eclipsing any humanity. The deaths of the two boys had only begun to whet his appetite.

Shadows from the two barrel fires whipped and danced on the tunnel ceiling. She turned again to call out to her friends, but he was there standing over her with a blood covered wicked smile. Her mouth contorted as her lips tried to form a scream.

The old meeting place was still; only the sound of embers crackled in the barrels. Down the hill were tire tracks from a large sedan or truck, evidence that would eventually point to a late model Chevy Caprice that belonged to Brad Johnston. It would turn up a week later at the Royal Scrap yard two counties east.

Chris Clemens, the only survivor, gave the police little to go on.

"Maybe one of the boys killed the other because he wanted his girlfriend, then he went nuts at the sight of what he's done and offs himself," Deputy Dan Gossen pitched to his partner.

"But this other kid, maybe gets bashed in the face with the bottle because he's caught in the middle, or tries to stop the boy with the knife," Deputy Dan Gossen continued.

"Helluva thing, Dan. It would take a lot for someone to almost slice their own head off with a knife," remarks Deputy Jerry Hagstrom.

"Last, that leaves us with the girl, Beth Williams, who ends up being mauled by a bear that just so happens to come along after all this shit goes down," mused Deputy Dan Gossen.

"Not so fast, you're forgetting the missing vehicle that everyone rode in on. That makes a fifth person. The Clemens boy said that someone threw a bottle at him, but there are no houses within miles, and he didn't see the person. I'm betting there is another school kid involved. We need to find that vehicle," said Deputy Jerry Hagstrom.

* * *

Although Lester could neither hear nor see anything to give evidence of his surroundings, a deep sense of home swaddled him as he slept. As with days prior, no dreams came, all he was left with was a dark void. His body, uncontrollably animated, crawled out from beneath the earth.

The space at first seemed confusing; it was not the same as under the young woman's house. Familiar items that belonged to him, various gardening tools, the winch off of his old Jeep, were all scattered around him, where he last left them.

He crawled to the middle of the far wall to a rough opening where water pipes rose upward to the kitchen sink, while drain pipes descended. Just as his body dug its way from the earthly burial in the corner of the crawl space, he was driven to claw upward. His nails, which had grown long and sharp, carved deep gashes into the already rough opening around the pipes.

A distant memory of coming home drunk a few years ago rattled in his mind. He could hear his wife Marion telling him, "Get out." The memory was so vivid it was as if it were playing on the TV and he was now watching it, hearing her voice. He sat back, listening, but it did not come again.

His mind continued to waver. Visions of past events and joyful times became tainted as twisted paranoia seeped in. His gentle human qualities were now distorted into sadistic longings. He was caught in the surf of his mind, lost in a tide of madness that was growing ever deeper. Thoughts of seeing Marion were his last hope to regain his sanity.

After staring at the wall, his daydream broke like a fever. Half standing he began again to claw at the hole above him. With a greater sense of urgency, larger chunks of wood broke free until he was able to pull his upper body through the hole. The sink cabinet doors were obstructed, but he managed to push them open and enter the kitchen.

Hearing soft footsteps coming down the hall, he moved to the corner of the room and turned to the wall. *Marion must not see my face.* He could feel her in the doorway. Her heart was racing, her flesh smelled familiar.

"Marion," he spoke her name.

With reassuring ease, he heard her say his name in return. Fear and guilt clenched at him. When she turned on the light he fled to the shadows of the crawl space. Marion's voice cried out his name once more as he pushed to the dark corner and into the hole where he had slept. Beyond the primal hunger that drove him to commit violent acts the previous nights, another hunger grew, one of loneliness.

When Lester arose from his burial, he saw that his secret entrance to the house was now blocked. There were planks nailed in place to secure the rough carved hole, the portal to his Marion's world. Too weak to remove the barrier, he tested the outer doors to the crawl space. They were loose, held only by a steel padlock on the other side and hung on aged hinges. After a brief struggle he managed to push them ajar, the rusty screws screeching like mice being trampled. Outside, he watched the wind animate the trees, although the wind seemed to avoid him, refusing to caress his face. He walked to the edge of the yard next to the old apple tree and contemplated letting go of his past life. Only seeing Marion for that brief moment increased his desire to remain. He longed to tell her the hell he had been through and to seek her comfort.

He then saw his old friend Herbert in the window. *Well, son of a bitch, what the hell are you doing there, in my home.* His thoughts boiled with rage, allowing no room for logical consideration. A memory of the couple he first came upon, their late evening passion was now an easy conclusion. As he watched Herb in the window, he saw Herb's expression changed from a vacant stare to one of fear. His body felt like it was on fire; he just wanted to tear off his clothes and tear out his hair at the betrayal of his wife and friend. He pulled his shirt off and clung to the base of the tree, his fingernails digging into the soft bark, his shirt catching on the tangled branches.

When he looked again, Herb no longer stood at the window. Lester heard the side door hinges creaking, so he slipped into the shadows on the opposite side of the house. He heard Herb's voice call out, "Anyone out there?" Moving along the side of the house, he came to Marion's window. It was open with only the screen covering it. With gentle hands he removed the screen, like a hunter bending a branch to clear his shot. Hunger gnawed and bitterness clouded his mind. He wanted to end both of them this evening. Only tender reminders of his wife's kindness, even to those who wronged her, shamed him. *She belongs to me,* his obsessive contemptuous thoughts demanded. With resolved conviction Lester knew that he would have Marion. Once again she would be his bride, wife, and soon his dark companion.

Enveloped by the shadows, Lester's body slid upward and into the open window. He stepped silently from the darkness and stood beside her bed. Marion turned in her sleep as moans of horrific anticipation left her open lips. Her face contorted as if witnessing someone being tortured while her hands gripped at the bed sheets.

Lester watched as his wife moved on the bed, her soft pure flesh pulsating and radiating with life. Glistening droplets of sweat pooled in the notch at the base of her neck. Her chin was stretched out and exposed, like one animal yielding to another's dominance. He could no longer bear the weight of his hunger or ecstasy to consume her. Drawn to the light within her, he kissed her flesh. Her life, her soul, everything flowed into him, down into emptiness. As she began to fade within his arms, a distant flicker of humanity caused him to release her. He turned away and slipped out the window as she lay lifeless.

Herb was no longer in the yard, so Lester returned to his earthly bedchamber without confrontation. The ground beneath the dark crawl space felt like warm sand on a summer's day. His dirty flesh did not rot. Insects and rats knew to stay away from his dead body, which was already claimed by something far more sinister than the most grotesque creatures that Mother Nature could conjure. Within his silent tomb, he neither dreamt nor held any thoughts, a privilege held by the living.

After last night's reunion, Lester's mind only entertained thoughts of evil. His anger and hunger had put things in motion. Visions of Marion falling from a cliff and landing on jagged rocks brought a wicked smile to Lester's face. Dried encrusted scarlet flakes fell from his curled lips. He could not bear to wait any longer. Strong workman's hands now employed by the Devil himself pulled the wooden planks to expose the hole in the kitchen cabinet. Rising like black smoke from a tapered chimney he entered the room above.

Moving into the living room, he saw Herb sleeping on the couch. Sliding against the wall he slipped into the shadows of the darkened corner, watching as Herb turned about in his sleep, a bad nightmare about to become real. Herbert's eyes opened, as he was jostled from one hell to another. Lester moved to the end of the couch and demanded that Herb leave. He bellowed, "Only one man in this house."

Herb cried out, "Lester?"

Hearing his name felt like a distant dream, a cloudy childhood memory with details washed out over time. Herb was talking to him, there was fear in his voice, but Lester could not make out the words.

"Leave this house, fornicator," Lester demanded.

Herb fell from the couch, trying to crawl away. To Lester, it was evidence of Herb's guilt.

With ease, Lester was on him with his hands around Herb's neck, driving him up against the wall. To Lester, Herb's body weighed as little as a ten-year-old boy, and his neck was frail and delicate within Lester's hands. He watched Herb's face contort from simple fear and confusion to the panic of one attempting to escape death. When Herb's eyes bulged then became vacant, Lester released his grasp and Herb's limp body slumped to the floor in a half seated position.

Marion's room was empty; unknown to Lester, she lay in a hospital bed after his previous night's visit. With her whereabouts unknown and the night coming to a close, Lester's body took over, ushering him to the crawl space and his resting place.

Each waking night he clawed up through the earth, he felt alive, reborn until the hunger set in. His hands trembled and reminded him of the chill of past winters. Tonight his path was unfettered. The rough opening was exposed, giving way to the kitchen, then to an empty living room and an open bedroom door.

He floated up and across the ceiling, shadows carrying him like a leaf on a breeze. Marion lay peacefully on top of the bed covers; her arms were out to her sides in a welcoming pose. He descended down to her like a cloud of gentle falling snowflakes. The sharp point of his forefinger ran down her nightgown like a box cutter, exposing her. As his body covered hers; she trembled and her lips shivered at his cold embrace. She stared upward, beyond him, beyond the bedroom ceiling, perhaps looking to God. Her essence flowed into him and was warm and comforting. Only she understood him, and even now he felt she would come to accept their new union.

Lester heard someone in the house, so he floated to the ceiling and into the shadows. He peered down, watching as Herb entered the room carrying a heavy wooden axe handle and kneeling beside Marion. Flowing within the dark band of shadows across the ceiling and down the wall to the floor, he stood behind Herb who was now covering Marion's body with the bed sheet.

He grasped Herb's shoulder in an icy iron grip and threw him into the opposite corner of the room, smashing his body against a wooden rocking chair, shattering it. He hoped that Herb's bones were as internally broken and splintered.

Lester looked at Herb, who was like an animal in a trap, broken on the floor, in pain, unaware how close death was. Herb was slow to get to his feet, but was armed with the wooden axe handle. Lester moved dreamlike around the bed. With the confidence of the Devil, he knew that this simple man could not harm him. He stopped the heavy blow intended for his head in one hand, and grasped Herb's shoulder in his other, bringing him to his knees.

"You're not coming with us," he told him.

Herb gave in to his pain and released the axe handle, which Lester tossed aside. Lester drew near, preparing to end his once old friend, but he was struck and forced backward. An object projected from Lester's chest; it was part of the rocking chair. Before he could react, Herb was on him, driving the splintered wood deep. Both men fell to the floor.

Lester crawled under the bed; he felt no pain from the impalement. The view under the bed reminded him of looking under the woman's broken down car just beyond the rest stop. His last thought was wondering why he had stopped that night.